The Water Beetles

The Water Beetles

a novel by
MICHAEL KAAN

GOOSE LANE

Edited by Bethany Gibson.
Cover and page design by Julie Scriver.
Cover photograph "Breeziness," by Visoot Uthairam, 500px.com.
Incidental illustrations by Dover (lotus); seamartini, istock.com (beetle)
Printed in Canada.
10 9 8 7 6 5 4 3 2 1

Library and Archives Canada Cataloguing in Publication

Kaan, Michael, author
The water beetles / Michael Kaan.

Issued in print and electronic formats.
ISBN 978-0-86492-966-2 (paperback).--ISBN 978-0-86492-967-9 (epub).--
ISBN 978-0-86492-968-6 (mobi)

I. Title.

PS8621.A263W38 2017   C813'.6   C2016-907039-5
                                             C2016-907040-9

We acknowledge the generous support of the Government of Canada,
the Canada Council for the Arts, and the Government of New Brunswick.

Goose Lane Editions
500 Beaverbrook Court, Suite 330
Fredericton, New Brunswick
CANADA E3B 5X4
www.gooselane.com

To the memories of my father, 簡子怡,
and my grandmother, 簡歐陽月勾.

And to R, M, and G.

I even learnt German, after a fashion, so that I could read what the Germans themselves had said about the bombings and their lives in the ruined cities. To my astonishment, however, I soon found the search for such accounts invariably proved fruitless.

— W.G. Sebald, *The Rings of Saturn*

Guangdong Province, Summer 1942

I'm watching the beetle. Not the beetle I wish I was, but the bigger one who wants to kill it. Mine is golden-green, small and easy to spot. Just behind it is the larger one with a shiny, deep-black carapace, so black it seems to drink the light right from my eyes. The big one hasn't struck mine yet, it's only watching, and it tastes the air ahead to see when it should act. I can see it will strike and win, and the beetle I wish I was will die. Like everyone else, it is at war, which means its every move is inevitable and prescribed.

I don't know why I chose this beetle. I was just resting in the shade. I was trying to forget. Then I saw my beetle's stubby horns and the crisp gold-green wings that might take it anywhere, so I wanted to become it. I wanted to escape. But now the other beetle is crawling up the stalk, and I see how small mine is, how short its horns are, and how terrible the big one is. I still love the colour of its wings. And if I still love this beetle, even when I can see that it will die, I wonder if I'm just unlucky — or worse, foolish.

The people we're walking with talk a lot about foolishness. There's the folly of not listening and of not watching.

There's the folly of speaking at the wrong time, and the folly of eating too slowly. If something goes wrong—and so much has—people get angry and shout at others and call them stupid, and then they fight, we fight. Sometimes I hear laughter or feel the slow peace of boredom, but it never lasts long. Beyond walking, hiding, and eating, no one really knows what to do. We are somewhere, and we are lost.

The road we're on seems endless, and the world alongside it a long descent into oblivion: whole villages abandoned or burned, fields of grain left behind to rot or feed the birds, temples smashed and insulted. I fix my eyes ahead so I won't see the bodies lying by the road, though in my mind I hear them wailing beneath their drapery of flies, begging to be recognized and buried. So many of the adults walking with us are parents who've lost their children, and yet they turn on us and shout at us for nothing. Often the wind blows, and it smells tender with greenery or rain, and other times it carries the stench of smoke and bloated flesh. People get angry if they think someone's been foolish, like when my little sister tripped and dropped her bowl. It rattled terribly in the dark. But anyone who looks around will see only one thing: bad luck—bad luck and terrible deeds. And no one wants to talk about that.

We're stopped because it's another hot day, and even the Japanese soldiers forcing us to march agree we should rest. We've stopped by a dense bamboo grove. Despite the soldiers' warnings to stay visible, I want to be alone, so

I'm lying close to the grove's edge. If I lie on my back and look up, I can see only a small patch of sky, the bamboo stalks are so dense. I can also see the two beetles climbing up a stalk. The little green-and-yellow one that is me, with one leg hooked into the crook of the stem, doesn't seem to care that he's being followed.

The greenery reminds me of our grounds back home, of the beds and potted plants that the gardener used to touch so carefully with his tools. It reminds me of the gardens at school and in the city parks, and other things that I worry are gone or I may never see again. At the moment I'm surrounded by plants, the wild and the farmed exploding next to each other in the light. There's nothing gentle about cultivated plants—they dig and drink, and push upward as hard as the wild ones. But I prefer the gardens to this. I prefer my memories to what is happening now. We have a garden on the roof of our house where my brother and I used to play a lot, before it became unsafe to be up there. It has a chicken coop and a vegetable plot, or at least it did when I left.

My older brother, Leuk, and I were up there one day last summer, playing marbles under an orange tree. We scratched a circle in the fine gravel and shot the marbles across it. Thick white clouds sailed quickly over us all day, casting the gravel in and out of shadow. The marbles darkened and brightened, and then a different shadow broke the light. I looked up, just as one of the first planes flew overhead.

The air is very dry today, and the ground is hard against my back, wicking off the sweat through my thin shirt.

"Chung-Man, what are you looking at?"

I roll my head over with a jerk, feeling a pebble scrape against the side of my head. Wei-Ming, my little sister, looks at me with a clutch of flowers in one hand.

"Go back to the others. I just want to lie here."

"We have to go soon. Yee-Lin said so."

"I don't care what she says."

This upsets her a lot. When you are a child yourself, you have no sense of how young children really are. My sister is eight.

"We have to *go*." She starts to cry.

I look up at the bamboo stalks again for a second and sit up. I catch a last glimpse of my beetle, just a dark shape. Shouting in Japanese erupts close by.

I take Wei-Ming's hand and we walk through the grove back to the road. My brother Leuk and a girl named Ling are sitting in the shade on the opposite side. In the middle of the road where the sun pours down, her calm face washed in sweat, stands my sister-in-law Yee-Lin. All five of us are exhausted and starving.

"Chung-Man," she says patiently. "We need to go."

Wei-Ming looks up at me again and pulls me towards the road.

"Can't we just stay in the shade?"

"No. You know they won't let us. Come on." She gestures to all of us and we draw ourselves into the sun. All around us the others are doing the same, drifting out of the grove as though they'd been caught hiding. A farmer strikes the papery sides of a water buffalo that the Japanese have allowed him to keep, and it rises slowly, looking sideways into the trees through the stricken wetness of its eyes.

The soldiers shout at everyone. We get back into a line and they walk down it, whipping bamboo switches through the air. In the heat their shirts cling to their skin and their gun barrels shine like wet teeth. We start walking and quickly catch up with the rest of the prisoners. People have slung bags across their backs and some have filled. their canteens from a well in a nearby field. A man and his wife shout at each other. They argue about whether the water is poisonous and then about who should taste it first.

Yee-Lin walks ahead, behind her Leuk holds Wei-Ming's hand, and Ling and I walk behind them. Despite the heat, the five of us cluster together. Among the many dozens of us who are captives, there may be pity but there's very little trust, and once we're all exposed again to the sun, other people's grief becomes a burden. A minute after we start marching again, I realize how exhausted I am. I ache from my feet to my scalp.

But I am here, every day, cinching and re-cinching my belt while I try to keep my load balanced. What else can I do? More than anything, I know that I must watch my little sister, and keep my head as clear as possible, and I must listen very well, even to my older brother. I match his step, I time my breath with his to keep us close, and I think of how this last fragment of my family, this vestige, has yet to come apart.

ONE

Hong Kong, Spring 1935

Rainwater ran downhill through the stone gutters of Wong Nai Chung Road, scattering into trickles that clouded with debris before vanishing through the gutter's cracks.

Leuk and I liked to play by the gutter when it rained. We picked up leaves and twigs and dropped them into the rushing water, higher up the street, and watched them sail down the gutter like little boats. When we were very young, we had to run to keep up with them. We played this game even as we grew taller, strolling alongside the little vessels. But then we started to get bored with it, even to find it a little embarrassing, and we gave up racing. That was just before the war, when many things ended.

In April 1935, I was five and Leuk had just turned seven. We could always play in the gardens or the front courtyard of the house, but if we wanted to go out to the street and throw leaves into the gutter, someone had to open the gates for us. If it wasn't raining and he wasn't busy cleaning the cars, that was Chow, our driver. On rainy days one of the maids had to let us out.

I should say that *maid* isn't really the right word. There were two women who took care of us the most, and they both called our mother "older sister." The younger of them had a long, graceful face like a peeled almond, and her hair was always neatly tied back. I often thought she could read my thoughts, because she had a way of tilting her head and catching my eye when I was tempted to be naughty. That happened a lot, at least when I was very young. She was younger than my mother and came from the same village near Foshan. Her name was Ah-Tseng, and whenever she opened the gate for us, she would say, "Don't get your shoes wet!" She was my favourite.

The other one was Ah-Ming, who was the same age as our mother. I think this was why she saw it as her job to discipline us when my mother wasn't around. As I look back, I have more sympathy for her. She often went around with a rolled-up newspaper tucked into her belt, a useful tool for swatting both flies and children, and she had no problem using it for both in quick succession. More than once I corrected myself when she raised that instrument at me, not because it really hurt, but because I saw the fresh innards of a dead fly stuck to the end.

In Kuala Lumpur, where I live now, in 2015, maids are foreigners and their employers mostly ignore them. They don't pay these women extra at the Lunar New Year, or talk to them in the kitchen, and they never ask them about their families back home. I have a maid—that's the right word—in my flat now, a Filipino girl, and I rarely know what to say to her. Once I was watching her unpack the shopping, and when she took out a chicken, I started telling her about the time my brother was two and ate a pile of chicken shit in the garden. I was laughing, but she looked as though I was ordering her to give me a bath, so I stopped. Life now is so different, manners are so obscure — I sometimes find it strange to see myself living in the present. Once in a while, out of politeness or real interest, younger people ask me about my life and what it was like before the war. They may even have read about the war. My usual response is to throw out anecdotes, some intriguing pictures of a life in a vanished world — trams, games, newsreels, colonial pomp — and it's usually enough. Once in a while I meet people who recognize what those pictures really are: a bluff. And they're also perceptive enough not to ask any further.

The old house on Wong Nai Chung Road was directly across from the racetrack and the Jockey Club, where my father and mother were members. The racehorses were kept not on the grounds of the Club itself, but in stalls on a road a short walk away. This road was linked to the main road by a short ramp, a sloping path that was too narrow for cars, and Leuk and I used to run down there sometimes in the mornings or evenings to see the horses being moved in single file to and from the racetrack. When they were being led to the track, we'd follow them there, though we stopped short of the entrance to the Club. Our father had warned us all that we were to be seen arriving at the Club only by car, never on foot. So Leuk and I bypassed the Club gates and continued down the road, following its gentle slope downhill. We always stopped at a certain corner from which we could see, just a block away where the road narrowed almost to a dead end, an old ruined house half concealed by vines, trees, and the intersecting poles of laundry that extended from the windows and balconies of neighbouring buildings.

. . .

One warm spring evening, Leuk and I were inside, sitting in the main-floor library, which looked even gloomier than usual because of the brilliant sunset coming through the narrow windows. Leuk had just learned from our father that in the fall he would be going to boarding school. This put him into a desperate, distracted mood. He told me he didn't want to go away and was afraid of being a boarder. We had two older brothers—Sheung and Tang, aged fifteen and sixteen—who were in their final years of boarding school, but we rarely saw them and knew little about what went on there. Leuk had pulled a dozen or so books off the shelf and kept stacking them into a tower and then knocking them down. At first I thought this was funny, but then the noise started bothering me and I was worried Ah-Ming or our mother would hear and get angry with us. I kept telling Leuk to stop, but he ignored me. I didn't understand then that he was afraid.

I looked at the clock on the mantelpiece: it was seven-thirty. I kicked the heap of books away before Leuk could strike it down again, and told him the time and said we should go upstairs. We went up the stairs to the second floor, where my father's study sat at the front of the house, with a view of the Jockey Club. The door was shut. We took off our shoes and I looked around to see if our mother was near. All we could hear was her voice far off on the third floor, talking to our baby sister Wei-Ming, and from our father's office came a faint sound of ticking.

We crept up to the study door and Leuk put his eye to the large keyhole, while I lowered my ear to the jamb. I closed my eyes and whispered almost inaudibly.

"I can hear it ticking."

"Me too." Leuk pressed his face harder against the lock plate, until his forehead bumped against the door handle with a faint click. We both jumped back and sat on either side of the door, ready to run, though there was no sign our father had heard the noise. A moment later I said it was my turn.

I put my eye to the keyhole. On the metal plate I smelled the tang of polished brass and the garlic from Leuk's dinner breath. Inside the study, the evening light washed through sheer curtains with a bluish hue, and all the surfaces of the room, polished wood and glass, glowed with the end of day. The large mahogany desk sat empty beneath the windows. On a small table nearby stood the machine. It had a heavy brass base topped with a glass dome nearly a foot high, and inside it whirred an elaborate mechanism like the innards of a clock. Wires ran from the base to an electrical socket in the wall. On the opposite side of the base, a roll of narrow paper hung on a little frame. The gears turned and the paper slid through an opening, and a small printer clattered information onto the paper before it emerged on the other side. Through the door jamb I heard the machine firing sharply like a miniature gun. Leuk and I just called it the machine, though years later when I saw one in a history book I finally learned the English term, *stock ticker*.

Next to the machine, sitting on a porcelain stool with his legs crossed, our father inclined his head to scan the emerging paper. A tray with his evening meal, untouched, stood on a folding table beside him. It always took me a moment to see him. The glass and metal of the ticker seemed to soak up and throw back most of the scant evening light, while our father, in the black padded jacket he always wore in the evenings, his face turned down towards the paper, was a mere shadow beside it.

Five nights a week our father would stay up to scrutinize the ticker's messages, and those nights he slept very little. Even when his cough was bad, he sat up drinking tea and sometimes dabbing his lips with a white handkerchief, which he then examined for blood. One night a few weeks earlier, I had watched him there through the keyhole. He was sitting cross-legged on the porcelain stool, hunched by the machine and coughing. He held a handkerchief dotted with little blood rubies between two fingers in his left hand, as though he were holding a cigarette, while with his right he nursed the paper that shuddered from the machine. He stared at each new scribble as it crossed his open hand. And then the paper strip, having lived a life measured by the width of his palm, fell to the floor like a dead snake. In the morning, the servants threw it into the fire.

Chow was responsible for the machine and for replacing the paper every second day, making sure it was ready by the time of the evening when the New York exchange opened. Once each roll was down to a quarter or less, he replaced it and gave us the remnants. Leuk and I loved to run around the rooftop garden, unravelling them and trying to crack them like whips.

Leuk wanted to see through the keyhole, but I told him I wasn't done yet. My father looked as though he had been posed on his stool by an artist, and there was something eerie about even the smallest movement of his head or limbs. Leuk insisted and reached up to push my head away from the keyhole. I whispered at him to stop and pushed his hand away, and then he grabbed my collar and pulled me down onto the floor with a thump.

Our mother also knew the importance of this hour. It was this kind of remote silence in my father that had made us rich. She heard us from the third floor, and in a second she was rushing down the stairs, one hand holding up her dress to keep it from swishing. Leuk and I scrambled to our feet. Our mother rushed over with a belt rolled up in her other hand, speaking in that angry whisper that frightened me.

"What are you doing here?" She grabbed us both by the collars and pulled us away from the door. I felt the belt against my neck and the pin from the buckle scratched me just below the ear. She hurried us down the stairs, and when we were far enough from the study, she warned us never to disturb our father at this hour again and threatened to hit us with the belt.

Maybe I shouldn't have introduced my mother that way. I know I must have tried her patience, and she had a lot to deal with for many years. Later I came to realize that she must have often been lonely, even with Ah-Ming and Ah-Tseng to keep her company. Children may offer love, but they rarely offer companionship, especially boys. So I don't mention the business with the belt because I resent it, it's just one of those little things that I remember, a part of that world that has mostly vanished. She lived a life of great luxury back then, but she was still at heart a village girl with no education. Despite everything she had, she saw her main job as keeping our family in order and together. Years later, I think she was troubled by the belief that she had failed at this.

Leuk and I retreated to the library, my mother's warning ringing in my ears. We looked at the books I had kicked across the floor earlier and started cleaning them up out of boredom. I stacked a few of them into a squat tower and cast him a look, thinking he might resume his game of knocking it down. Instead, he stood at the window at the library's far end, craning his neck to get a particular view. The library jutted out a little from the back of the house, so that if you looked through the window, you looked onto an enclosure at the back, bordered by Ventris Road. This was a small yard used mostly for rubbish, just off the kitchen door. The window my brother was staring through had a small ledge outside where we used to conceal toys.

I squeezed my face next to Leuk's. From this angle it seemed the back of the house was a separate building. Above the rubbish yard, through a window on the fourth floor, we could see my mother talking to Sheung. It wasn't his current room, but part of a suite that formed an apartment set aside for him when he married, with the other half of the floor for Tang. The fifth floor, which was mostly empty, had been similarly marked out for Leuk and me.

When I think of our old house, I recall a photo of our family taken in front of it when I was still a baby. I lost my only copy of the photo sometime in my thirties, and time has retouched the memory accordingly. I see my mother sitting in the centre, with me on her lap and all the other children behind her, and my father standing at the faded edge. Of course, we would never have been posed that way in the original. My father must have been seated in the centre, flanked by my mother and the oldest sons, with the younger boys seated at the front. When I left for university, I had the photo stored in a frame that I bought from a shop near our house, and while the frame survived the long journey overseas and was otherwise never moved much, it must have been a flimsy piece of work. It came apart one day when I picked it up while cleaning, and the photograph of my family, which landed in a bucket of soapy water, was ruined.

In August, a month after my sixth birthday, I got out of bed early in the morning to go pee. As I walked down the hallway to the bathroom, I heard a commotion on the main floor, so I continued towards the staircase. I listened for a moment and started back towards the bathroom, and then I heard someone crying. I ran back to the top of the stairs and listened. I held my legs together and grasped myself with my left hand through the long cotton nightshirt I wore to bed.

I went down one flight to the landing and crouched behind the railing. In the front hall five adult figures clustered near the door, each moving awkwardly as though uncertain whether to leave or stay. To the left of the door stood my father's doctor and a British officer, in black and khaki respectively, each toying thoughtfully with the hat or cap he had removed. They stared at the floor while Chow, beside them, translated for my mother and Ah-Ming, who stood to the right. My mother shook and cupped a hand across her mouth, containing her sobs so masterfully that they were almost inaudible against the steady rhythm of Chow's voice. I had never seen or heard an adult weep, and it was nothing like the full-cry wailing of a child. She choked back every sob, all her effort focused on the pressure of her hand. It was all binding and discretion, containment, the labour of self-consciousness. As Chow finished speaking, he gently touched my mother's arm.

I liked Chow. He came from a nearby fishing village and had been with us since he was fourteen. Between the fidgeting of the two men on his right and the sorrowing women on his left, he seemed to hold the unlikely gathering in balance, starkly ceremonial in his black jodhpurs and white shirt. I had caught the last few, strangely formal words in his translation. As he released my mother's arm, the officer—who seemed relieved to be going—put the cap back on his head and gave a brisk nod to my mother and Dr. Carrick.

Just as the officer turned, I stood up from my hiding place and snapped to attention, clapping my slippers loudly on the marble stairs, and shouted my best imitation of a sergeant-major's bark. I thought it would be fun to surprise them. I threw my right hand up in salute, still clutching my penis with my left.

My mother looked up first, and then everyone was staring at me. I think the officer smiled briefly, then turned and nodded quickly to Dr. Carrick before dashing out.

Dr. Carrick picked up his bag. There was silence for a moment. Then Ah-Ming, her cheeks flushed with anger, flew up the stairs and seized me by the ear.

"What are you doing? Don't you know your father has just died?" She raised a hand to slap me, but my mother intervened.

"Chung-Man, go back to bed!"

I stared at her for a moment, and then the meaning of Ah-Ming's words became clear to me.

I turned and ran up the stairs, the slap of my slippers' leather soles echoing in the hall. When I got back to the third floor, I stopped and looked down at my clothes. I had peed myself like a baby. My white nightshirt was stained down the front, and the stairs, of greyish-white marble the colour of boiled bones, were splashed with a trickle of bright yellow piss.

Of my father's funeral I have patchy memories of black horses with ostrich plumes, of droning choirs and endless lines of visitors. My only vivid memory is of the Hong Kong Police brass band playing a march on the church grounds as we filed out in our dark clothes. I clapped my hands in time with them and sang as though it were a parade, before Ah-Ming told me to stop.

Sheung and Tang were named as the inheritors of the business in my father's will, though a board of governors, and not my mother, was to hold it in trust until they had both turned twenty. Starting in the fall, months after the funeral, Sheung and Tang spent more and more time with my father's associates, learning the details of my father's enterprises. Until late October they had most of their talks in a small pavilion on the grounds, because my mother declared my father's study off limits to everyone but her. The garden by the pavilion was full of vines and trees that had a wild sheen when it rained and on sunny days hung like the damp and unkempt hair of ghosts, laying an unsettling shade over the rattan furniture.

My father had been so little involved in our everyday life that his departure barely rippled in our routine. Leuk began boarding school in September, and our governess returned to instruct me in reading and writing while also watching Wei-Ming. I felt Leuk's absence more than my father's. Over the Christmas holidays my mother explained to me that I would be leaving for school next fall too.

We were in the library the morning she told me. I was sitting by a window that looked onto the courtyard, playing with a globe that showed the British Empire coloured pink. I had a paper bag of roasted peanuts from the hawker down the street and was laying the empty shells in a circle around the globe's base. My mother sat next to me and showed me the confirmation letter from the school. I recognized its red-and-gold emblem from a certificate that hung on Tang's bedroom wall and asked her if the letter was about me.

I was excited at first. I had always imagined the school as a single room identical to our library, full of uniformed boys reading our books and eating snacks prepared by Ah-Tseng. My mother explained to me that I would live there with three hundred other boys, that it was on the other side of the harbour, and that she would visit me only occasionally.

I spent most of that day almost inconsolable, clinging to my mother and crying until she sent me to my room. Tang tried to distract me with my Christmas presents and stories about how fun the school was. All I could do was beg my mother not to send me. She dragged Leuk into my room, thinking he could set my mind at ease, but he had only just spent his first term there, and when he saw me sobbing and begging to stay home, he started crying too and said he hated being sent away to school.

Finally, Tang and Sheung separated us and my exasperated mother gave us all money to go to the afternoon movies. Her only request was that Leuk and I shouldn't sit together because she didn't want us to cause a scene in public. My older brothers took the two of us out to the local theatre, and they each sat with one of us in separate rows. I sat beside Tang, noisily managing the three bags of candy he'd bought to keep me quiet.

As Chow drove us home, Sheung pulled out a copy of the school magazine to show us that it could be a fun place. I flipped through the dense and unreadable English text in search of photos, which were few, until a drawing in an advertisement caught my eye. It turned out to be a regular notice in the magazine, and I would return to it again and again over the years as I worked on my English. Around the periphery of the image ran the words of the insecticide advertisement I eventually learned to read:

Keep your books free from the ravages
of Cockroaches and Silverfish
with FLIT

2 oz	*4 oz*
50 cts	*90 cts*

Obtainable at the Colonial Dispensary
Pedder Street, Hong Kong

At the centre of the notice marched an inexpressive tin soldier, his bayonet drawn and pointed at an immense cockroach. Unable to make out anything but the simplest words, I stared at the picture while we drove. When we got home, I ran in and showed the advertisement to my mother, thinking that the hunting of giant vermin was part of the school day. She waved it away in disgust and lectured Sheung for telling me stories. Worried that she would confiscate the magazine, I took it to the library and tried to conceal it on the ledge of the far window, but as I was trying to keep my balance, it slipped from my fingers and fell down into the rubbish yard below.

TWO

July 1936

Despite some of the stories Leuk told me about the Diocesan Boys' School, I thought of going there only as being sent away from home, and I was terrified. My older brothers' total lack of interest in saying anything at all confirmed my belief that my mother's decision was one of deliberate cruelty. The only time I heard anything close to consolation was when Sheung looked up casually at me from a newspaper and said, "Don't worry about it. You'll survive."

His bluntness only cemented my impression, and my fear, that the school was some kind of machine that blunted human feeling. I had seen a movie in which a man was lost in an immense, swirling crowd, and as he spun around, struggling to find his way, he was met only with the indifference of everyone around him, people drowning in their own chaos and fear. That was what I started to expect school would be like. Maybe nothing could have reassured me. And maybe, had I known what would come later, during the war, I would have understood that there were far worse things. But I was only seven.

For the moment, on this summer afternoon in 1936, I consoled myself by staring steadily at a photograph of my father. I was perched on a stool, trying to ignore the old tailor who was finishing my school uniform.

My mother had draped the framed picture in black crepe ribbon, as she had done in every room in the house. It had been, I learned later, a year of tumult and worry with the family firm. With the business held in trust and my older brothers still two years away from taking it on, it was as though my mother had riddled the house with images of my father to warn the world that his legacy could not be toppled. She didn't understand the legal complexities of the business and how it would pass to her sons—she was never consulted in such things anyway—and in the strain of losing my father and the void it created, she began to feel a formless dread for the integrity of her family. Twice she made my older brothers swear they would develop the upper-floor apartments for themselves upon marrying, rather than moving out, and reminded Leuk and me that we were expected to do the same.

The tailor fussed over a few final details. Then he nodded to Ah-Tseng, who left and brought my mother in. She looked me over and her eyes misted as she touched my cheek. I hated the uniform and it probably showed. I doubt she took much notice of the tailoring itself. Then she cleared her throat self-consciously, whispered something to Ah-Tseng, and left quickly. The tailor, a red-faced man with short white hair like a boot brush, bowed ostentatiously to her back.

Ah-Tseng handed the tailor an envelope of money as I fought my way out of the stiff woollen outfit. The tailor's apprentice, a boy of no more than twelve, helped me. During the fittings his main job had been simply to hold up a large portable mirror that he carried in on his back. I noticed each time how his hands were covered in cuts and bruises.

After folding up my uniform, the apprentice began to put away the tailor's kit and the tall mirror in its bamboo frame. He held the mirror with one hand while he fished a long leather strap out of his pocket, which I assumed was used for carrying it.

"Don't do that inside!" the tailor snapped, and he struck the apprentice on the side of his head. The tailor nodded at me and they left. I followed and watched them go down the front steps of the house to Wong Nai Chung Road. Once there, the apprentice took the strap and rigged the mirror onto his back with the reflective side facing outward. Then they hurried down the street, the tailor carrying in his hand his bag of tools and the apprentice on his back the reflection of clouds and airplanes.

Our father rarely involved himself in our lives, with the exception of getting us admitted to school. Leuk was the last son whose admission he'd overseen, and in my case the task fell to my mother. Over the past year I had caught glimpses of her struggling to master the forms. Of course, it was a given that I would be let in, but she was unable to handle the details of paperwork without help. The headmaster sent his wife to our house to assist her, and I sat beside my mother while she asked Mrs. Lo questions about the school, something she knew little about despite having three sons living there. She grew especially unsure of herself at all the talk of uniforms and rituals, of cricket, of the mysteries of boiled puddings for dessert. In later years I understood that it was my father alone who straddled the two worlds of the British and the Chinese. Without him, and with his business held in trust and her older sons away at school, my mother felt herself little more than a village girl thrust out among strangers, and the strain of maintaining face in this unbuffered world was slowly wearing away her confidence.

I left for school on a Monday morning in late August. Leuk had left a day earlier, while I got to have an extra day at home with my mother and Wei-Ming. At the front doors, my mother wept openly as I put my jacket on and Chow loaded my bags. Now I was in the car, wearing my uniform and holding a bag of plums Ah-Ming had given me. Chow's neat black driver's cap floated over the headrest. I alternated between looking out the window and watching my feet dangle over the seat.

I asked Chow if the school was far from our house. He said that no, it wasn't that far, but since I was going to board there, it didn't matter. He said all I needed to do was pay attention to the teachers and respect them, and to behave well. It was a very hot day and the windows were rolled down, and as the car sped along, I smelled flowers, rotting garbage, and now and then the scent of the harbour. We climbed a hill up Stubbs Road. We moved out of a neighbourhood of apartments and houses and onto a road bordered by high walls hung with vegetation. There were few pedestrians, and the thick, soft walls of vines and trees around us seemed to dampen the engine's sound.

The world seemed very bright and close. Ah-Ming had ironed a sharp crease into my shorts and I was wearing new shoes. The jacket didn't feel too hot. My mother had told me I must wear it so that I would step out of the car properly dressed, but I had other worries.

Chow drove through the broad gates of the Diocesan Boys' School. The car passed from the silent pavement to the soft crunch of fine gravel, up a drive that led to a large white building. I stepped out of the car and noticed a yellow-winged bird jumping around the base of a bush beside the front steps. There was a sign with the school's name over the entrance in Chinese and English. As I was sounding it out, Chow put my bags down beside me, and I turned to look up into his face. My hand was in my pocket and I fidgeted, then pulled it out impulsively. As I did so, I realized I was about to offer it to him to hold, and stopped myself. I adjusted my clothes awkwardly, then put my hand back in my pocket. I realized I'd forgotten to ask my mother when her first visit would be.

I took my hand out again and held both arms stiffly at my sides and looked straight ahead at the school's front doors. A minute passed in silence, during which neither Chow nor I spoke, and I felt heat climbing my scalp and neck in the late summer morning. The school entrance was flanked by ornamental bushes with an unfamiliar scent, mingling with the smell of dry gravel dust. I thought to steal another glance at Chow to see if he was watching me, if there was something I should do next, but then the doors opened. Mr. Lo, the headmaster, came down the front steps to greet me. He wore a suit the colour of wet limestone and his glasses caught the sun.

I moved into my current flat six years ago, in early 2009, just before my eightieth birthday. The evening I arrived in Malaysia from the United States, it was monsoon season in Kuala Lumpur, and as the plane landed, I looked out the window and saw the smeared image of a city drenched in weeks of heavy rain.

My daughter, Evelyn, picked this flat for me. It was sparely furnished, as I had requested, and I brought only a few things with me on the long flight over. Preparing for the move was more work than I'd first expected; the sorting of accumulations is a bit of a cliché for old people, but it's true. In the end I don't know what moved me to keep some things and discard others. Giving things away to friends and neighbours, in the belief they might be of interest, seemed more like an eccentric form of littering than preparation for a different life, and so the garbage bags filled quickly. When my daughter greeted me at the airport, I did indeed feel lighter, though that's a sensation one shouldn't overthink in old age.

It had been nine years since my wife Alice died, after her long illness, and though I'd adapted to living alone, I never quite overcame the feeling of living an uncentred life. For the first few years of her disease, when her hospital stays were mostly acute and she was able to travel and live her life in between, I approached her illness as a problem for us to overcome. But in the second stage it was less clear what was happening to her and why, and her illness exacted a more severe toll than we had expected. She changed. The disease merged with the woman who was my wife, altered her personality, and try as I might, I could see her only as a sick person. I felt pity, and resented feeling it. Leaving our old house, which felt changed, even invaded, was a relief after a decade of illness and another of solitude.

When Evelyn brought me up to the new flat, I looked around and appreciated its plainness and large windows, though the smells were what I noticed first. The building was then newly finished; all the way from the entrance the scents of paint and sawdust had trailed us in a growing eddy, and the chalky odour of cut stone and the last ghosts of wood polish and sealants followed me into the flat. My daughter had stopped by earlier to open a few windows, so that when we entered the flat I was struck by the rain-crisped atmosphere of all these fading residues. It must have been that scent, of freshness and the ancient sea-damp of my childhood, that impressed on me that this was the first place in my life where I would live alone.

A feeling of unease seized me at that moment, and to shake it off I walked over to the windows overlooking the park. The sky, bound in stony clouds across the landscape, surrendered endless rain onto the city, painting the roads and sidewalks in a dark gleam. I let the initial stab of loneliness pass and turned to help Evelyn direct the movers.

I had returned, if not to my old city, then at least to its corner of the world. To be close to Evelyn was good for both of us, though I knew we wouldn't have agreed to this had it not been, like a pianist's flourish, a gesture in service of the end. I didn't want to see this reunion as a portent of decline, even though that was what it was. Looking at Evelyn as she fussed over my things, I knew I should feel joy. Over the years I've known events in my life that others would envy: travelling the world, getting into medical school, marriage, children, a rewarding if truncated career. But too often I found myself unable to feel true happiness, only a sense of troubled relief, as though I were continually avoiding disaster. Only once, a long time ago, did I really feel that deep illumination, a great burst of happiness when I found someone I'd yearned for.

For years I told myself I should sit down and write a memoir of my mother, and a couple of times I went as far as to type a title at the top of a page, which I underlined decisively. I felt a desire, sometimes even a compulsion, to release a portion of myself, to set it outside myself. I thought I had to do this in order to be legitimate to others, even to confirm to myself that I was real. But I made little progress with the memoir, and in the cleanup for the move from Chicago I finally put the idea aside for good. As time goes by, I feel this failure lighten, knowing how little we can truly transcribe of what resides inside us.

Evelyn stood next to me at the window. Despite the heavy rain, she pointed out the nearby gardens where I could walk, a mall with restaurants, an Anglican church. I watched her finger draw a circle over the glass, tracing and retracing as though to reassure me with the smallness of its scope.

THREE

September 1941

I was now twelve and about to start my sixth year at Diocesan. My first months there in 1936 were marked by the pain of separation from my mother. I had no idea then that my misery was shared by the other first-year students. The intense routine at the school, and its many rituals of belonging, compelled us to talk and think about things other than our sadness. So I adapted as I had to. I learned that fear is made worse by thinking, and that survival often requires no thought at all.

We were one month into the 1941 school year. Each fall, after the holidays, the return to routine was like the snapping of a flag, sharper and sharper each September, so that it took ever fewer days for us to regain the persona of the student boarder who sang the school's official songs and rose in unison for its teachers. This time the transition was almost instantaneous, as though my summer break had been only a performance of some loud-mouthed youth who also carried my name and image. I was ready for the year.

Three large buildings made up most of the school: the dormitory, where three hundred boys ate and slept, the huge central building with the classrooms and theatres, and the residence at the far end where the headmaster and some of the teachers lived and where parents were sometimes received. These were surrounded by lawns, gardens, and an athletic track.

Sometimes, after class or in the evenings, Leuk and I met by a huge, ancient banyan tree at the edge of the property. We would sit or stand beneath the curtains of hanging roots, talking, speculating, testing each other with questions that neither of us could have answered. We talked about movies we would see or about snacks in the market and what food we missed most from Ah-Ming's kitchen. We talked about all the things we missed from home, but not about the centre of that world, our mother, whom we missed most of all.

Early in October, Mr. Lo called us into his office to tell us that our mother was coming to visit us in a couple of weeks. I was thrilled to hear it, though disappointed that it wouldn't be a weekend home. I met Leuk out at the banyan tree and we talked about her visit. We were almost desperate to impress her with things we had each made but were mindful of not doing anything too similar. Finally we agreed that Leuk would finish a painting he was working on, and I would show her my best effort in calligraphy.

One evening that week, I went to the teachers' library. The housekeeper said none of the teachers was using the library at the moment, and I could go in if I was quick. I found the volume on calligraphy that I needed and put it in my bag.

Outside the library, I heard agitated voices. I looked down the long hallway to the teachers' parlour, and in the yellow light I saw several of the teachers gathering close around the radio. Some looked right at it while others sat with their heads bowed in concentration. An older teacher, Mr. Yuen, held a book between the palms of both hands, worrying the page corners with his thumb. I couldn't make out much of what the radio announcer was saying, something about Japan and its emperor, Hirohito, and about the Nationalist government in China. At the mention of the Nationalists, Mr. Yuen looked up and smoothed his white hair back nervously, and then he leaned over and whispered to the teacher next to him. I heard war mentioned several times. Then the announcer mentioned Singapore.

"How can they abandon Singapore?" a teacher shouted, and the others hushed him angrily while Mr. Yuen reached over and turned the volume up. The previous week, two boys in my school had left suddenly for Singapore with their families.

Afraid of being caught, I returned to the dormitory.

We had all been hearing fragmentary talk of war by then, but until that night it had sounded only at the periphery of our days, like a far-off noise or an argument overheard through an open window. War appeared on the screens at movie theatres, during the newsreels about Europe, when we were busy talking and throwing peanut shells at each other. War was a word, another subject, tossed out by the same adult sphere that assigned homework, wrote Sunday sermons, and gossiped in the market.

In the past two weeks, though, something had begun to shift. Five boys' parents had come for unexpected visits, and within a day or two the parents had taken their sons from the school with all their belongings. Mr. Lo had been present at each departure, seeing the boy off with a lingering handshake, and at times I had seen him later in the halls on such days, wandering pensively or looking out over the grounds. I asked Leuk what he knew about these boys leaving, but he had no idea.

It was Sunday, October 19, the day my mother came to visit. I still recall the calendar posted at the far end of the dormitory over the sink, with all the Sundays in bright red. Every time I went to wash my hands or face, I looked at it and counted the days to her visit. On Wednesday evenings after supper, every boy in the school had to write his mother a letter in the dining hall, and these were delivered the following day. My letter the Wednesday before her visit had been a little longer than usual, and I had asked, with the mixture of formality and yearning that this ritual inspired, for a few extra items.

"Mother, could you please bring with you some sweets, but not too many as the headmaster doesn't allow them to be hoarded, but I need a few extra to give to my prefect. I also need socks and if Leuk hasn't asked you he needs some too. I greatly look forward to your visit. Can you also bring something to read because I'm bored? Your son."

The old Daimler gleamed as it pulled through the gates, up the gravel drive to the steps, where Leuk and I stood with Mr. Lo. He stepped forward first to greet our mother. Chow got out quickly to open the passenger door and our mother stepped out onto the gravel. I still remember the emerald green of her dress and her jacket of white silk running with embroidered willow branches. She beamed when she saw us. We ran past the headmaster to her, and as Leuk and I embraced her, I felt our arms cross over the ermine stole around her neck, her sole concession to Western fashion. The fur pressed into my cheek, and I smelled her perfume as she murmured words only my brother and I could hear. Chow ran around to the back of the car and lifted packages out of the boot.

Mr. Lo accompanied us into the parlour. It was an ornate and stuffy room, a mixture of European and Chinese furniture sinking into thick Persian rugs. A low coal fire burned in the brazier, and a photo of the missionary Robert Morrison hung on the wall, next to a much larger photo of King George. My mother settled herself into a sofa just beneath these images and passed each of us a small box wrapped in brown paper. Her eyes shone as we took them, and she pursed her lips.

We sat with the boxes on our laps, waiting to be told that we could open them. My mother looked at us for a moment with a smile, and yet I felt a slight disquiet, sensing that she was both happy and worried as she nodded at the boxes.

"Go ahead. After you open them, I only want to hear about school."

After we opened our packages and thanked her for bringing what we'd requested, she asked us about our schooling. Leuk brought out his painting, of three carp swimming in a pond in which the branches of a willow were reflected. I brought out my scroll and handed it to her excitedly. She was delighted with our work and pored over each one.

She told us about our older brothers and how well they were doing with the firm and asked us more about school. She seemed happy, almost relieved, to talk about our education and the good grades we'd earned. She talked also about Yee-Lin, the young woman Sheung had married that summer, and how pleased she was with her. Wei-Ming, who was now seven, had just started at a school nearby.

Though I was glad to see her, throughout the visit a question gnawed at me. I thought of the boys who'd left abruptly in recent weeks and worried she had come to take us home, or might soon.

I remember being conscious of every moment of her visit, fearing it was a prelude to our leaving the school. I had no idea where those other boys had gone, or what had become of them. School was where we surely belonged, and to be apart from our parents for a time, even our entire families, was a necessity of life. There was a time to separate; somehow I knew this, from my arrival here five years earlier, from the way we were induced to bond like little tribes, or from our growing lack of interest in writing home to our mothers. There had been nights when I wondered if the true purpose of our school was to break us from our families, and I felt shame at my enjoyment of my life here, even though I missed my mother terribly at times. But who were they, these women who lived in service to their own inarticulate power of love, to take us back when we were not yet men? I thought of being taken away while the other boys went on learning and bonding, studying the secrets of manhood. And if I were suddenly taken home, I knew I'd be both happy to be with my mother yet dangerously incomplete.

I was sorry the whole visit was taking place in the parlour. Everything else in our lives at school was somewhere else — the classroom, the theatre, the field, the painting studio — but I hadn't planned on showing our mother around. We ate lunch there and she talked a little more about Wei-Ming's school. At the end of the visit we walked outside, where Chow was waiting with the passenger door already open.

On the gravel drive, she put her hand on Leuk's shoulder and gave each of us a kiss. As she leaned over, I threw my arms around her and felt tears prick my eyes. When I did that, she moved her hand and brushed her fingers slowly over the clipped hairs on the back of my neck. My mother stood up again and I looked at her face.

"Over there!" I said. I pointed at the banyan tree in the far corner of the field. "Do you know what that is?" I asked.

"What is it?"

"It's where Leuk and I go to talk almost every day. Almost no one goes there. That's where Leuk told me you were coming to see us."

She glanced briefly at the tree. "Then I'm glad I came." She kissed me. "I'll be back before Christmas."

Mr. Lo was back and my mother returned his bow as he said goodbye. She stepped quickly into the car, and Chow got in and turned it around. I had been excited to tell my mother about the tree, to be outside in the sun again with her. It seemed she had just arrived. In the clear afternoon light, I imagined the parlour as a sombre box, a musty playhouse decorated by fussing old maids and colonial lawmakers, crammed with cold and over-polished wood. I thought that if I could only show her my scroll again, here in the sunlight, it would look better. But when the passenger door shut and I saw her face filtered through the greenish glass, tears welled up in my eyes, and I fisted my hands and held them tight against my sides. Leuk turned to look at me for a moment, as though he, being one year older, could surrender a few seconds of looking at our mother when I could not, and took my hand.

"Christmas," he repeated. "And who knows, she may come back even sooner."

When the car was out of sight, we headed back to the dormitory. I could smell autumn in the air again, blowing over and through us, washing out the scent of the parlour.

There was a reunion of my old class at Diocesan in August 1997. The joke among us was that it was the fiftieth anniversary of the year we *ought* to have graduated, not when we actually did. Of the original twenty-five graduates in our class, eighteen made it to the reunion, but the discussions about who was missing and why were strangely brief the first evening. Alice was doing better and could travel again, and I watched her mingle with the other wives. There was really only one she knew well, but she was at ease the whole evening. It was the first real break she'd had since her last stay at the hospital.

Of the seven former students who didn't attend, two we knew to be dead, one sent his regrets, and four others never responded. As might be expected of a group of men approaching seventy, we had difficulty keeping track of who had died and who was merely absent. One of these was Wing Kwok, who had gone on to become a teacher at Diocesan. He had retired ten years earlier and no one had heard from him since. Two of the school's current senior students joined us the first evening, but even they had only heard his name.

The two students and the current headmaster, Dr. Pak, gave us a tour of the school. Sometime after the war, new facilities had been put up and the old dormitory converted into classrooms. We walked through them, and I recognized the building from within only because of the entrance and the view from the windows. The entrance still had a distinct smell, not unpleasant, that I used to notice on my clothes when I went home on holidays, a mix of institutional laundry soap and resin, what I think of as the smell of echoing hallways. The grounds seemed much smaller than I had remembered them, and the old banyan tree was gone.

Vincent Lim, one of our group who helped organize the reunion, had surprised us all on the second day by giving us new blazers with the school crest on them. He and his wife handed them out and insisted we wear them. Alice gamely carried my jacket. I looked ridiculous in the blazer, as did most of my old friends. Stumbling into a lineup for a commemorative photograph, we looked like the inmates of some institution that used costumes as therapy, and I and a few others were quick to use the heat as an excuse to remove them by mid-morning.

Over lunch that day, in a Hunan-style restaurant at

a shopping mall, the conversation turned back to Wing Kwok. Despite returning to the school a mere five years after graduation and having taught physics there for over three decades, he had kept a low profile among alumni. His retirement was known to only a few of us, thanks to a brief notice in the school bulletin. My memories of him were shadowy: a reserved, gangly youth, the son of a senior police officer who was shot in the early days of the occupation. It was said that the school waived his tuition after the war because of this, though he tried to conceal it. A few others recalled how he had excelled in science and won the physics and math prizes two or three times. Someone said we should go check the honour roll boards in the main hall, but no one could remember where they were or if they had been moved during the renovations.

Vincent Lim drank heavily during the lunch. He kept his school blazer on and sweated despite the blasting air conditioner. He became sentimental and talked about "the missing boys," a phrase that seemed ever more grotesque as he flushed from the brandy and his lank grey hair stuck to his forehead. He ate rapidly and twice his wife discreetly touched his sleeve to get him to settle down.

Another classmate remembered an old rumour that Wing Kwok's mother was half Japanese on her mother's side and her father was a merchant who exported to Japan.

You know, said Vincent, I think I met her once when I went to the Kwoks' home. She had a little of that rounded face that Japanese women have. She was very quiet.

Who knows, said David Chen. David was sitting next to Vincent. The owner of a large factory, he was a driven and pragmatic man with no interest in reminiscence. He reached over with his chopsticks and picked up a choice piece of goose from right in front of Vincent.

A petty argument erupted between them, with Vincent defending the importance of remembering the old boys and David replying that he was just here to enjoy himself with his friends. Our misery is behind us, he said bluntly.

Everyone else had grown quiet. The tables around us were noisy, but our utensils clinked awkwardly as we picked away at the last of the lunch. We settled the bill quickly and went back to the school. As soon as Alice and I walked back into the main hall, where a display had been put up for our reunion, I inhaled deeply and took in that familiar odour of polish and camphor.

Even now, eighteen years later, I sometimes notice one of those old school scents in something, like a storage trunk full of old clothing, and I can almost see the light slanting through the windows of the dormitory or the dining hall. In the last months of my life, the world outside seems to be nothing more than a jumble of clues, too many to make sense of—street food, garbage, gardens, exhaust, a kitchen, a forest, clothes dried after soaking in river water, and dried blood.

FOUR

December 8, 1941

Nearly two months passed before the next part of my story, though what happened in those months I barely remember. There was a school play, maybe, and I have some recollection of failing a test. But I may be inventing that. When it comes to that period, I feel as though my mind is a cracked pot that has sat in a corner dripping water. A fog seems to have descended on the period just after my mother's visit, just as one can vividly recall a nightmare but not the moment of falling asleep.

During the first morning class on the eighth of December, there was a sudden commotion. The teacher, Mr. Lee, was late, and in the hall two other teachers ran from room to room, shouting at the students to get out. I was folding a paper airplane against the wall and thinking I would throw it out the window before Mr. Lee arrived, when Mr. Lo burst into the classroom.

"Go back to the dormitory!" He waved us out into the hall as I hid the airplane behind my back.

"Go back and pack your bags quickly and bring them out to the main entrance. You're all going home. If your families don't come to get you this morning, someone from the school will drive you."

We swarmed around him and asked what was wrong. Our delay seemed to terrify him.

"Do as I said!" he shouted. He sounded angry, but looked pale and under-slept. "All of you, get your bags. If you see other boys in the building, tell them the same."

I needed to find Leuk. I searched up and down the hallway and in every classroom. Other boys were racing past me to the dormitory, where I should have been by now.

As I was leaving for the dormitory, I ran into Mr. Lee.

"Chung-Man, what are you doing? Go get your things!"

"I can't find Leuk," I said. The students in the hallway were confused, some of the younger boys were crying, and the senior students were racing them back to the dormitory.

Mr. Lee fixed his eyes on me and took me by the shoulder. "He's here and he's heard the message. Don't worry, just get your things."

I hesitated again and looked past him down the hall. Then he shouted at me to go. I dropped the paper airplane and ran to the dormitory.

It didn't take me long to shove all my things into my suitcase. But the stairs were already congested. Boys raced up and down, hauling luggage or running back upstairs to get it, looking for friends or brothers. One boy looked out the window and shouted that he saw cars pulling into the drive.

"Hey, I think your dad is here!" His friend ran over to see, and then other boys crowded around the windows.

"Get away from there!" Mr. Lee's face ran with sweat in

the overcast daylight. "If you're ready, just go. Don't worry about your belongings."

And then it seemed every boy on the floor was panicking down the staircase, unbalanced and clumsy with suitcases and rucksacks. Someone grabbed me by the collar. It was Leuk, and he nodded at me, panting. Between us stood a younger boy of about seven who was holding his hand.

"Meet me at the entrance," he said and ran downstairs with the boy at his side.

When I got outside, there were already a dozen cars lined up at the entrance, none of them ours. Leuk ran ahead of me with the boy still gripping his hand. He turned to the boy.

"Do you see your parents or your car?"

"I don't know." He started to cry.

"Where's your teacher?" said Leuk.

The boy looked around and pointed to a man near the gates with several other younger boys lined up beside him. Leuk ran over with the boy and talked to the teacher. The teacher shook his head and pointed somewhere towards the school. Leuk said something and the teacher repeated the gesture, and Leuk started walking back towards me, still with the boy. He was wailing now, clutching his backpack and pulling on Leuk's arm as if he were ringing a bell. I stared at the boy.

"Who is he?"

Leuk got angry at me. "I don't know. I found him in the dormitory on the main floor, and he asked me to help him carry his bag."

I asked the boy what his name was, but he was crying so hard I couldn't understand him. His jacket was too big for him, and his right sleeve was laced with fresh snot. I forgot for a moment that I also had no idea what was happening. Cars kept piling into the driveway even as others raced out the gates. Then the sound of an explosion roared over the school grounds. It rolled upward from the harbour. The trees around me erupted with sparrows fleeing northward.

Adults who had been walking children to their cars now ran with them over the gravel towards the vehicles. The boys still inside threw their suitcases out the dormitory windows, and I thought with horror of the crush on the staircase. I looked away from the school doors. A car pulled up close to us, and a woman dressed as a maid or governess stepped out of it. She shouted at us. The boy cried out and ran towards her, his backpack swinging from his arm. Leuk ran with him. The woman grabbed the suitcase from my brother, threw it into the back seat, and helped the boy in. The last I saw of them was the woman leaning over and struggling with the handle as the driver swung the car over the gravel towards the gates.

I stood next to Leuk and watched the cars come and go. "Is Chow coming?"

More blasts tore through the air, and planes droned somewhere, far away but coming closer. We stared at the gates. Air sirens began to blare, rising and falling out of time with each other.

What I learned later was that Chow had left the house as soon as the radio announced news of the invasion. He had asked my mother which school to go to first; Wei-Ming was at the one across the valley from ours. Much later he told me he decided to get her first because he knew how brave the boys would be. When I asked my mother, she always looked away and said she didn't remember everything about that day. Nobody ever told the same story. Perhaps no one remembered.

Fewer cars were arriving now, and only a small group of boys were left. Leuk and I stood with our bags and watched the gate and road. Nobody could tell us what was happening, and I began to think no one would come for us. My skin felt as though it had been immersed in freezing water. I looked at my brother and saw the same thing in his face.

Mr. Lee asked us if our car was coming.

"I don't know," said Leuk.

"It's too late. I'll take you both. The trams are still running." He picked up my suitcase and ran with us to the gates. The school was in a normally quiet part of the neighborhood. Now I heard cars tearing down the streets, their tires screaming wildly against the slow, resigned chanting of the sirens.

We ran down the pavement to the tram stop on the main road. I was sweating and my backpack straps were pulling my jacket down. Mr. Lee was ahead of us and kept looking back to make sure we weren't falling behind. Leuk turned to me and took my hand, pulling me down the slope.

We stood at the stop and waited as if we were going to the races, and I thought we must look absurd standing patiently while the tram stuck to its route. Mr. Lee looked at his watch.

"It comes every five minutes at this time of day. It should be here soon."

A massive boom rolled over us from the harbour. Someone screamed in a nearby house, and planes droned louder in the distance. Machine guns fired somewhere far off, in long, explosive bursts like cracks tearing open in the earth.

Mr. Lee was pale and wiped his brow with a trembling hand. Just up the road, the tram bell rang lightly. He took some coins from his pocket and picked up our suitcases.

The tram arrived, moving pathetically at its usual steady pace. The driver waved us in while the few other passengers on board watched us anxiously. As the tram trundled down the hill, I watched the trees and buildings pass as I always had. I wanted to tell the driver to hurry up, to tell him we had to get home to our mother. But when I looked at him, he was sweating profusely at the wheel, a look of terror on his face. On the top of a nearby hill, I noticed one of the air-raid sirens, a spindly wooden tower dwarfed by the surrounding trees.

Mr. Lee stayed with us all the way to our stop. Leuk and I shouted our thanks to him and leapt off the tram steps onto the sidewalk. I caught a last glimpse of my teacher through the dirty glass, wiping his brow as the tram rattled forward. We ran up the street and found the gates open, and my mother waiting fearfully at the door.

Wei-Ming was already home. Once we were inside, my mother shut the doors. The house itself was silent as a tomb, and the noise from outside echoed through the halls. Warplanes roared overhead, and I listened to heavy trucks and police cars tearing over the streets. Leuk, Wei-Ming, and I stood close to our mother, motionless at the foot of the stairs.

Higher up the hill, from a wooden tower pinioned to the rock, a siren cast its long, declining cry across the valley.

FIVE

Warships had been closing in on Hong Kong since late November, and lone airplanes had flown over the harbour in the evenings. First they flew very high and were unmarked, but from late November into December they had begun coming lower and displayed the Japanese insignia. The British had reinforced their troops throughout Hong Kong, preparing for an onslaught from both the sea and the mainland. But until the attack on the eighth, everyone still went to work and walked to the market, old men sitting at their tables with teacups and birdcages while their wives chatted. No one seemed to be concerned. It seems to me that people wandered through the days plunged into a thick syrup, complaining about the price of goods or the noise of trucks in the street, gossiping, their mouths and eyes and every other orifice filling up with the cloying ordinariness of life as though wanting to be buried in it.

War is a hammer in its opening act. The invader brings it down and everyone is stunned to see buildings fall, roads blown open to expose the primitive earth beneath their feet. It's as if people don't believe their world can be destroyed.

In the second act, a strange, corrupted underlay of normalcy emerges from the broken world. The trees and wind still smell the same, there's no change in the weather or birdsong. Then suddenly, even when things seem peaceful, the smell of scorched buildings or rotting flesh blows in. Guns fire randomly near and far. Shots ring out and there's no reply, no ambulance siren, no firing back.

Sometime early in the second act, a few days after our return from school, we were sitting down to the midday meal. My mother was at the head of the table. Sheung was there, but Tang was at the factory, and Yee-Lin was sitting across from Sheung. I was in my usual spot between Leuk and Wei-Ming. The doorbell rang and we froze. Everyone looked at Sheung to get up. He adjusted his seat awkwardly, letting it scrape against the floor. Then Chow ran out of the kitchen. Since the invasion, the servants had taken to eating together in the kitchen at the same time as we ate. He was carrying a flashlight because we had pulled all the curtains shut. In his right hand he held the gun he kept with him at all times now, and he strode to the entrance as Sheung settled back down in his chair.

When Chow returned, the gun was tucked safely in his belt. "Mrs. Leung, there is a family outside asking a favour."

"Who is it?"

"The Yee family, ma'am. The father was with Mr. Leung's bank."

My mother and Sheung looked confused. Embarrassed now that he hadn't gone to the door, Sheung rose. "What do they want?"

Chow glanced hastily at my mother. "They want to live here."

Leuk, Wei-Ming, and I turned to our mother. Sheung started to object, but my mother stood and walked out of the dining room with Chow. They returned with a family behind them, a woman, two girls, and a boy.

Mrs. Yee stopped near the head of the table. With porcelain-white fingers she brushed a stray lock from her reddened eyes and nervously smoothed her skirt. The three bewildered children with their dusty rucksacks trailed her like the attendants of an exiled queen. As she met our eyes, she looked ashamed and pulled her children close. I knew the boy, Shun-Yau, who was a year behind me at my school. I looked at him, but when he recognized me, he frowned and stared at the floor.

My mother remained standing. Sheung rose from his chair.

"Everyone," said my mother. "Please welcome Mrs. Yee. She and her children will be staying with us."

She asked Ah-Tseng to set four more places at the table. We all said hello and Mrs. Yee told her children to introduce themselves. The girls were Shun-Lai, who was sixteen, and Shun-Po, thirteen, then Shun-Yau. He and Shun-Po nodded nervously.

"Thank you for your generosity," said Mrs. Yee. Chow and Ah-Tseng took the family's bags upstairs. Mrs. Yee bowed and left quickly with the children to find their rooms.

"Her husband is the manager at the bank where we do all our business," said Sheung.

"Mr. Yee is dead," said my mother, looking down at her plate. Leuk clattered his spoon in his bowl. "He was shot three days ago. The Japanese have taken their house and car. They walked here from Wan Chai with just their suitcases."

I looked up at the wall where a photo of my father hung, still wrapped in black crepe. Ah-Tseng laid out four settings at the end of the table near the large windows, where I was sitting. She put one of the settings next to me, and as she set the last dish down, she leaned over and spoke quietly to me.

"The little boy can sit next to you, Chung-Man."

The thought of it made me sick.

Mrs. Yee and her children returned. She tapped her shoes delicately over the marble as though to escape notice.

"Please sit," said my mother. Yee-Lin got up and spoke to the two girls, trying to reassure them. She rested her hands on Shun-Po's shoulders for a moment, as the girl's eyes darted nervously between her dishes and her mother, and then she returned to her seat.

The Yees sat at the end of the table, with Shun-Yau between me and his mother. He perched on the stool several inches too far from the table, his hands tucked under his legs, and stared at his knees. Mrs. Yee and the girls pulled themselves in. She looked at her son for a moment. Her eyes darted nervously around the table, always back to my mother and Sheung. Finally she leaned over and touched Shun-Yau's sleeve.

"Please sit properly," she whispered. Shun-Yau didn't move. I stared at the fish on my plate. "Please." Shun-Lai and Shun-Po sat upright in their chairs with their hands folded in their laps.

"Girls, please eat," said my mother. "Leuk, pass them some vegetables." He reached over for a plate of cabbage and passed it to Shun-Lai, who took it with a whispered thanks. My mother called Ah-Tseng back and asked her to prepare an extra dish of vegetables. Yee-Lin got up again and poured tea for Mrs. Yee, whose eyes were fixed on her son.

"*Shun-Yau.*" Mrs. Yee leaned towards him. Her eyes jumped back and forth between him and my mother, who looked down at her bowl and said a few trivial words to Yee-Lin.

Mrs. Yee bit her lip. She reached over again with a trembling hand. Shun-Yau stared at his knees, glowering. His face had gone red as blood.

"Please sit properly," she said. "And eat." Then she touched his arm again. He jerked violently and her fingers flew from his jacket. Shun-Yau's eyes rimmed with water and he blinked hard several times. Across the table, Shun-Po coughed weakly. Her head was bowed over her rice bowl so that her hair partly concealed her face.

Shun-Yau made a few quick noises in his throat, bowing his head deeper until his chin was nearly on his chest. He made a low groan as though he was about to vomit. Mrs. Yee put her hands on the edge of the table and leaned over again.

"Shun-Yau. You must sit like everyone else." He held his breath and looked up, daring us to look into his red-rimmed eyes. Then he pulled his stool up to the table.

Mrs. Yee watched him for a moment, but when their eyes met, she looked away to her dish. I reached over and picked up a plate of fish and set it before the Yees. Mrs. Yee took some, and I offered it to Shun-Yau. He hesitated for a moment before pulling the dish towards his bowl. In it lay thin steaks of halibut, brown and crispy in salt, and with the large spinal bone still in the flesh, the way it was always served.

Mr. Yee, who would never sit at our table, had been wealthy and well-connected like my father. But unlike my father, he died in the street, watching the Japanese throw his family from their house at gunpoint. He had seen his children's faces as an officer pointed a revolver at his temple. He was buried without ceremony, maybe in one of the smoking corpse heaps I'd heard my brothers whispering about one evening.

Two days later, the doorbell rang again. I was in the library with Leuk and Shun-Lai. I had invited Shun-Yau, but Shun-Lai told me he never left his room except for meals. I ran into the hall, where I found Chow and Sheung by the door. Sheung shouted, "Who is it?" through the door, and a woman replied. Chow tucked the gun back in his belt and opened the door, just as my mother came down the stairs.

I recognized Mrs. Wong from the neighbourhood. She and her husband owned a large jewellery shop and their son was the clerk. They bought gold from one of my father's factories. She had a suitcase and her daughter with her, a girl of about fifteen. Once the door was open, she pressed a handkerchief to her mouth and sobbed. My mother took Mrs. Wong's hand, and told her and her daughter to come in.

They weren't the last. As the world outside descended into violence, the house filled up. It became a place of jostling children and harried servants, of dislocated adults drifting through the halls. Wei-Ming was happy to have other children her age to play with, and I think it consoled my mother to see my sister running and laughing around the house again. I helped set up their rooms and beds, and tried to keep the other children occupied, showing them where they could study in the library. They kept me busy. But sometimes I stood back and looked at that crowd of grieving and broken families filling the halls, and their noise and clutter hammered my brain until I ached. I saw them as a second invasion, a leaderless army bearing fear as its weapon.

Despite the caution of the adults around me, I caught bits of their conversations and fragments of radio broadcasts, and throughout December I pieced together what had happened to Hong Kong. On December 8, the Japanese Imperial Army, who had invaded northeastern China several weeks earlier and were working their way south, crossed the Shenzhen River that separated the British colony from the mainland. This left them only about thirty miles north of the mainland portion of Hong Kong, and so about forty miles from where we lived on Hong

Kong Island. The Allied forces that had assembled there either succumbed or pulled back from the onslaught, and eventually the Japanese penetrated the New Territories into Hong Kong itself. Even as the Japanese moved inward on land, they had already bombed Kai Tak Airport on the eighth, weakening the British. The blasts we heard at my school that morning were the sound of the airport being shelled, the sound of a fatal blow.

I'm recounting this quickly, as if I were reading from a history book, but at the time I knew even less, and the adults around me didn't know much more. We had no idea where the fighting was or what progress the Japanese made each day. We only heard of it as one hears of a change in the weather, that a hurricane or typhoon is coming.

The truth is that one never knows enough. Looking back into the past is a lonely game of self-delusion, watching people and events move with an inevitability that never was. The history books tell everything with such certainty. But at the time, nothing seemed inevitable to me. Some things were impossible or unlikely, some things expected, but most of all, beyond the routine of daily life, the world was a mystery. We knew little until it happened.

A few days after the Wongs arrived, I found Sheung and Tang sitting in my father's study—my mother insisted we still call it that—listening to the broadcast in English. I caught something about American planes and Kai Tak Airport. My brothers spent a lot of time by the radio but rarely had anything helpful to report.

Throughout the house, people sat idly or paced the halls and rooms, busying themselves with minor tasks and conversations in our little island of ignorance. Mrs. Yee and Mrs. Wong, when they emerged from their rooms, talked only about what their children should eat and how long it would be before they resumed their studies. The three girls from these families played together but avoided my sister. Shun-Yau stayed in his room.

I got mad at Leuk one evening when he broke a model plane I had put together a couple of years earlier. I banned him from my room and refused to talk to him. But after an hour I realized that I wasn't as attached to the plane as I thought I had been. I was bored and decided I would coax Shun-Yau from his room. Trucks had been barrelling down the street all that evening, but it didn't worry me—the walls of the house and the leaded windows had a way of muffling street noise.

I went down to the second floor and stood outside Shun-Yau's room. His mother and Shun-Po were in one room, and Ah-Tseng had converted a small disused study into a space for him. I put my ear against the door, then knelt down and tried to listen under the jamb. It was a plain room without rugs and had little furniture, and sound echoed easily against the walls and marble floor. I heard pages turning and then bedsprings creaking as he shifted on his bed. I paused, and then I knocked on the door. At first he was silent.

"Mother?"

"It's me, Chung-Man. Do you want to see something?"

He didn't reply at first, and I heard a few more pages flip. The door behind me creaked on the opposite side of the hall, and I turned to see Mrs. Yee peering through the half-open door. She gave me a look of tragic, almost beggarly gratitude underlined by a weak smile, and then she retreated into her room and quietly shut the door.

"No," Shun-Yau said. I heard him shift on the bed again.

"Come on. I'm bored. There's something you should see. It's an animal."

The springs creaked again, and I was about to walk away when the door opened a few inches, framing the right side of his face.

"What is it?"

"Just come out." I drummed my fingers on the door. He opened it, showing an impressive cowlick on the right side of his head, as if he had been lying in bed all day. I nodded to him to come. He opened the door all the way and stepped out. We walked towards the stairs, and I heard his mother's door creak open as we passed.

I took him down to the cellar. To get there we had to walk down to the main floor, through the entrance hall into the dining room, and then through the kitchen to a storage room near the back of the house where the servants kept pickled vegetables, rice, dried fish, and a small icebox where the maids put fresh meat and fish every day. At the back of that room was a plain wooden door.

In the storage room by the kitchen was the sharp, pungent odour of dried seafood and fermenting vegetables. The cellar air carried a damp smell of earth and dissipated fetor, and it wafted up the stairs and mingled with the storage room odour. The cellar air was milder but not fresh. I turned the light on and told Shun-Yau to follow me down the stone stairway.

At the bottom, I hit the next switch, and we went down a short passage lined with empty containers, tools, and crates. We turned into a room lit by a single window fitted with iron bars.

In a corner near the window were three large wicker baskets, each about three feet high and fitted with tight wicker lids.

Shun-Yau blinked uncomfortably in the gloom. He looked at the window, then the baskets, and then turned back to look at the door and the passage lights.

"What's in here?" he asked.

I shrugged my shoulders. "Just those baskets."

He stared at them. "That's it?"

"Don't you want to see them?"

"Maybe."

I stood beside the first one. He started as I left his side, but he didn't follow me.

"Don't worry," I said. "Just come here." Then I pulled a small flashlight from my pocket.

Shun-Yau fidgeted and took a few steps towards me. I turned the flashlight on and loosened the basket lid. As I worked it off, a soft, shifting sound came from inside, like a hand brushing over a wall. Then the lid was free and I took it off.

"Look inside," I said and shone the flashlight down.

At first I saw only the tight weave of the wicker. Then I heard the shifting sound again, and two small yellow points gleamed back into the light: eyes. Shun-Yau caught his breath but didn't back away. I turned the flashlight to its highest power. A brownish snake, flecked with pale green, slid slowly around the bottom of the basket, flicking its tongue as it tasted the changed air.

Shun-Yau's eyes widened, and he smiled.

"Wah! Is that the only one?"

I shook my head.

"He's big!" he said. He took the flashlight and reached as far down as he could. As his hand moved closer, the snake drew up against the side of the basket and drank in the light.

"It doesn't scare you?" I asked.

"No," he said. "We have this kind in our garden all the time, but not this big. When I get back home, I'll have to catch one and grow it in a cage like you."

"It's not a pet," I said. "We buy them every November from the market and my older brothers host a big dinner in December like my father used to. When the snake butcher comes, he grabs one by the tail and cracks it like a whip to kill it. Then he takes a big knife out and *fffff*"—I ran my finger down my arm—"he slits the skin and pulls it off like a sleeve."

By now Shun-Yau had reached in with his other arm and was coaxing the reptile to taste his fingertips. The sight unnerved me, and I shuddered. Shun-Yau snickered.

"I just ate a cookie. He must like the sugar." He wiggled his fingers at the snake. "Let's see the others."

I let him keep the flashlight as I put the lid back on the basket, and he helped me loosen the next one. "I thought there'd be two in each one," I said. We worked the lid off, but there was no sound from within. Shun-Yau tilted the basket as he thrust the flashlight down.

At the bottom lay the stiff curls of two dead snakes. I caught a faint whiff of rot as Shun-Yau moved the light over them. One snake was bent in the middle, covered in bite marks. Their skin was dull and greyish.

Shun-Yau shone the light closer on the bitten snake and shook the basket a little. The bodies slid over and a few maggots crawled out of one of the wounds.

"Yuck," I said. "Let's put this back on."

We put the lid back and looked at the third basket. Shun-Yau held the lid and rocked it a little. Something slid over the bottom.

"Let's not bother," I said.

He crouched down and held the flashlight close to the bottom side of the basket.

"If they're still alive, maybe they'll see the light through the cracks," he said. He waved the light over the basket. There was no response, and I pulled on his sleeve.

"They're probably all dead. Let's go."

"What about the one that's alive?" he asked.

"Just leave it." I wanted to get out of there.

He shone the light at the bottom of the first basket and waved it back and forth. Inside, we heard the last snake move slowly across to catch the glimmer. I imagined the light piercing the wicker, like sunrise shining through the grass, and I felt sorry that this would be the snake's last memory of light.

. . .

Ah-Tseng frowned at us when we walked back through the kitchen. "Where were you? It's suppertime. Go wash your hands and sit down. Your mothers are already there."

Shun-Yau tugged my sleeve quickly before running to the bathroom. "Thanks for showing me that," he said.

After supper, I went upstairs. As I passed the second-floor landing, I noticed Shun-Yau's door was closed again. Mrs. Yee was arguing with one of her daughters in their cramped room across the hall, and I could hear them all the way up the stairs.

I went to the fifth-floor parlour at the front of the house. We rarely used this room, and most of the furniture was covered in cloth to keep the dust off. There was a set of very high windows that looked down into the front courtyard and the street, and you could see all the way to the racetrack from there.

I opened the windows into the room and was preparing to push open the shutters when I heard trucks coming down the road. I left the shutters closed and peered through the slats into the street. The Japanese still permitted the street lights at night. The moon was up on my right, but it was a thin sliver of new moon and too weak to illuminate the room.

Through the broken light of the slats, I saw three British trucks turn onto our street. The first one halted and the others braked abruptly. A soldier jumped out of the first truck's driver's seat, ran around to the back, and shouted. Five or six soldiers climbed out of the back holding rifles. The driver barked something at them. But when artillery suddenly rumbled in the distance, they all looked around and more soldiers jumped out of the third truck. A couple of them pointed up at our house. I knew they couldn't see me because I had the lights off.

The guns rumbled again. The driver barked orders, the others got back into their trucks, and the convoy raced down the street. Now the street looked again as it always had. A faint sheen of water trickled down the gutter under the street lamps, and in the silence I heard the blood in my ears, *fffft, fffft, fffft*. I shut the window. It would be a long time before I was inside that room again.

SIX

I had begun to wear my father's watch. Sheung gave it to me after cleaning out some boxes of our father's belongings. The crystal was marked with a light scratch, and I soon developed a habit of running my fingernail over it while I was thinking.

At night I took it off and put it on the bedside table. One night its ticking seemed unusually loud. I woke from a noisy dream and noticed the ticking in my ears. I put the watch on and looked at it: 4:05, December 15.

I sat up and went to the window. I lifted it and opened the shutters, and the silence ended. Before me was a new world. My window looked northward towards the mainland, and though it was dark, the city was lit up. Everywhere buildings were on fire. Trees blazed like torches, and smoke rose in red and orange columns like banners of conquest. There was no sound of fire trucks or ambulances.

Northward over the harbour, I thought the stars had lined up in rows. It was the glint of reflected moonlight on the bomber planes harrying the waterfront where the ships docked. As if acknowledging my witness, they unleashed their cargo, and I watched the bombs fall. They were far enough away that I heard their explosions only as a gentle thrumming, like fingers tapping on my door.

The heavy gunfire came closer. It was the first time I heard it unfiltered by the walls of the house, and with every blast I imagined a building collapsing under its force. My hands and scalp went cold. I closed the shutters and ran into the hall, where I found Tang.

"They must have crossed the harbour," he said.

That meant the mainland was lost and the British were cornered on the island. I asked him what we should do. He turned away and ran down the stairs to the main floor.

I followed him and found my mother already at the doors with Chow and Ah-Tseng. I ran to my mother and she looked at me and took my hand.

"Where are Leuk and Wei-Ming?"

Another blast shook the air and a tall porcelain vase rattled on its wooden stand. Chow turned the heavy bolt on the door. Other families came downstairs now, including the Yees. Leuk came down with Wei-Ming and she ran to my mother.

Chow looked out each window and gestured for us to keep away. "There's nothing we can do. Just wait inside."

Another blast went off and there was a low roar of something large collapsing. Mrs. Yee covered her face and began to wail.

"Mrs. Yee, please return to your room," said my mother. She pitied Mrs. Yee and looked anxiously at her three children. She spoke impatiently to the elder daughter. "Shun-Lai, take your mother and siblings back upstairs. You are safe while you stay in the house."

Shun-Lai took her mother by the arm and walked her upstairs with her sister. Shun-Yau wanted to stay with us, but his sister ordered him up.

We quickly brought more chairs into the front hall and sat close to each other and listened to the fighting. Sheung had the radio on in the parlour with the volume at its highest, but Yee-Lin was so terrified she begged him to stay with her in the front hall. He held her close on a sofa while she sobbed. The air trembled around the house, blasting the walls in louder and louder waves. And we sat. The blasts drew closer and we didn't move. Wei-Ming was on my mother's lap with her thumb in her mouth and a doll in her other hand.

Then the blasts began to move away, and a minute later they were far off again, less frequent. The receding blasts were replaced by screams outside. Women, men, children, their voices separate or rising together. They called out names, cried for help, screamed that they were burned. It was worse than the bombing. I covered my ears and rubbed them with my palms to keep the sound out. And I listened to myself sob. My mother reached over to hold me and said my name, and I uncovered my ears so I could hear her voice.

Everyone in the house was now gathered in the front hall, and as the screaming raked the air, we sat or stood in silence and stared at the floor. I listened to the rapid, shallow breathing of a man next to me who clutched his daughter's hands. None of us dared to part the curtains and look out the windows, and I knew what everyone was thinking: that a face might appear in one of them — torn or blackened, distorted with pain.

From the radio in the parlour down the hall, we heard only odd cracklings of Japanese as Tang tested the dial.

. . .

I woke with a start to hear the front door almost cracking in two. Someone was pounding hard on it. Wei-Ming was still asleep on our mother's lap. Chow rose; he had been sleeping on a mat in front of the door, with his revolver tucked into the back of his belt. He stood warily by the door and motioned for us all to stay quiet. The person outside pounded the door again, and then a man shouted that he was a British soldier, demanding to be let in. Sheung ran up and shouted back.

"What do you want?"

"Let us in."

"I can't."

Then several men shouted back at him, and they pounded against the door with something hard, like a rifle butt. Sheung looked at my mother and explained what had been said.

"Let them in," said my mother. "Maybe they can protect us." She picked Wei-Ming off her lap and passed her to Yee-Lin, telling her to take my sister upstairs.

Sheung opened the door. Three British soldiers stood at the threshold and a truck engine revved outside the gates. A tall officer with a narrow face streaked in engine grease leaned through the opening. Behind him, a younger soldier coughed violently. Four others waited behind, a few feet from the door, carrying two massive artillery guns between them. The officer squinted in the darkened entrance and asked Sheung if he was the master of the house.

"We need your house, then."

Sheung asked him why.

"The Japanese have bombed the harbour and crossed the water. They're flying sorties over the island now. You've got the tallest house in the Valley. We need to put our anti-aircraft guns on your roof." The soldiers behind must have heard only "guns on your roof," and they pressed forward carrying the heavy weapons.

Sheung and Chow jumped back at the sight, and the men again mistook this for agreement. In the confusion, my mother rose and yelled at them in Cantonese, and the officer told his men to stop. Behind me, most of the refugees ran to the back of the house.

"You can't bring this in here," Sheung said as he eyed the massive weapons. "The Japanese will locate them and bomb our house."

"They're going to bomb it anyway. You should get out. We have other guns up on the hilltop, but that's all we have right now."

Sheung waved his hand towards the smoking ruins. "And go where?"

The officer didn't answer. Outside, ten more soldiers were carrying another four anti-aircraft guns onto the grounds. The lock on the gate was broken and they were bringing their truck onto our drive. Machine guns erupted in the distance and planes roared overhead. The soldiers looked up at the dawn sky.

"For God's sake," shouted the officer. "They're going to bomb this area any second. We need to get up there."

My mother seized Sheung by the arm. "Where will we go? There's nowhere for us. Tell them they can't."

The officer cast her a hateful look.

"I'm very sorry," said Sheung, and he put his hand back on the heavy brass door handle.

"You bloody fool," screamed the officer, and I knew he was desperate, not angry.

Tang pushed Chow aside and spoke to Sheung. "Let them up there. What else can they do? It might save the city if we let them up there."

"Who's going to thank us while we wander the streets? Who'll take us in? No one. Let them in here and we're all dead. We'll stay together here." He pushed Tang back, gave the officer a final apologetic look, and shut the door.

He slammed it hard and the sound echoed through the front hall. More guns fired in the distance. My mother sat in silence with her hands trembling on her lap, as though awaiting a visitor.

We spent the rest of the morning in uneasy silence until the distraction of awaiting the midday meal. Tang moved the radio into our father's study upstairs and listened to it there, where the rest of us wouldn't hear the news. The shelling died down and sounded farther away. I moved uneasily from room to room, trailing Sheung or Chow as they tried to keep busy. Ah-Tseng and my mother were preparing the lunch, mostly from the preserved foods in the pantry: salted vegetables and pork, dried oysters, rice.

Mrs. Yee did not come down. I heard her wailing in her room, screaming for her husband while Shun-Lai, who was also crying, tried to console her. The younger girl, Shun-Po, ran to Shun-Yau's room and shut the door. When Mrs. Yee failed to calm down, her children came downstairs with drawn faces and red eyes.

They sat at the table and picked at their food. Shun-Yau and the younger sister started to bicker about how much rice was left in their bowls. She said he left too much behind and was wasteful, and he said the same of her. She said their father was watching them and would be disappointed.

He started to count out the remaining grains with the tip of a chopstick. "One, two, three, four…" he said.

Then Shun-Po reached over with hers and stirred the grains around. He ignored the taunt, nudged the bowl away from her, and resumed counting. A plane flew overhead. I was sitting between Shun-Yau and Leuk, and we decided to count out loud with him.

"One, two, three—"

At "four," the air in my chest suddenly compressed. The dining room window shattered as a blast tore through the air. I heard it for only a fraction of a second before everything went silent, followed by a painful ringing in my ears.

The blast knocked me backward off my stool and I hit the floor headfirst. The thick rug under the table saved my skull from cracking on the stone. The room spun for a few seconds, and I stared at the ceiling as a handful of reddish leaves blew in through a hole torn in the wall.

Shun-Yau lay beside me. He blinked at me as though I had just woken him, and for a few seconds we lay next to each other in shock. Then Leuk struggled to his feet and I sat up.

Wei-Ming screamed next to her broken chair as my mother ran to pick her up. Far off, I heard another explosion. The sound was oddly gentle, like the rolling of a giant drum, very far away. My mother cast her eye over the Yee children, who stood jammed in a corner by a cabinet. Shun-Lai held her younger siblings.

"Shun-Lai," my mother said. "Your mother should come down now."

The girl ran up the stairs and I heard the bedroom door open with a bang. Moments later Mrs. Yee and her daughter hurried down. As they entered the dining room, another explosion sounded. Her two other children ran to her and she held them close as she collapsed against a wall, crying that they had nowhere to go, that there was no safe place anymore in Hong Kong.

We moved away from the window. The heavy curtains had caught the flying glass, but the window and part of the wall around it was blown out. Ah-Tseng produced a first aid kit, and she and Yee-Lin checked everyone for cuts. Incredibly, no one was hurt. Chow looked out through the hole in the wall, where a large part of the grounds and outside wall lay in ruins.

The fighting continued sporadically all day, though it never came any nearer to our house. Chow and my older brothers found some boards to nail over the hole. When they put the last board up, the room returned to darkness, and their hammers drowned out the muffled shelling in the distance.

My mother told us all to sit together in the living room, away from the main entrance. I sat with Leuk on one of the sofas. I wanted to start a fire in the hearth because it was cold, but Chow said that would be too dangerous. Mrs. Yee sat on the sofa next to mine, her face a bloodless grey. She stared into nothing as Shun-Lai held her hand. Shun-Yau sat with Leuk and me. He looked over at his mother for a moment and then turned and whispered to me.

"What do you think happened to him?" He looked around to see if anyone was listening.

"Who?"

"The last snake. I wonder if the explosion burst the glass in the cellar. Or it could have knocked the basket over. Maybe the last one got out."

"I don't know."

"If he got out, what if the floor's covered in broken glass? He was already in pretty bad shape."

I tried to imagine the snake, suddenly liberated in the chaos, crawling through the gloom over the broken glass. I could hear the fine dust abrading its scales and imagined its lightness would protect it from injury.

"No, I think he'd be all right," I said confidently. "I think they ... they have a special sense, a special ability that lets them detect danger. That's why they're so good at hiding, like those snakes that wait in trees."

He looked at me very soberly while he took this in. "It must be dark in there," he said, and he looked at a scroll hanging on the wall, a painting in ancient script that none of us could read. "Maybe the window wasn't blown in. Is the cellar window on the same side of the house as the dining room?"

I furrowed my brow and with my finger tested out a little map of the house on a cushion. "Here's the dining room wall, so the kitchen is over here. When you turn to go down the stairs, you end up here...and here's the cellar...then that little room...No. No, it isn't." I wasn't quite sure I'd got it right, but I didn't want Shun-Yau to know that.

"All right," he said. He looked relieved. "But when everything's cleared up, let's go back down there and check on him. Maybe he doesn't need to be there anymore. He could stay in my room. There's an empty box in the closet, and we could feed him crickets."

I nodded. "You're right, there's no point to leaving him there."

We talked about it for a while, and in the end we decided that the snake shouldn't live in our house anymore. We agreed to head back to the basement later, and if he was still alive and it was safe for us to do so, we'd let him loose in the garden. We talked a little more about the snake and how best to help him. I looked at my watch: it was eight thirty, and I was tired. I thought of my bed but stayed on the sofa with everyone else.

The last time I took Alice to the hospital was in late July 2000, a single day that seemed to claw back all the energy I had recouped since my retirement a year before. I didn't miss my work much, even though I'd retired early to take care of her. If I saw news stories about hospitals or developments in medicine, I felt little connection to that world. Television dramas set in hospitals baffled and irritated me, they seemed devoid of anything familiar. When I brought Alice into the emergency department that

Thursday night when she could barely talk, I was wearing a pyjama shirt over my walking shorts and was still under the haze of a small whiskey I'd drunk an hour earlier. In the waiting room, I fumbled with my new cellphone as though it were an alien artifact. I wanted to act, to seize the splintering world and punish it. Instead, the world receded from my grasp, taken by a tide that even my wife was drifting into. I cursed the phone and drew stares as I broke it on the floor. Then a young doctor, a former student of mine, recognized me and called Evelyn and Chris for me from his office.

Over the next week, as it became clear there was nothing left to do for my wife but keep her comfortable, I consoled myself with long walks around the hospital and along the water by the old port. My children stayed at the house but were mostly in the hospital with their mother. Chris had been out to Chicago frequently in the last year. Evelyn, having a family of her own and living on the other side of the world, hadn't been for two years and had limited her information dutifully, almost lovingly, to Alice's self-censored letters about her illness. When she arrived from Malaysia and saw her mother, she was unprepared for the change in her appearance.

One afternoon in the family room on Alice's ward, Evelyn confronted me and said she believed more could still be done. She said we should get another opinion, consult someone from another hospital, order more tests.

You must know people, she said. Call them. Why haven't you done that?

I didn't want to get angry with her. Chris tried talking to her, but she wouldn't listen to him.

You don't understand, I said. Her lungs are badly damaged. She's in renal crisis. All mom's defences are gone.

Evelyn gave me that old look of dismissal, the fourteen-year-old cutting down her blowhard dad. Then she went back to Alice's room. Chris stayed with me and I dozed in a chair.

Around five that evening, they both went down to the cafeteria for some dinner. I went out for a walk. I crossed the road and in a few minutes was at the old port. Parts of it were semi-ruinous, where decommissioned small- or medium-sized shipping vessels were stored before being hauled off for scrap. Most of this section of the port seemed ready for the junkyard, while canny developers had already set in on the other section, opening garish bars and fast-food restaurants that catered to the young.

I sat on a bench and looked onto the lake. By the pier to my left a trio of shuttered vessels tossed sluggishly in the water, creaking against their heavy chains like wounded bears in a terrible old circus. At my left a half-dozen young men strode towards me, headed for the bank of new bars and restaurants to my right. I could tell they were military men on leave, given their haircuts and physiques, and the loud, rambling one-upmanship of their talk. I tried to imagine them in their uniforms, armed or wearing medals, or helmeted and shielded for combat. I imagined them wielding tanks and rocket launchers. In their T-shirts and shorts they appeared lost and reckless.

The scant cloud of the afternoon had grown to an impenetrable overcast, and a light rain started misting down. The sun, still two hours from setting, glowed coolly behind it, a pale and distant disc. The young men shouted and waved at me as they walked past.

Evelyn appeared next to me on the bench. She said she wanted to sit with me and let Chris be alone for a while, and I smiled because we both knew how typical that was of him. She apologized for being sharp with me earlier. I put my arm around her, and for a moment I imagined she was a child again and we were at the old duck pond near our house. We sat there and chuckled at the young recruits as they attempted to get into a bar that wasn't open yet, trying to bluff the impervious owner into letting them in.

In time the mist became true rain. I pulled the hood of my windbreaker over my head and Evelyn opened her umbrella. Even as the rain began to blow harder, we stayed sitting on the bench. The bars opened and the army of revellers finally got in to start their night of drinking. The pier was a little quieter as the interiors of the bars lit up. And while we watched the water, Chris was with Alice in her room, and he was with her when she died.

Evelyn and I were only a short walk away at the time. At the burial a week later, I couldn't watch the coffin descend. I closed my eyes and relived the moment of death as I had known it: a lightless sun, an army without weapons, a port of rusted cargo vessels creaking in the rain.

SEVEN

The shelling and gunfire went on into the evening. Sheung came downstairs and said it seemed, from what he caught on the radio, that most of the fighting was happening near the harbour. Tang likened it to what he'd heard earlier that day, and the two of them sat at the dining room table and compared notes. They were still in their business suits, arms folded soberly while they talked, as though they were about to be consulted on the war's progress. I thought they looked silly, because I couldn't yet understand how responsible and helpless they felt and how much they had to force themselves to look and feel competent.

One week later, on the twenty-third of December, my elder brothers' effort of will collapsed. The pounding of the heavy guns had grown over the past two days, and Sheung said very little about what he heard on the radio. I began to doubt that there was much being broadcast.

That afternoon, while Shun-Yau was sitting with his mother, Leuk and I went into his room. Because it was originally a spare room, it looked out onto the less attractive back of the house on Ventris Road, which in those days was more of a lane than a true street. A portion of the concrete wall that surrounded our house was lower there—perhaps four feet high—so that any adult walking past it could see into a small enclosure where the servants threw the rubbish. A truck approached and its engine ground and banged to a halt. It was a British army truck and badly damaged: the windshield was gone and part of the back was torn off. There was blood splattered on the hood and the military insignia on the driver's door was burned away.

The driver stopped behind our house. Even while the brakes were squealing, three British soldiers jumped out of the back, followed by the driver and a fifth soldier in the front. They peered over the back wall of our house and gestured and shouted at each other. Three of them ran to the back of the truck and started gathering up guns. They quickly picked up rifles, pistols, even machine guns, and started throwing them into the rubbish yard. The driver shouted at them to hurry. Two soldiers picked up a heavy gun like the one the British had carried up our front step nearly two weeks earlier, and hurled it over the wall, where it struck a steel barrel. Ah-Tseng went running out of the kitchen. She shouted at the soldiers to stop, but Chow brought her back in.

The soldiers ignored Ah-Tseng. Through a hole in the side of the truck I saw a wounded man laid out. His chest and left arm were wound in bloody bandages. He wasn't moving. One of the soldiers checked on him while the others finished disposing of their guns.

Once they had discarded the larger weapons into the yard, the soldiers climbed back into the truck. The driver started the engine. It struggled and let loose a few bangs like gunfire. Smoke crept out from under the hood and swept into the cab. After another quick effort from the driver, the five soldiers got back out of the truck. One lifted the wounded soldier out and carried him on his back, and then they ran down the alley. The abandoned truck roared with orange flames behind our house.

I wanted a closer look. Leuk and I ran down the stairs, through the front hall, and into the kitchen, hoping to get a glimpse of the piled-up weapons. Tang stopped us and told us not to go out. I asked him if he had seen the guns being thrown into the yard.

"Of course I did. If the Japanese see that, they'll think we're storing weapons for the British. We have to get rid of them."

Chow came back inside. He looked more afraid than I had ever seen him. "There's no way we can lift all of those, and it's more dangerous to bring them inside."

"Get a tarp and cover them," said Tang, and Chow retrieved a large canvas roll from the cellar while Tang paced nervously around the pantry.

"If the Japanese see the tarp, they'll wonder what we're hiding," said Leuk. So we agreed to cover the tarp with garbage.

"Gather all the garbage you can find into these," said Chow. He pointed to two large wicker baskets he'd brought up from the cellar, the snake baskets.

Leuk and I ran through the house with the baskets and gathered everything we could—waste paper, dead house plants, broken toys, rags—and hauled them down to the kitchen. Tang and Chow took the baskets from us at the door and went outside and scattered the garbage over the tarp. We took vegetable scraps, bones, and all the other kitchen garbage and added it to the pile. Then Chow took a rake and stirred the refuse around so that the tarp couldn't be seen. They tore up dead plants in the yard and threw them on top with their soil. Leuk and I helped them, tearing up weeds and clumps of dirt to cover the canvas.

Back in the kitchen, Chow looked anxiously outside at the smoke still climbing from the hood of the truck.

"We can't do anything about it," said Tang. "Someone will move it, though, and it won't be the British coming to reclaim it. From now on, no one goes out this door." He shut the back door. It was a flimsy, plain wooden door with a simple lock, unlike the heavy, church-like doors at the front. It would have been easy to kick open.

After hauling all that garbage and dirt to cover the weapons, I was filthy. I went up to the bathroom by my room to clean up. I looked at the grime and dirt on my hands and forearms and the dark smears all over my face where I'd wiped off sweat.

I turned the faucet handle. When only a small trickle came out, I turned it again. The thin stream weakened to a drip, the pipes trembled behind the walls, and after the last drop of water a thin hiss came from the tap. I went to my mother's bathroom and turned the taps there — nothing. In the kitchen I found Ah-Tseng at the sink, frantically trying to wring water from pipes that sent out an airy sigh.

I ran down the hall and found Sheung. We went to my father's study, where he scanned the radio for a few min-utes to confirm the obvious. The Japanese had captured the water reservoirs on the island and were slowly shutting them down.

The water shutdown affected us as nothing else had. To hear gunfire through the walls and barricaded windows simply confirmed to us that we should stick to our plan: stay indoors and fortify the membrane of our life with flimsy patches of wood, old locks, tarps, and dimmed lights. It was as though the invasion were a typhoon, a force directed by air masses and ocean currents rather than human evil, and would eventually pass over us. We could convince ourselves that our barricades were useful.

The loss of water was different. The pipes lay hidden behind every wall throughout the house, and whenever someone tried a tap or the pressure changed, we heard it. I might be in the kitchen or my room when the ghostly sound of trickling water or air would emerge through the plaster walls. No blast, no roaring engine, just the sigh of life being choked off by a distant hand.

The water still flowed weakly over the next two days. We saved it for drinking and washed very little, and the grime that crept over our skin even in the winter chill also reminded us that things could still grow worse. Soon, it seemed, a messenger would come to announce the next phase of life.

On Christmas Eve, the message was delivered. I was waiting in the kitchen with the other children for a drink of water, after a meal served cold because Ah-Tseng and my mother no longer boiled or steamed our food. I was hungry in the bored way of children, thinking of the seafood dinners we used to eat on Christmas Eve: abalone and fried shrimp, crab, stewed clams with lotus root, and cuttlefish. I wandered upstairs and found my way into my father's study, where the lights were out and sheets hung over the windows. I pulled the sheets open a crack and the moonlight shone on the mantelpiece and cast a sliver of light over a photograph of King George that the governor had given my father. The room seemed not just still but frozen, a monument to a vanished time and life. Then I looked through the crack in the curtains towards the harbour. I heard planes overhead and took in the widening orange glow of fire spreading across buildings. A cluster of bombs fell from Japanese planes into the shimmering orange light. I thought they looked like goldfish.

It was still dark when I woke early on Christmas morning. I got up to get some water and walked down the hall in bare feet, hearing the raspy breathing of my family through their open bedroom doors. We all slept on the third floor now. Wei-Ming groaned in her sleep as I passed. At Sheung and Yee-Lin's room, I stopped to listen to their paired breathing until I could tell them apart. Their room had heavy curtains, around which a thin rectangle of faint light glowed. I grasped the small flashlight I had brought with me and turned it on inside my pyjama pocket, to muffle the click. I withdrew it slowly with my hand over the light and then carefully uncovered it on the face of the hall clock. Four thirty, Christmas Day. I covered the light again and prepared to put it back in my pocket, turning to go downstairs.

I nearly screamed when I turned. In front of me was Mrs. Yee, her hair undone over her long white nightgown and her hands clasped over her belly.

"Is that you, Chung-Man?"

"Yes." My heart pounded so hard it hurt. I started flicking the flashlight switch nervously in my pocket, causing my right pyjama leg to flicker weirdly in the darkness.

"I am often awake," she continued. "I get up sometimes to check on my children." She looked down at my leg where the clicking emanated. "Thank you so much for keeping Shun-Yau busy. Without his father he's lost, I'm afraid. Boys need other boys to play with. Please keep it up, he needs a friend."

The shock of our meeting in the darkness made me start to hyperventilate. I placed my hands over my stomach in an instinctive imitation of her posture. Behind her, at the end of the hall, a silhouetted figure rose to a seated position. It was Chow, lying on a cot at the top of the stairs.

"Please don't cry," said Mrs. Yee. I wasn't. It disturbed me that she misunderstood what I was feeling. A low groan sprang from my throat.

A pair of slippers clicked rapidly towards us. My mother took me by the shoulders and looked me quickly in the eye. Chow stood up from his cot. In an angry whisper my mother asked Mrs. Yee what she was doing.

Mrs. Yee looked at me. "I'm sorry...I don't sleep very well at night — I was up again — when I heard Chung-Man ..."

My mother sent me back to my room. I stood inside the doorway and listened.

"Mrs. Yee, don't wake anyone else up."

"How can you sleep?" she replied.

I heard Chow's footsteps and then his voice, a low, consoling tone. My mother was losing her patience, and Mrs. Yee began to cry.

Across the hall, Wei-Ming groaned again and called out. My mother said something in a short, angry voice, then I heard Chow intervene and tell Mrs. Yee to return to her room. I climbed back into bed and listened to my pulse pounding in my ears.

This was just the start of my mother's growing impatience with Mrs. Yee. Later that day we all stuck together in the library, where it was easiest to stay warm and conserve fuel, and the books helped distract us a little from hunger. My mother avoided Mrs. Yee as much as she could. I think Mrs. Yee, having lost her husband, sometimes felt that she had something in common with my mother, and of course she did in that regard. A few times I heard Mrs. Yee say, in a low voice, things like, "You know what it's like..." before alluding to her husband or my father. But my mother recoiled into silence every time, and in fact I didn't see them as very alike, either. Over the time they were with us, I sometimes came to resent Mrs. Yee, a feeling I also detected in my mother. I felt she was somehow to blame for her husband's murder and her homelessness. I felt sorry for her children.

Finally that evening, while my mother was ignoring yet another of Mrs. Yee's overtures, I went over to the library mantelpiece and took down the photo of my father. I set it on a table and began to read in front of it, as though my father were supervising a school lesson. I looked up once. Mrs. Yee was watching me, and I looked back at her and held her gaze for a moment. I almost felt, in a frightening way, that I had her in my power then. I turned and saw my mother staring at me, uneasy, almost sorrowing like Mrs. Yee, and she hurried over and put the photo back on the mantelpiece.

EIGHT

Two days after Christmas, we met in the library with the Yees to discuss if it was safe to go outside. We were living off the dwindling store of food in the pantry and Ah-Ming guessed we had about a week of it left. The meals were already smaller and I noticed how little my mother and the servants ate. The night before, my mother had sat at the table and taken nothing but water.

After the meeting, Tang and Chow went into the streets to see if any markets were open. It was the first time in two weeks any of us had left the house. I was in the front hall with Shun-Yau when Tang and Chow returned. As they shut the front door, a cold breeze blew in, metallic with stale smoke. Their shoes and the bottoms of their trousers were covered in ash, as though they had been wading through it. They gave a grim report on the city: crumbling apartments, blackened storefronts, bodies. They said nearly all the shops had been raided and there were few farmer's carts on the streets, but there were signs of people returning to the market. Tang caught me staring at his shoes. He turned and looked at the trail of grey dust behind them, and both of them stood by the door and knocked the ashes off their clothes. Tang took out his handkerchief and wiped the ash off the floor, and then he smiled at me.

"I'm afraid that's all I brought back."

Throughout the night, gunfire erupted in the streets. After one episode I heard the tires of a large vehicle screeching over the pavement, and then a crash and a muffled explosion. I thought of the truck that had burned in our back lane, of a hundred such vehicles, of burning buildings, all dusted in ash.

The next day, my older brothers went out again to the market and returned with a small amount of dried vegetables and sweet potatoes.

The following day, my mother said others should take turns going to the market. Ah-Tseng volunteered and I quickly offered to go with her, and we went to the kitchen, where she kept her shopping baskets. As we prepared to leave, she adjusted her sleeve where she hung the basket on her left forearm, and I realized I had seen her make that gesture a thousand times over the years. As soon as she slipped her arm through the handle and held it to her stomach, it was as though we were back in the summer before I'd left for school and the past month had never happened.

Ah-Tseng and I walked down to the market street. We turned the corner onto a larger avenue that was empty and silent. She was very nervous. I'd volunteered to go out with her because I wanted to help and felt badly for her, but when I sensed how close she walked beside me — a twelve-year-old boy — I didn't want the responsibility.

The market was gone. The stalls and carts had been smashed and were strewn across the street like kindling.

On the posts of the buildings where the hawkers and farmers used to stand there were posters in Japanese and Chinese saying the markets were disbanded and rationing was being imposed. They bore yesterday's date. I read the sign out to Ah-Tseng. She was fairly literate, but I think her eye first hit on the Japanese characters and she was so frightened that the rest of it confused her.

"Chung-Man, we should go home."

"Maybe we should walk around a little more and see what we can find. There might be some shops on the side streets."

She took my arm and hurriedly turned back homeward.

We turned onto a street where more people had ventured out, mostly women with empty shopping bags in hand. A few took note of us walking away from the market street with nothing to show for it; rest stared anxiously ahead as they hurried through the chill.

Then I heard shouts, formal and rhythmic, almost like dogs barking, and what first sounded like applause. A troop of about fifty Japanese soldiers marched around a corner towards us. They held their rifles tightly over their shoulders and their boots struck the pavement in unison. In an open car at the front of the troop, two officers rode in the back seat. They had identical thin moustaches over which they stared past the black-helmeted driver, a man whose sunglasses, white gloves, and grip on the steering wheel seemed crafted to project an image of supreme impersonality.

Everyone on the street backed into the doorways of the buildings behind us. But this was pointless. The Japanese knew we were there and that there were others on the streets ahead of and behind them and people hiding inside buildings asleep or sick. We were all of us, every resident of the city, under watch and swept into a single glance as quick and sharp as the snapping of a flag.

At first their perfect marching and the barking of the sergeant over the engine were unsettling. But it was the flag that awoke my fear. The white banner with the radiant red disc sailed from the car and from poles carried by the soldiers in the lead. I had never seen it before. It looked like the Union Jack, its cool naval blue torn off to make a banner of pure heat and searching fire.

A quartet of soldiers brought up the rear in another car with a long rope tied to its back fender. In contrast to the timed marching of the soldiers, the rope swung awkwardly over the pavement. Tied to the rope, around the corner a man in a bloody shirt appeared, and then behind him walked a line of prisoners, bound at the wrists and necks by cords. I guessed there were forty men and women of all ages. To those of us pressed into the doorways and crevices, their bodies offered up the promise of the coming days: heads lurid with bruises and dried blood, hair torn out in fist-sized gaps, arms enlarged and loose from broken bones, mouths gaping. In their eyes was the vacancy of those who understand they are about to be forgotten.

About a third of the prisoners were women, and they were clustered in the middle. Like the men, they stumbled quickly over the pavement in shoes or bare feet, and the sharp pull of the vehicle rippled through their shoulders.

Most of the women were young like Yee-Lin. Their faces and limbs were badly bruised, and some looked as though they'd had their teeth knocked out.

The prisoner at the front stumbled when the car lurched, and he nearly pulled the men behind him to the ground. In the back of the car, one Japanese soldier sat with an arm craned over his seat as he looked back, the only one in a casual pose. He laughed when the man stumbled and at the disarray it caused in those behind him. When the prisoners regained their step and quickly caught up with the car, restoring the slack, he shouted and shook his rifle at them. Then he leaned over the back of the car and hooked the rope up with his bayonet. He stood quickly and gave the rope a violent pull. The man in front fell down onto the road and was dragged forward on his side. The others staggered, bound wrists brought down as though in supplication, and they bent their knees to stop from falling, so that they had to waddle like ducks. Two men near the front tried to help the fallen man back up, until they stumbled against the force of the rope and the captives bumping into them from behind.

The soldier watched. In particular he watched the first man, whose face and torso left a long brushstroke of blood across the road, which the prisoners behind stepped over. Maybe that man cried out as he was dragged over the pavement, but I was spared the sound of it where I stood because of the noise of the vehicles and boots. I felt a cold pain bite into my side. Ah-Tseng gripped my upper arm, her other hand pressed over her mouth. Airplanes soared above us with the red disc on the underside of their wings, birds of prey surrendering to the lordly sun. Like the soldiers' boots, they moved across the world as though it were rusted metal for them to crush.

When Ah-Tseng and I got back from the market, we found a family sitting in the front hall with their belongings rolled up in a single blanket. They said their house had burned down and they'd heard ours was safe and that my mother had let them in. That evening an old couple arrived, followed by their son and his family. Over the next four days, at least fifty people showed up at our gates. My mother took them all in.

By the fifth day, the number of people staying with us was becoming dangerous. The house was crowded with refugees, sleeping on blankets and mats in every available space. The constant foot traffic and the noise were noticeable from the street, and my mother and elder brothers feared it would make the house a target. Tang shut the front gates just as another family was approaching, and he and my mother had to tell them to go somewhere else. The father shouted at my mother that he had nowhere else to go. He tried to climb the gate, and Chow pushed him off it. A grandfather with two children also begged to be let in, a crowd forming behind them. Finally, Chow took the pistol from his belt and waved it in the air. In a cracking voice, he threatened to fire it. The refugees scrambled into the streets. My mother ran back into the house, her hand twisting the dress at her heart.

I shared my room with five younger boys. At bedtime,

after Leuk and I came in to sleep, they darted back up from their blankets on the floor and ran out to find their parents where they slept in the hall or other rooms. All night long there were children wandering tearfully through the house until they found their parents. Finally I gave my room up to a family of six. The Yees slept in a single room. Leuk, Wei-Ming, and I moved into my father's study. We found it comforting to sleep in a triangle around the old stock ticker with its glass dome still intact, an emblem of a quieter world. A childless young couple and the husband's parents joined us there at night. Sometimes I opened my eyes and saw the wife sitting up and watching us with her hand resting on her belly.

Wei-Ming, who was now seven, hated losing her room. The first night we slept in the study, she refused to lie down and would only sit on her blanket and beg to be taken back. Leuk was asleep. I moved over and sat beside her with my back against the heavy wooden legs of the stock ticker table. I decided this was the time to do something adult, so I took her hand. She pulled it away and whispered that she wanted to go back to her room.

"You can't. Other people need it now. There's a family with a baby and a grandmother."

"I want my room back."

"Go to sleep."

"I want to sleep in my room. Why are they here?"

I knew an adult in my place would have invented something. I told her to go back to sleep or our mother would be angry. She started crying at the mention of her and got up and ran into the hall. She shouted in the hall and up the stairwells, and immediately there came the clattering slippers of parents who mistook her for one of their own. I lay down and stared at the moonlight bending over the glass dome. An hour later, Ah-Tseng came into the study with Wei-Ming asleep on her shoulder and laid her back down beside me.

The following morning, I ran to the window of my father's study when I heard a noise. Two Japanese military vehicles, a truck and an officer's car, appeared at the gates. A dozen soldiers jumped out of the truck, and at a shout from one of the officers the truck, reinforced with a heavy grille, backed up and smashed through the gate. I ran back out to the landing to look for my mother and stopped as the soldiers broke open the front doors. They stood in the doorway, the dawn light spreading around them with theatrical power.

An officer stepped forward, followed by a civilian in a black suit. The civilian looked around with an air more commanding than the officer's. Sheung ventured towards them and tried to speak, but they ignored him. The senior officer turned to the man in the suit and spoke to him in Japanese. The civilian was neatly turned out in his clothes and polished spectacles, and he looked around authoritatively as he spoke.

"This house is to be vacated by midnight tomorrow. Those remaining will be arrested or shot." He was Chinese.

Sheung stepped forward and addressed the civilian. "Sir, I am the—"

"The military government is assuming control of all large facilities and buildings," he continued, parroting the officer. "Chinese civilians must relocate within the curfew period. All goods, including money or other valuables, other than personal belongings, must be left behind in this house. The resident family of the house may stay but must move to one of the upper floors." The officers looked around the hall, while the civilian made a point of looking people in the eye.

One of the refugees, a newlywed who had arrived with his wife and her parents, rose angrily. He stepped over mattresses and jumbled clothes, moving towards the door and shaking his fist at the interpreter.

"You are Chinese! How can you—"

A soldier came forward from behind the officers. He swung his rifle around and butted the man's face with the wide steel cap of the weapon. The man staggered back and tripped on a mattress, and even as he fell, the blood was already pouring from his ear and mouth. He landed on a suitcase and no one touched him.

"A guard will now be placed on this house," the civilian echoed. "Unauthorized persons must start leaving it immediately." Then the officer turned and left.

A woman crawled sobbing over the piled belongings on the floor and cradled the wounded man's head. She gently touched his hair, ignoring the blood soaking into her dress.

. . .

Within an hour, four more truckloads of Japanese soldiers came to occupy our house. The refugees tried to clear out quickly. My family and the servants were moving our possessions up to the fourth floor. We couldn't help the refugees anymore.

The family living in Shun-Yau's room came down the stairs. The father and sons carried heavy suitcases and bundles tied awkwardly with mismatched straps and cords. The mother walked slowly between two ancient grandparents. She held each of them by the arm as the grandfather gripped the railing tight. The grandmother had a huge goitre on her neck, and she wobbled down the marble steps as the woman tried to keep her steady. The grandfather had a bamboo cane hung over his wrist where he held the railing, and it swung and ticked against the banister as they descended. His face was red and screwed tight as though he was in pain, and his bone-white hair hung limp around his skull.

The soldiers brought in supplies and quickly scouted out the kitchen and bedrooms. Yee-Lin and Sheung stood together against a wall in the parlour near the staircase. Two soldiers strolled past them as they looked around. One of the soldiers stopped and stared at my sister-in-law. He smiled and said something to the other soldier that made them laugh, and then said something to Tang. Yee-Lin held his arm. My brother darkened in humiliation. He stood silently and avoided their eyes. They laughed again and went on exploring the house.

The woman and the grandparents were nearly down the stairs. The daughter looked angry as she tried to keep them all steady. The grandfather's face was strained and he stammered through pursed lips. The woman hushed him with a few short words as she concentrated on their feet going down the steps. Then he stopped and grimaced, stammered a single, desperate syllable, and twitched. Standing at the base of the stairs, I heard the shameful sound of his rectum opening and caught the foul scent spreading through the air. I backed away and kept my arms stiffly at my sides as though I could protect his dignity by not covering my nose. The grandfather hung his head and made strange swallowing sounds while the grandmother asked why they had stopped.

Between them, the woman stared at the hall floor only two steps away. Her chest rose and fell and she shut her eyes for a moment as though remembering something. Then she took a breath. She walked the grandparents down the last two steps just as her husband returned from outside, and they crossed the front hall and left the house.

As many people left as could before the curfew, preferring the burned-out streets to a house full of Japanese soldiers. Tang bravely convinced the Chinese collaborator that the Yees were our cousins, and so they would be allowed to stay. When morning came and the curfew lifted, the last of the refugees left. A few bowed to my mother and thanked her as she stood by the door. She bowed back to them and said each time, "We will meet again soon." Then a soldier warned her away with a shake of his rifle. We ran upstairs as he slammed the front doors shut.

NINE

All of us—my family, the Yees, Chow, Ah-Tseng, and Ah-Ming—now lived in the fourth-floor parlour. The only furniture was a single chair, and we slept on blankets and mats.

Every day, the servants and my older brothers went to the market and were harassed by soldiers on the street. Tang came back one day with a black eye but said nothing about it, and Ah-Tseng refused to go outside without one of the men. I doubt they felt they had much safety to offer. Daily we heard shots and the sounds of people being arrested or beaten. At night, violent sounds broke in from outside. There were shouts and cries and gunfire. And I heard the screams from encounters between soldiers and women in the streets, and in the dying terror of their cries I conjured images of teeth.

We were still permitted to use the toilet down the hall. One evening, a week after the Japanese took over our house, I went down there after our meagre supper. It was dark in the hallway as most of the windows were shuttered. I stayed in the bathroom a few extra moments, savouring the privacy and the small space, and examined my teeth. My gums looked red and I wondered if the coarse food we ate was harming me, and I touched my gums and teeth carefully with my fingertip. I grimaced and made faces in the mirror, until a noise outside reminded me to return to bed. Then I opened the door.

I jumped back and hit the door, which flew back into the wall with a bang. A soldier was standing in my way, one hand resting on his hip. He looked at me and said something in Japanese.

I froze and met his eye. I don't think he liked that, because he shouted again. I stared at the floor and tried to control my breathing. He spoke again. Thinking he was angry at me for not looking at him, I raised my eyes, and he barked at me and stamped his boot on the floor. Behind the door to our room down the hall, I heard scuffling.

Even though I had just been to the bathroom, my bowels started churning. I set my hands over my stomach and held myself, fearing I would lose control and make things worse. He shouted louder and slapped my hands away.

I thought saying something, anything, would help. I took a breath with an audible shake, but all I could manage was a stammered, "Excuse me…"

He yelled and grabbed me by the top of my hair and pulled hard, and I screamed. I thought my voice was echoing strangely, but then I realized it was my mother screaming through the parlour door.

Still holding me by the hair, the soldier dragged me down the hall. I thought he was taking me back to the room, but he passed it. I stumbled and my scalp burned under his grip. As we passed the room, I heard the door rattle and bang as though people were fighting behind it.

My mother shouted at me and I called back to her, and then I heard Chow telling my mother to move back.

The soldier dragged me to the top of the stairs and put one boot on the first step. He pointed to the bottom of the stairs and said something. I pleaded with him to let me go. He began to swing his arm back and forth, and I stumbled and slipped onto the first stair. I knew he was threatening to hurl me down the stone steps, and the pain began to radiate down my neck all the way to my feet as I braced myself to be thrown.

The door opened and Tang hurried out. He crouched in supplication with both arms out, nodding and bowing at the soldier as he crept forward in a waddle.

"Please, sir, let him go. Tell me what you want, but don't hurt the boy."

The soldier yelled back at him. With a last, decisive swing of his arm, he hurled me away from the steps towards the door. I screamed as I felt my scalp tear and my shoulder hit the hard floor. I heard another thud, and at the same moment my mother and Chow ran out and pulled me into the room. The soldier kept yelling. A moment later, as I was sitting by my mother clutching my scalp, Tang staggered back in. His nose was broken and he clutched his groin, and Sheung helped him to the chair. The soldier appeared in the doorway, shouted, and spat on the floor before slamming the door shut.

Two days later, our food was nearly gone. The Japanese had instituted rationing on Boxing Day and the quantities were hardly enough to live on. They allotted 6.4 taels of rice per person per day, about half a pound, and a small amount of peas or beans. I had recovered quickly from the assault in the hallway, but Tang's face was a mass of bruises. Because Sheung had been the last to go out, Leuk and I offered to get the rations.

As we prepared to go out on our first errand alone, Sheung had us repeat the route in detail. When we were done, my mother asked us if we were sure we wanted to go, but Sheung interrupted her.

"It's all right. They can do it." He waved us off.

We hurried down the stairs carrying old rice sacks. I didn't look at any of the soldiers, keeping my eyes on the floor until we were out the door.

We stood on the sidewalk and I looked down at the dry gutter. The wind lifted the lapels of our jackets as we walked. All the way down Wong Nai Chung road, we clutched the rice sacks and they flapped around us, twisting as the wind deflected off the buildings. I saw a man walking down the other side of the street. He carried a large box tied with a string handle, and from the way it swung I could tell it was empty.

Across the street, an old couple hurried, clutching bags of rations. Most of the windows in houses and apartments had the curtains drawn, and the streets were nearly empty. It had been a long time since my walk with Ah-Tseng and I felt sorry that she had been made to go out so often since.

We passed a butcher shop we knew. Its windows were smashed and the meathooks, still smeared with grease, creaked in the wind. We passed a Buddhist temple where many of my friends went. The gate was open, but it looked empty. The incense rings swung coldly from the beams and the statues loomed in the shade. Then I caught a glimpse of a monk between the columns. His slippered feet moved slowly over the flagstones while a hanging banner veiled his upper body.

We turned down a lane towards the ration centre. This was the sloped road that ran past the stables where workhorses and racehorses for the Jockey Club were kept. The stables had large wooden doors with grated openings on top. In the summer we avoided that road because of the smell, but otherwise we liked to walk down it and see the animals in their stalls. Today the doors were all shut, and as Leuk and I walked, I noted the deathly silence.

"I wonder if they took the horses," Leuk said.

One of the stable gates was open. The large green panels of its doors had been drawn wide, and a man leaned against the frame smoking a cigarette. When he saw us coming, he straightened up but left the cigarette between his lips. He watched us as we approached, and stepped back into the shade of the doorway.

There was a large cart in the stable, the kind farmers brought their goods to market in: flat with low sides, usually filled with cabbages or bamboo crates of ducks. But this cart was piled with corpses. At first I saw only their empty faces, resting on their sides or hanging upside down, pressed together but registering no discomfort. An image of cabbages tumbling off a cart came into my mind, and of a farmer's wife standing by it, weeping at the ruin of her goods.

I knew it was wrong to think like that, to daydream while I stared at these lost faces. But the image came quickly. More and more it was becoming my habit to see one thing and envision another, to transform the world's images as they opened up to me. Until now I never knew I had this ability—not to change the world, but to remake and reduce it to my vanished world of gardens and school-yards, of the kitchen and the library. And then nothing might be remembered, only retold. For there are times when we absorb the world as we grow and learn about it, but others when we make a dark exchange with it, casting out memories, pocketfuls of time, and future selves as its brutality marches into our lives.

I began to shake, and Leuk gasped and gripped my arm. There were men and women and some children. I had seen the marbled discoloration of death once before, in a beggar who had died behind our house. These bodies were smooth-skinned and clear, newly dead, but they bore the vestiges of fear: a hint of distress in the caving of the mouths and cheeks, the closed and unclosed eyes, the limbs pushed around in ways ridiculous or intimate. Though the cart was stationary, I heard it creaking on its axle as though it were being drawn away.

Inside the doorway, leaning and immersed in shadow strung with sawdust, the man stood very still and smoked and watched us.

A faint, sweet smell of drying manure drifted from the stable. The rice sacks hung weakly on the crook of my little finger, ready to blow away into the wind. I shifted uneasily where I stood. The cobblestones seemed sticky. My right leg shook uncontrollably.

"You probably didn't know them," said the man in a slow, level voice. He was a local too, just like the civilian who'd come to our house with the Japanese. "Not from this neighbourhood." When he stopped speaking, the ash on his cigarette glowed like a serpent's eye.

The wind was chill and damp, but I felt sweat seeping into the back and collar of my shirt, and again I sensed the stickiness of the ground beneath me as I shifted where I stood. I couldn't move. I stared at the dead faces. I wished for all those bodies to be somehow…dry. Bloodless maybe, or undamaged, as though they had been gathered up in silence from the roadside after entering eternal sleep.

I seized my brother by the arm, closed up my coat, and ran with him to find the street. We looked back only once, to see if anyone was following. But there was no one in the lane. We were running from nothing. As we turned into the street, I turned around again and caught a last glimpse of the black hole we had gazed into.

"Wait, just wait!" shouted Leuk. He grabbed the back of my shirt to stop me the instant we turned the corner. He seemed winded, but he wasn't breathing hard. He leaned back against a wall and looked up, squinting.

"What is it?"

"Just wait. I feel sick." He held his stomach and leaned over. I thought he was going to vomit on the pavement, but he just hung there for a moment. Then he straightened up and rubbed his eyes.

"Did we get away from it?" I asked.

"From what?" Leuk was squinting again. He rubbed his eyes furiously as though dust had blown into them. He opened them and squinted again and started rubbing hard, grinding the knuckles of his index fingers into his eyes so hard I worried he would injure himself.

"Stop that!" I shouted. Then I envisioned the cart and smelled the stable air, a dry mist of ground manure and human bones. I choked and retched. Bile burned my throat.

"It's so bright," Leuk said. "My eyes hurt. Give me a minute."

He passed me his rice sack as I coughed, and he leaned against the wall with his hands cupped tightly over his face. My coughing slowed. It was very quiet in the street, just the sound of the sacks crackling in the breeze. I heard vehicles and voices somewhere, though everything seemed far away.

Leuk dropped his hands. His eyes were red and watery, but he wasn't squinting anymore.

"I'm all right now." He took back his bag, an empty thing that flapped crazily in the wind, as though to plead that it didn't belong there.

After that, we stuck to the main roads on the way to the ration centre. The Japanese had set it up in an occupied post office, where we waited in line with dozens of others. Inside, the young soldiers looked down at us with stony boredom as they dropped small bags of rice into our sacks. They all displayed the same contempt and sternness, as though trying to appear older. I saw them as infinitely dangerous, indifferent to violence. We avoided their eyes, and Leuk and I didn't speak until our house was within sight.

As we walked up Wong Nai Chung Road towards the house, the bags of rice exerted a satisfying tug on my wrists, and I realized how tense I was. I swung my arms at my sides and liked the way the weight of the bags pulled on my shoulders.

I couldn't help seeing all those faces, like sleepers frozen in a moment of nightmare. I tried to understand it, like a hand grasping for a light switch in a dark room. I tried to focus on the sensations of my body: the pull on my shoulders, the string handles of the rice sacks cutting around my wrists, the warmth in my shoes, and in my left ear the stuffy, nasal breathing of my brother as we tramped up the dirty pavement.

I recall this moment as the first time I became aware of the changes that had started in my body. I sweated more and my voice was breaking. I woke up in the middle of the night or in the morning with an erection, or one appeared suddenly as I dressed. I had grown a little taller and had just inherited some of my older brother's clothes—the first time any of us had ever worn hand-me-downs. Wearing them was like pretending to be another person.

As we walked up the last stretch of pavement, Leuk stopped and looked up at our house.

"Who's that?" he said.

It was late afternoon now, and a few illuminated windows in the house stood out against its soft grey walls. A girl in silhouette stood in a third-floor window. The curtains were drawn, but the yellow light of the lamps threw her form crisply onto the cloth. She was brushing her hair with steady strokes like a rower on a lake in summer. We stopped and watched her for a moment.

"It's Shun-Lai," I said finally. "What's she doing there? That's where the Japs are staying."

As soon as I put my hand on the gate handle, I knew something was different. The sentries were gone, and the front courtyard was empty.

We hurried through the courtyard and up the front steps. Leuk pushed hard on the door and we nearly tripped over each other getting in. The lights were on, but there was no one in the front hall. As I looked up the staircase, I felt my face flush and my hands turned cold. It was so quiet, and I thought of the stables.

Then my mother appeared. Her shoes clicked evenly over the floor and the yellow lamplight washed over her shoulders. The sight was so familiar that the past few weeks were almost erased. When she saw us, she hurried over, shut the door behind us, and put her hands on our shoulders.

"They've left. An officer summoned me an hour ago and said they had been told they don't need the house. They've taken all their things and left half an hour ago. We have our house back."

We brought the rations into the kitchen, and my mother shut them up in a cupboard as though she were putting ivory into a vault. We told her we were starving, so my mother warmed some gruel for us. We ate quickly and went upstairs.

On the second floor, a door near the landing opened and Shun-Lai stepped into the hallway with a hairbrush in one hand. The news about the Japanese had made my head swim and I'd forgotten about seeing her in the window. She was in her pyjamas and a soft grey flannel bathrobe. She turned to me as I got to the top. She knew where I had been and asked how it went, and we talked a little about how good it was to have the house back.

She smiled, and her brushed hair glowed in the faint hallway light. I had seen this girl so many times, but now in the yellow light she looked different: the pale cotton, the dark bristles of the hairbrush, the wintry flannel, all lifeless things and yet painting a picture of life. Suddenly, I found her beautiful. As I thought of this, she wished me good night. I echoed her faintly and walked to my room, slightly confused.

Once in the darkness of my room, I remembered the stable and the cart. I couldn't believe I had forgotten those people in my brief talk with Shun-Lai. I shut the door and sat on my bed as shame overcame me, and I cried quietly until Leuk came in.

That night, I lay in my old room again, with Leuk in the bed next to mine. I shook the sheets a few times because I was warm, and I felt them sink slowly downward as they expelled air over my face. The bedclothes settled on my abdomen, revealing the profile of my new body. I was thinner.

Was there less of me? I pondered the question for a while as I listened to my older brother breathe. I felt overloaded and burdened, and my head ached. My brain was turning into a crowded landscape of pictures and sounds, and my own thoughts were becoming indistinguishable from the noise I absorbed from the world around me. I felt exposed, unable to conceal my chaotic inner world.

I shut my eyes and tried to focus on the sound of Leuk breathing. Then I gave up and turned to look at him. The shutter slats were still open and the moonlight glowed on the sheets. I glanced at the clock — half past midnight. I had never lain awake so long before. Leuk was lying on his side facing me. He was quiet, his breathing hushed and tidal in the bluish light, defiantly calm. I turned away onto my side and gave in to the ticking of the clock.

TEN

It was now February 1942, and we had just two things left: our house and each other. When the weather began to improve that month, I felt life in general should improve, as though the invasion had been timed with winter and so must die with it too. But food was in even shorter supply, and instead of returning to school, I had to endure the constant drone of propaganda in the streets and on the radio. The cruelty of the Japanese bit harder.

A strange thing began to happen in the evenings. Sometime before dark, usually around six, a low ringing of bells could be heard in the street. The first time we heard it, Leuk and I were sitting in our room playing cards. I put my cards down and accidentally exposed them to his view, ending the game. I opened the window and listened. At first I heard what sounded like horns blowing from far away, and then I realized it was a gong being struck — not a large temple gong, but a smaller one like the one we used to call everyone to dinner. I looked out into the dark streets and tried to track the sound, and Leuk silently joined me.

The sound faded and came closer, then moved farther off again, until I could distinguish many gongs being struck at once. They rang just loudly enough to be heard, as though struck with extreme care. The gongs seemed to ring in triplets now, fading in and out over the streets, quick but unpredictable, like a school of fish darting through water.

The bedroom light went out, and I turned to see Ah-Tseng hurrying towards us. She pulled the shutters closed, lowered the window, and drew the curtains over it.

Leuk asked her if she knew what it was. She stared nervously at the curtains and brushed a strand of hair behind her ear.

"It's a warning." She seemed distracted. She reached over and fingered the thin white cloth of the curtain as though to reassure herself. "To get off the street. You hear it more during the day, before the curfew starts."

I caught the vagueness in her voice and I watched her. She looked away and her voice turned blunt.

"It's a warning to girls and women," she said, "that the Japanese are off duty. Don't you hear the screams at night?"

She put her hand over her mouth and bunched a dust cloth tightly in her other hand.

I backed away from her. My voice dropped as though in apology. "I do. I hear them."

She looked quickly away from the window as though a gong might sound again any second. She smoothed her skirts and said that dinner would be ready soon.

The next morning, I slept late. As I roused myself and took in the mid-morning light, the clock read a quarter to ten. I was embarrassed. Leuk was gone and his bed was made, and I imagined he'd been up a long time. I dressed quickly, worried that others were up cleaning or running errands to the ration centre. I hadn't gone to bed more tired than usual or exerted myself the day before, but when I pulled my belt through the buckle, I was reminded of why I was so tired: the pin ran an inch past the last hole. My stomach grumbled while I took the cloth belt out of my bathrobe and ran it through the loops. I pulled it tight, fixed a careful knot, and tucked the loose ends into my waist to conceal them.

Mrs. Yee's door was open and her room was empty. From far downstairs I heard the distinct quaver of her voice, beaten thin with distress and calling for her elder daughter. When I got downstairs, I found her by the front doors, rigid with dread and yelling at Chow. My mother and Ah-Tseng stood next to him.

"She was supposed to be back by now! Where is she?" she shouted. "You sent her out there and told her it wasn't far! She wouldn't get lost. Go and find her! Bring her back before they take her!"

She reached out to grab Chow by his jacket and he moved awkwardly away. She stood frozen, her hands clawing the air, a pantomime of utter helplessness. Then she caught me staring at her. Her eyes paused on my improvised belt before flitting away. Then she started wailing. Twice Chow and my mother had to drag her from the front door. Mrs. Yee staggered back and collapsed at the bottom of the staircase, where she cried over and over again, "Go get her! Bring her back!"

Earlier that morning, Shun-Lai had argued that she should be allowed out to line up at a nearby vegetable stall. Mornings were safer, as the Japanese were assembled in their headquarters at the French Convent School. Her mother had agreed only if Chow went with her, but when he arrived, she had already run out on her own. It was eight o'clock when she left, nearly two hours ago.

Mrs. Yee sat on the bottom step, staring downward in despair. Her hair had come loose and she splayed over the marble like a large injured insect. At the top of the stairs, Shun-Yau and Shun-Po appeared. They made their way down tentatively, first holding each other by the hand, then letting go when they reached the bottom, where their mother shook and sobbed, unaware her other children had come to her.

Shun-Po crouched down and extended a hand towards her mother's back. "Mama, please—"

Mrs. Yee shivered and raised her head, until at last she looked up and took her daughter's hand. She looked into her daughter's face. "Please, go find her."

Shun-Po froze and her brother stepped forward. "Mama, come back upstairs. Shun-Lai will come home." He leaned forward but didn't touch her.

Mrs. Yee didn't respond. My mother turned to Ah-Tseng and told her to take some tea upstairs. Then she walked over to the stairs and gave each of the children a quiet nod; they stepped back with visible relief. Leaning forward, my mother took Mrs. Yee's wrists in her hands and spoke to her in a quiet voice.

"Mrs. Yee, I'm sure you cannot be comfortable here. I will send someone to look for your daughter, but you must go back up to rest. Now, children," she said to the Yee children, "go with Chung-Man and Leuk to the library, and do your studies. Ah-Ming will find you a snack." She stood back and Mrs. Yee rose with her, her face distorted by tears. She was exhausted and her sobs had shrunk to dry, hollow whispers.

"My daughter…" she started, and my mother put one arm around her and helped her back upstairs as Shun-Yau and Shun-Po stepped quickly away. My mother wrapped her arm close around Mrs. Yee's shoulders, holding her like a child so that Mrs. Yee inclined her head towards her. My mother turned her head and looked back at the four of us one more time.

"To the library, please," she whispered.

I scanned the street from the library, thinking I might pick out the form and movement of a sixteen-year-old girl among the few people out. But the picture in my mind was of a body moving carefree and lightly, and there was nothing like that in the world before me. Chow and Tang said they would go out to look for Shun-Lai, but by midday the soldiers were everywhere. My mother and I sat down on a sofa and looked out the window together. Japanese troops paraded nearby, the thrum of their boots and martial calls beating the air. A trio of transport vehicles rode down the street, wrapped in canvas and dark paint, their back ends bristling with young arms clutching machine guns. The sidewalks emptied.

I asked my mother if she thought Shun-Lai would be found. Of course, I knew that if she could have come back, she would have. There were no distractions left out there for a girl: no market, no chance meeting of friends. My mother put her arm around me.

"I don't think she will. But no one knows anything, and we mustn't say things like that to Mrs. Yee."

I leaned against her, pressed my head on her shoulder, and she reached up and touched my ear. I didn't want to move now, and my mother was very still. I looked up at her when I felt her shake. Her eyes were shut and tears ran down her face, and she had pressed her lips together tightly, believing I wouldn't notice.

Three days passed, and Shun-Lai did not return. Mrs. Yee fell into a kind of trance, silent and haunted, as though she craved to rejoin her daughter. I felt pity for Shun-Po and Shun-Yau as their mother receded from them and became a ghostlike creature who wandered the halls, her face sunken and lost inside her knotted hair. The only sounds she made were the shuffling of her feet and the rustle of her clothes. Her clothes almost drowned out her voice as she whispered to her children in fixed phrases throughout the day: *wash your hands, come and eat, don't go out.* Her son and daughter drew back from the woman who recited these words with feeble gestures, a woman who seemed no longer there.

After that day, each time we gathered together, we were confronted by the cruel contrast in our fortunes: the Leung family remained intact while the Yees diminished. From the servants and even Mrs. Yee, I heard superstitious whisperings about the meaning of this cruelty. Sometimes at night I imagined ancestral voices muttering bitterly about it from their cold seats in the afterworld, denouncing the stacked evils of homelessness, husband-lessness, and poor eating, as though they couldn't see the changed world outside our walls. But here among the living we were assailed by events that seemed to have no explanation, and our connections to the past grew weaker every day.

Over the next two days, I tried to fight the gloom pervading the house. Leuk and I managed to coax Shun-Yau out into the courtyard with us, and then his sister joined us, though they were withdrawn and never stayed for long. But Leuk and I revived all the quieter games that we could play outside without drawing too much attention from soldiers on patrol.

That was how we spent our last days in the house: hemmed in by our ornamental walls and our invaders, re-enacting the fragments of our former life, waiting to be thrown out into the world.

In November 2001, I went to visit my son Chris at his home in Seattle. I remember the halo of street lights at the city's edge, porcelain white like in a surgical theatre, though softened by the rain. I had decided to visit him after the anniversary of Alice's death, and from my first day there I felt a loneliness that followed me through his house like a python. I am not a lonely person by nature, but his house imposed it on me through its quiet greyness. He's always been a man with little to say, withdrawn and unhappy. I was glad to see him, but I felt I needed a break. So I went for a drive and then hiked through a small suburban park until almost sundown, and in defiance of the temper of that house I climbed in my unsuitable shoes up the wet grass of a hill, pushing off an irritable mood.

I slipped a lot. My god, I thought, you're past seventy now, get back down there. But I kept climbing, gripping trees or anchoring my feet over rocks to pull and push myself upward. The misted air collected on my face in the twilight, and I breathed harder. Then I reached the top. I leaned over, bracing my hands on my knees, and paused for several minutes.

The hilltop wasn't much to look at, for all the effort of the climb: a derelict bench sat next to an old garbage can lying on its side, braced by tall grass. The hilltop was the size of a small yard, and the view of the city was obstructed by trees. A few yards ahead I found a statue half hidden by a sprawling yew, and I went over to inspect it. There was a rusted plaque on its base, almost illegible except for the initials W.B. and some dates. And the stone, of whatever kind, was pitted and broken over its surface, and everywhere worn to indistinctness by the weather. I ran my fingers over the statue's face, the lips a mere rippling interruption in the lower half, the nose gone. I yearned for my son's house again and felt bitterly cold. A sudden sharpness pierced my chest, I leaned against the statue in the wind, and I saw how much this little spot looked like a graveyard.

And those other small parks, the ones in my old city where memorials were put up here and there after the war, what did I recall of them, and what can they say to anyone who sees them now? Like the statue I touched that night, those memorials can only whisper, their granite has been set over a mountain of oblivion. Living memory is barren: it has no descendants or inheritors. It is a reservoir from which no channel can be struck. Where are Shun-Lai and her mother? Where are the tailor and his apprentice? They have crumbled like statues before time and the rain, and the ground they once walked has grown thick with forgetting.

The hilltop made me uneasy. I felt the inadequacy of my old walking shoes against the wet grass on the hillside. Clumsily, I made my way back down and cursed myself, frightened of the park's emptiness in the near dark, and on the drive home in the rental car I blasted the heat and shivered in my wet clothes. Old fool.

It was late when I returned to find my son nervously pacing the driveway in the rain, a mobile phone against his ear. He met me with such a worried look that he seemed likewise to have aged that evening.

ELEVEN

Late in the afternoon of the twenty-third of February, my mother summoned us all. She sent Sheung and Tang to gather us up from around the house, both families into the library. Mrs. Yee entered leaning on her son's arm. I hadn't seen her for two days and was shocked at her appearance—though I'd also been avoiding my own face in the mirror. I was tired, my clothes smelled, and when I touched the contours of my face in bed at night, I could feel how thin it was getting.

My mother sat stiffly on a chair next to my elder brothers. Wei-Ming ran over to her, and my mother gave her a quick kiss and had her sit by Sheung. She looked around at us.

"Children, you all see how bad things are. We've held up in here as best we could, but there's little left for us to eat. I know it must be safer in the countryside." She looked at me and Leuk with these last words. "Boys, you and Wei-Ming can go to live with your uncle. You'll be safe there. Yee-Lin will take you, and the rest of us will stay here. But don't be afraid, it won't be for long."

She said this in a very flat voice, as though she couldn't believe she was really saying it. I looked at her and nodded. I believe she saw me. I need to believe that she saw I understood. Even now that moment has a sharpness, like the day I heard my father had died. I still see the evening light fading behind her, and the orange trees trembling in the windy courtyard. In the chilly air of the library, a small draft of warm air drifted up from my shirt and passed under my chin. The stale odour of our clothing hung over me and Leuk; and staring numbly past my mother at the rows of books, I thought of the scent of their pages. I longed to retreat into them, to become someone whose pain was just a story.

How the others responded, I don't remember. But we all got up and returned to our rooms to prepare.

The plan was simple and terrible, and it was the only one my mother could devise. We would break up into three groups. Mrs. Yee and her children would have to leave for her sister's in Wan Chai. As for my family, my elder brothers and my mother would stay in the city, where the danger was greatest. My older brothers expected the Japanese would want to confiscate our firm and keep them on as slaves to run it, and if they disappeared with us, we would all be hunted down. Yee-Lin, Leuk, Wei-Ming, and I would leave for our uncle's house in the countryside, where we would be safer and could perhaps attend school. My mother said we would reunite as soon as we could.

I didn't know what "as soon as we could" really meant. No one did. It could mean when the war was over — but what if the Japanese won? I imagined us retreating into China, deep into its mythical West, where I imagined the

Japanese might never go. That evening I stared at a map of Guangdong, trying to grasp what my mother had said and where we might end up. It was incomprehensible. Even the nearest villages seemed far away.

I had so little to take, it took only a few minutes for me to pack my bag. Ah-Tseng helped me, keeping her back to me as she leaned over the clothing on my bed. I caught a brief glimpse of her face, swollen with tears. Everything fit into my backpack, the same bag I'd taken on trips to the park or market. She packed clothes for me, some soap and a toothbrush, and a small paper package of dried fruit and sweets.

Then I went downstairs with it, and set it down next to all the others, which were propped against the wall by the front doors.

My mother and older brothers gathered Leuk, Wei-Ming, and me, and told us that Yee-Lin would guide us to our uncle's house in a village called Tai Fo. My mother reminded us that Yee-Lin was nearly twenty and we should listen to her as though she were our mother. As if to emphasize this, my sister-in-law and Sheung brought out a map and began explaining the journey to Leuk and me. We would go up the Pearl River at night by boat, to Tai Fo, a town I'd never heard of. Sheung wrote the names of my uncle and aunt on a piece of paper, folded it, and put it in Yee-Lin's bag. He couldn't spare the map, so he had meticulously made two copies of it on plain paper, which he gave to Leuk and to Yee-Lin.

Sheung called Leuk and me into my father's study and said he had something for us.

"I know your pants aren't fitting very well these days," he said. I was so hungry that I felt angry at his attempt at humour, but I didn't say anything. He instructed us to take off our cloth belts. We stood there holding our pants up by the belt loops while he went to a small cabinet and took a few things from it.

"Here's a new belt for each of you," he said. "If you're careful, it will do more than keep your pants in place."

I unrolled my belt and puzzled over it. Its leather was even more worn and scratched than my old belt. But the buckle was different. In my hand it weighed more than the rest of the belt. It was solid gold. Leuk's was the same.

"We'll give you a little bit of money," said Sheung. "But that's for ferries or small favours. The buckle is for when you're really in a bad spot."

I started to loop the belt around my pants, but he told both of us to wait. He knelt down in front of Leuk and took a small bottle and a cloth from his pocket.

Sheung tipped the bottle very slowly over the cloth, and a small silver ball rolled out. It was the first time I'd seen mercury, and I was fascinated. He cupped the cloth to keep the little ball from rolling out of his palm, and then he took Leuk's buckle and carefully rubbed the mercury over it. Almost instantly the gold turned a dark, dull brown. He made sure to cover every spot, including the pin, and when he was done, the buckle was as ugly as the belt itself. Then he took my buckle and did the same. He put the bottle and cloth away and told us to put the belts on. Now that they were stained and scratched, the belts suited our old pants and also fit well.

"You're wearing more money than any villager will earn in a lifetime."

I cupped the buckle in my palm. The gold was still warm from being rubbed, warm like skin. "If I need to sell it, how do I get it off?" I asked.

"Only do that if you have to. Scratch it carefully, and do it in secret. Smash it up with a rock so no one knows how it was disguised. If someone knows one of you has gold hidden, they'll guess the rest of you must too."

By the time all these last details were taken care of, it was late in the afternoon, and we realized it made no sense to leave when it was nearly dark. My mother agreed that we would stay in the house one more night.

That evening, I sat at the dining room table with my small bowl of millet dotted with chopped, salted turnips and a sliver of egg, listening to my family eat as slowly as they could. I hadn't expected to stay another night. In the house sealed like a tomb, and with my belly shrunken, listening to Yee-Lin weep at the thought of leaving her husband, I could still touch the smooth white floors and see the faces of those I knew, and believe that I was lucky.

I knew it would be hard for me to sleep that night. I sat in the library facing the garden and looked outside at the trees, which seemed to have grown. In the countryside, I thought, there would be trees everywhere, wild and taller, impenetrable walls of forest along the road. I felt cold and wanted to find Leuk, but didn't want to leave my favourite seat in the old library.

Around ten, I heard the familiar tentative click of Mrs. Yee's shoes and others walking behind her. She and my mother came into the library, talking in low voices, while Shun-Po and Shun-Yau trailed behind, all three carrying bags. I moved to leave the room, but my mother said I could stay. She turned and took Mrs. Yee's hands in hers.

"Mrs. Yee, I would never want to turn you and your children away. I wish this were the safe place it used to be. Maybe one day soon it will be again."

Mrs. Yee thanked my mother for taking her family in. "My sister's home in Wan Chai isn't far. On quiet days I may be able to walk back here." I knew what she meant when I looked at Shun-Yau. He was carrying two bags over his shoulders: his own and Shun-Lai's. The handle of her hairbrush was sticking out of a side pocket like a signal, as though she had merely forgotten the way home.

"Please be safe," my mother said and called me over.

I bowed to Mrs. Yee and wished her good luck, and then said goodbye to Shun-Po. I shook Shun-Yau's hand. "See you back at school, I hope."

"I hope so too," he replied.

My mother and I walked them to the entrance. Chow was waiting to walk them all the way to Wan Chai, and had plotted a safe route for himself back to the house. He checked the street and then ushered them outside, past the broken gates.

TWELVE

Tang touched my shoulder and I opened my eyes. He looked worried as he turned to rouse Leuk from his sleep.

"Time to get up," he said. He opened the shutters, revealing grey skies.

"I don't want to get up." I thought this would be funny, as though Tang were trying to get me off to school. Instead, he bit his lip and blinked a few times before he spoke.

"Come on," he insisted and took me by the arm.

I got up and dressed and went downstairs with Leuk. My mother and Ah-Tseng were having tea and had set the table for Yee-Lin, Wei-Ming, Leuk, and me. There were small bowls of steamed millet mixed with rice, and on a plate in the middle were two salted duck eggs sliced into quarters, and a dish of preserved vegetables with a little salted pork fat.

I waited until the others were sitting before I picked up a slice of egg with my chopsticks. I paused and looked at my mother.

"Don't worry, I've already eaten," she said.

Yee-Lin ate very quickly with trembling hands. I heard her breathing in between mouthfuls, and she sipped her tea slowly as though trying to calm herself. Sheung sat down next to her and stared vacantly at the empty plate in the middle of the table. A small pool of brine where the eggs had lain glistened on the cream-coloured pottery. I reached over with my chopsticks and dipped the ends in it, and then I brought them to my mouth and tasted it. I looked over at Yee-Lin and she did likewise.

My mother put down her teacup and looked at her. "It's time for you to go," she said.

Sheung walked with us to the road, looking carefully around for soldiers. Holding my bag, I thought our departure would draw stares. I imagined people pointing us out in horror, as though the last fortress of the city had fallen.

But nobody cared. The streets swarmed with homeless and distraught people carrying bags and cases not worth stealing. No one would notice us. I realized, after looking with pity at the people in the street, that I was one of them. I clung tightly to my small bundle, fearing someone would steal it, but I didn't see anyone who would have had the strength.

The number of people in the streets was growing. On the front steps of abandoned and vandalized shops, people sat silently as if posed there by a painter. Many had patchy, discoloured swellings on their limbs that were otherwise as thin as poles. A skull-faced boy Wei-Ming's age drew his hand up to his face, moving as though half frozen, and chased a fly off with fingers covered in red sores. Many years later, unable to forget him, I guessed that he had beriberi. His hopeless eyes locked on mine, seizing me with a power that was monstrous in proportion to his shrunken frame. I felt as though I were sinking into a pit of cold mud that climbed up my chest, threatening to fill my mouth.

We were headed for a small harbour to the east where fishermen kept their junks near the river mouth. It was a long walk through the damp spring air. We quickly left the crowded areas and were in the poorer parts of the city, where few people showed themselves. The buildings were old, encrusted with posters, and coloured only by the masses of hanging laundry. Stray dogs fed well on garbage and rats. Up ahead, fishing boats bobbed in the harbour. It struck me only then that I was leaving home.

We reached the harbour in the early evening. I was starving and thought about announcing it, though I knew the rest of my family probably were, too, and didn't need to be reminded. Unlike the main harbour, which was lit up all night for the ships, the lights at this port were rationed, and in the twilight the docks and fish huts had a ghostly feel. The old wooden vessels creaked softly as the water lapped against their oiled hulls. Fishermen and their families shuffled over their boats, silhouetted by coal fires and dim lanterns.

We waited near an old brick building. Yee-Lin took a sheet of paper from her purse and squinted at it in the inconstant yellow light. I asked her what it was.

"The name of the man who's going to take us," she said quietly. She held the sheet close. "He's supposed to meet us here. His name is Kwan. Chow made the arrangements. He's already been paid. I don't know much else."

We bought a little food from a hawker — small packages of sticky rice and shrimp — and ate standing in the dark. We stood apart from everyone else. The hawker, a woman with a tanned face bound by a scarf whose ends were tucked into her winter jacket, took the coins from Yee-Lin and jingled them curiously in her palm for a time before locking them up in her cash box.

A man in a plain black suit approached. He looked us over and spoke to Yee-Lin.

"Come this way, Mrs. Leung," he said. She asked if he was Mr. Kwan and started to reach into her purse for the paper, but he gestured abruptly for her to put it back. We finished our food quickly and followed him.

The boat was moored at the harbour's edge, far from the fishermen. The captain, a tough-looking man with a shaved head, stood at the prow. Two parents and their daughter, who looked about fifteen, were already seated in the boat with their baggage. Although the boat could have held over a dozen passengers, there would be only seven of us. When I saw the girl, I thought of Shun-Lai.

"Everything is arranged with the captain," Mr. Kwan said. "He will take you to Tai Fo where your aunt and uncle live. Your husband has written to alert them, but he didn't use your names in the letter." He looked at Yee-Lin's hands and pried the folded paper from her fingers. "Don't keep such things on you," he said and walked over to a hawker and threw the precious paper into a brazier. He looked at us all. "Once you cross over into China, you'll be safer, but you can expect the Japanese to be patrolling the border heavily. Let the captain deal with them."

Mr. Kwan helped us into the boat, and Yee-Lin got on last. The other family was sitting near the back, so we sat in the middle. We didn't speak to them.

The captain leaned against the side of the boat. "That's it?"

Mr. Kwan nodded, and then he unmoored the boat and heaved the rope on board as the captain started the engine.

The pier receded as we moved downriver. The harbour lights dimmed quickly and the silhouettes of crouching figures on the wharves disappeared. All I heard was the engine and the river sloshing against the vessel. In the dark, only a single lantern mounted at the back of the boat shed any light. The parents behind us whispered quickly back and forth, and each time the girl said something, the mother urged her to be quiet. I looked back at them. They were huddled on the bench with a large blanket spread over their knees.

When we were in the middle of the river, the captain suddenly slowed the engines and turned to us. "Do you have any valuables?"

Yee-Lin stiffened next to me. "Yes," she said.

"You don't want the Japanese to take them. We'll be stopped and inspected for sure. Give them to me and I'll conceal them for you." He looked over our heads at the family behind us. "You too."

Wei-Ming leaned over and whispered into my ear, "Don't give him our stuff." She had one hand on my shoulder and pulled hard on it as she whispered, her lips running so close to my ear that her words blurred into anxious puffs. Yee-Lin looked cautiously at Leuk.

"It's all right," said the captain. "I don't want your things. You can bet we'll be stopped, though. The better I hide them, the shorter the delay. I do this all the time. Look." He opened a small wooden locker on the side of the boat and took out a few oilcloth sacks. "I'll put them in here and tie them up and hang them over the side with a small weight. The hook goes under the waterline, so they won't see it. Do you have something?"

"Yes," said Yee-Lin at last and looked at the three of us. "Come on, give it to him." She took out her cotton bag full of coins and banknotes, and another one with jewellery, and we each took our money bags out of our pockets.

Each time we handed the captain something, he said, "Good," before shoving them into the sacks. He tied the sacks tightly with a leather strap. "Anything else?"

My right hand fell on my belt buckle. I rubbed it lightly, fearing that in the dark the mercury stain had somehow worn off. "No," I said. I looked over across Yee-Lin and saw Leuk fiddling with his belt. His eyes caught mine. He pulled his hand away from the buckle and looked up at the captain.

"Nothing else," he said.

The captain looked at us searchingly. In the lantern light I discerned the lean contours of his face. He shut his eyes for a moment and ran his free hand over his shaved head. "Okay, then," he said. "Leave the belts on."

He tied up the last sack and moved on to the other family. They made a real fuss about it.

"We don't have much," the mother protested.

"You may not want me to hide your valuables, but it's better for all of us if you do."

I heard a lot of shuffling and the jingling of coins and jewellery, while the parents whispered to each other over the rumble of the engine. The captain walked back up to the helm as he tied the last of the sacks. Then he took a pole with a hook on one end and reached over the side of the boat. He pulled up a long chain that banged against the hull as it came up, and he secured the oilcloth sacks to the end before carefully lowering it back into the water. Then he turned to us with a quick grin, showing a mouth only half full of teeth.

"Very good!" he said, as though he'd just won a bet. He returned to the helm, one hand rubbing the back of his head, and revved the motor. In my seat I rocked with the movement of the boat. I leaned against my sister-in-law and fell asleep.

I woke with a start. People were shouting and a loud horn blew twice. I opened my eyes as the boat chugged to a stop and a bright light shone in our faces. Men shouted at us in Japanese.

The woman behind me spoke rapidly to her daughter; her husband told her to be quiet. A patrol boat had pulled up next to us and shone a searchlight onto our deck.

The captain turned and extended an upraised hand towards us, telling us to stay calm. He said a couple of words in slow Japanese, over and over again as the officer shouted, probably the only words he knew. The Japanese threw a rope across our starboard side and the captain took it and pulled the two boats closer. One of the soldiers leapt into our boat. The captain looked at us reassuringly.

"Inspection, that's all." Another soldier boarded. They looked over every surface with flashlights and then shone them in our faces. Wei-Ming squinted in the light. Yee-Lin raised her hand to shield her eyes, and the soldier barked at her and slapped her hand away. He let the flashlight linger on her face as she blinked and stared into her lap.

They opened everything, the chests, our bags, the boxes of fishing gear stored under our seats. They bantered back and forth, and in their voices I recognized the boredom of the young soldiers who ran the ration centre in Hong Kong. They made us empty our pockets and take off our shoes and shake them over the deck. When they were done with us, they moved to the other family.

The routine was the same. I wanted to look back but didn't dare. I just sat and blinked my eyes repeatedly to flush the burn from the flashlights. The family shuffled their bags and I could hear the young girl breathing hard. Then one of the soldiers spoke sharply to the other. Their voices quickened and rose. One of them barked, and the mother and girl screamed. I jumped in my seat and gripped the edge of the bench. Wei-Ming grabbed me with a shaking hand.

They dragged the girl away from her parents and took her into their boat. The father got up and I heard the click of a rifle cocking, and then his wife pleading with him to sit.

We sat for a long time, hearing only the rumbling of the engines and the two boats knocking against each other. I couldn't see where the soldiers had taken the girl. It was a much larger boat than ours. Of the four soldiers I had seen on it, only two remained on deck. One swept a spotlight downriver with his rifle in one hand, and the other one faced us, resting a boot against the side of the boat, his rifle still cocked. I looked at our captain. He was leaning against the wheel with his arms folded. I met his eye for a second, and he looked away into the blackness.

A cabin door opened and the girl came back out with one of the soldiers. He shouted at her and gestured towards our boat. She clambered over the edge and ran back to her mother. The soldiers on our boat returned to their vessel, unlashed our boat from theirs, and they pulled away. All the spotlights but one went dark, and their boat roared off downriver towards the city.

Our boat rocked in its wake. The girl was crying and I turned to look at her. The captain leaned over and talked to her.

"Did they touch you?" he said.

"No," she said. "But they took the money belt I had under my dress."

The captain looked at the father and cursed him. "Idiot! You should have given it to me." He went up and revved the engine and gave us all a quick look. "We'll be out of their reach soon."

I woke to the sound of the engine sputtering as it shut down. It was early dawn, very clear, and I caught the scent of kitchen fires. We had docked in Tai Fo and the captain was securing the boat.

Wei-Ming was still asleep. She was on the deck next to me with her bag under her head. I sat up and shook her. Yee-Lin and Leuk were already awake. The captain fished our possessions out of the water with a grappling hook. The other family was gone.

The captain handed us our bags. "They got off earlier, at Wan Yue." He took some of the money Yee-Lin paid him and bought food from a hawker, then sat on the ground with his back to us and ate. Leuk and I picked up all four bags.

The air was clean, and I listened to the river washing against the dock. No guns, no trucks, no Japanese. I tried to feel some kind of relief. After months of near confinement in our house, I was out in the open. I tried to tell myself leaving for Tai Fo would be just like leaving home for school, except that I was older and should be better able to deal with it. Leuk and Yee-Lin didn't seem troubled, and Wei-Ming was just tired, leaning against my sister-in-law as Yee-Lin got her bearings. When I looked at them, I told myself everything would be all right, and that someone, a voice from up the river, would call us home soon.

THIRTEEN

We walked from the boat landing to a wide dirt road.
Fishermen working in trios were headed the other way,
down to their boats, and paid no attention to us. Yee-Lin
told us our aunt and uncle lived nearby.

There were few people on the road as we walked into
Tai Fo. Some of the houses and shops were in poor repair,
others bright with new paint and coloured banners. In
the compact public square across which two larger stone
buildings faced each other, a policeman sat asleep on
a folding stool with his cap tilted over his face. Yee-Lin
spoke to him. Without getting up, he rubbed his eyes and
pushed his cap up to look at her. She started telling him
what she could recall from Sheung's letter, but the officer
ignored her and responded with a quick, vague gesture
indicating the way. Then he went back to sleep.

We moved quickly down another dirt road. Other than
the birds, the scuffing of our feet was the only sound in
the air. Leuk walked ahead of me and his bag knocked
against his legs as it swung. The sight irritated me and I
told him to carry it over his shoulder.

"Don't tell me what to do," he said without looking
back and let his bag knock even harder against his legs.

We arrived at a small house with a banyan tree leaning
towards it. The red trim around the doors and windows
looked newly painted, and banners hung from the eaves.

I had forgotten it was almost the New Year. I heard the thin metal of cooking pots rattling inside the house and the scrape of a chair.

Yee-Lin set her bags down and knocked on the door, and a lean-faced woman in a grey padded jacket opened it and peered out. I was struck by the ease of her gesture, as though she would never expect to see armed men or refugees at her door. The lightly silvered hair near her temples blew over her face as she listened to Yee-Lin. The woman looked straight at her, and then she smiled and reached out and lightly touched her hand. She stepped outside and spoke warmly to us. Leuk and I bowed to her.

"Your father and my husband were cousins, but I never met him. Come inside now. I've been expecting you but didn't know when you'd arrive." She reached over and picked up Wei-Ming's bag. "Very cold today," she said and made a rubbing gesture on one arm. We let the girls walk with her, and Leuk walked beside me. He looked exhausted; dark rings hung under his eyes and he shuffled through the gravel to the doorway.

Our aunt told us to put our bags down and sit at the kitchen table. She served us rice porridge with fish. She must have known from our faces that we hadn't eaten like that for a long time. I ate everything. We ate from big earthenware bowls, and when I scraped my spoon against the side to wipe off the last smear of porridge, Yee-Lin warned me not to be rude. So I moved the spoon slowly over the side and held my hand against the dish to tame the scraping of the earthenware bowl.

We shared a room at the back of the house and slept on mattresses on the floor. None of us had slept well on the boat, so we all lay down. I woke within half an hour and lay on my back, listening to the others doze. A fly crossed the ceiling and made its way towards the window. It stopped on a chip in the red paint of the frame before crossing over to the glass, and there it skated noisily over the pane, knocking itself against the leaded grille. The bedroom door was open.

For a time my aunt shuffled over the floor directly overhead, and I listened to the clapping of her slippers. I tracked her movements around the upper floor, down the stairs, and through the hall. I didn't want to get up and pulled the quilt up to my nose. The fly rattled against the window as it warmed in the sun. It must have been the middle of the afternoon.

I made my bed carefully, mindful of what my father would have thought of me as I prepared to meet his cousin. I smoothed the quilt carefully before returning to the kitchen.

My aunt was sitting at the table picking over a pile of vegetables, separating the rotten leaves from cabbages and excising black spots from radishes with a small knife. She looked up at me.

"Chung-Man?" I bowed a second time. "You can help me here. Your uncle will be home soon for supper." She extended her foot and pushed a stool out from under the table towards me.

I sat down and started trimming the vegetables. A pile of leaves and soft black excisions from the radishes built up at my elbow.

"The school is closed today," she said. "But the three of you can go there tomorrow and sign up."

At the mention of school, my heart lightened. It had been three months since Leuk and I had run to the tram stop with Mr. Lee, and all I'd done since was read half-heartedly and poke through my math books.

"Is it a big school?"

She smiled but didn't look up. "Not too big — good enough, though. Both my children went there. You should be fine. Your brother sent school fees ahead for at least a few months."

My fingers went stiff. The paring knife slipped in my hand, and I cut my thumb with it. My mother hadn't said anything about being gone for months.

"Be careful," said my aunt. I looked up and saw both her worry and her irritation. "Come clean your hand." She washed it carefully in the sink, which had an old-fashioned pump rather than a faucet, and wrapped a bandage around my thumb.

I sat down again and picked up the knife, but a terrible chill spread throughout my chest. I sat silently at the table for several minutes, fumbling with the knife and vegetables as a mess of decayed trimmings piled up before me. My eyes pricked and I blinked rapidly.

"Did my brother say how long we'd be staying here?" I asked.

She didn't look up. "No. But you're welcome to stay for as long as you need." She stopped her work and looked at me sympathetically. "I'm sure you'd rather go home," she added.

Then I felt it in my face: a terrible loosening of muscle and a sudden heat beneath my eyes. I took in a sharp breath and clamped my jaw hard, pressing my legs together on the stool. I squeezed my eyes shut for a few seconds, then opened them and tried to keep up with the peeling.

My aunt got up quickly with a scrape of her stool and tossed her trimmings into a basket destined for the yard. She stood over the sink with the paring knife tucked into her belt, her back to me. I hoped she would be distracted by the swaying of the banyan outside the kitchen window.

"Come here, Chung-Man," she said without turning.

I got up and let the noise of the stool mask the sound of my throat clearing, wiped my eyes, and stood beside her.

The banyan tendrils were moving softly in the breeze, and I stared at them too, the leafless and naked whips of the massive branches hanging sadly in the late winter air, tracing weak lines in the dust.

An hour later, Yee-Lin joined us and asked if she could help in the kitchen. A few minutes later Leuk and Wei-Ming stood nervously in the doorway, looking at me seated at the table as though by special permission. By then my aunt was making supper with Yee-Lin, who told my siblings to come in and gave them each a cup of tea. When we were all sitting together, I forgot the shock of what my aunt had said about school and started to feel better about being in her house.

The four of us were sitting in the kitchen when the front door opened and my aunt announced that our uncle was home. The three of us immediately stood up while Yee-Lin wiped her hands on an apron. A middle-aged man dressed in a black winter jacket, white shirt, and dark pants stood in the entrance, rubbing his hands together as though washing them. He grinned broadly and welcomed us as my aunt removed his jacket, and we all bowed and thanked him for taking us in.

I was amazed at his likeness to my father. There's no similarity more jarring than to someone who is dead. He took only three steps into the kitchen before I recognized my father's gait and the particular slope to the crown of his shaved head. As the evening went on, I caught myself staring at him from time to time and watching his movements. It reminded me that my memories of my father had been reduced to the geometry of gait and gesture, like the memory of a shadow puppet.

Unlike my remote and preoccupied father, my uncle had a warm, informal manner. After dinner we sat in the parlour sipping tea and eating from a small plate of sweets. My aunt sat in her chair and watched the coals glow in a brazier in the corner. Other than the stove, this was the only source of heat in the house. Still in the jacket he'd worn outside, my uncle sat back in a large chair with his teacup balanced on the knee of his crossed leg and entertained our questions. Leuk did most of the questioning.

"What do you do?" This ought to have been rude, but our uncle looked pleased.

"I'm the district magistrate." He said this with the assured drabness of someone with high status. "Do you know what that is?"

Leuk and I said we didn't. Wei-Ming was nearly asleep on the sofa beside Yee-Lin.

"It means I listen to people argue all day!" He clapped his hand on one armrest to lend weight to this depleted joke, and his teacup rattled in its saucer. "Who would want to do such work? But it has to be done. People never stop fighting."

"Do you know when it will stop?" said Leuk.

Our uncle looked at him. "How could it? Today I had to listen to all kinds of nonsense, and it was the same as ten years ago when I first started." He looked into the brazier and cracked his knuckles.

Leuk paused. "No, I mean the fighting in Hong Kong. The Japanese. Are they going to leave?"

The dim glow of the coal brazier held our uncle's eyes. "I don't know," he said finally. "Someone has to defeat them, and get them out of China for good." He turned back to us and gave a firm nod, as though this bit of advice had been missing from the British strategy.

I wondered who was powerful enough to do that. Not the British, who had left, nor the Chinese army, who I'd been told were barely hanging on to China itself. I knew nearly nothing about the Americans. From what little I'd heard of Pearl Harbor, they seemed no better equipped to dispose of the emperor's armies. I had no answer, and in my uncle's parlour the question didn't seem to have one.

The following morning, we got up early and our aunt gave us breakfast and walked us to school. Yee-Lin came along to learn the way. My sister-in-law had packed each of us a lunch in a tiffin box, and I tucked mine inside the front of my jacket to feel its warmth. My aunt wrapped a yellow scarf lightly around her head to preserve her hairstyle, and we followed it to school like a beacon. We shuffled over the gravel past dormant shrubs and bamboo, over a bridge that crossed a small stream, and into the village centre.

In the village, we passed through the same square where we had met the policeman the day before. He was still there, though when he saw my aunt he got up from his chair and straightened his uniform.

"Good morning, Mrs. Leung."

She nodded at him as we passed. At one end of the square was a large, well-kept building that stood out against the shabbiness of some of the others. The paint was fresh and gleamed in the cool morning light, and the large black wooden doors reminded me of our own back home. Our aunt said it was the courthouse. I imagined my uncle at his desk in there, leaning into the elbows of his dark jacket as people arrived to involve him in their time-consuming arguments and the grievances of village life.

Our first day at school passed quickly. I couldn't focus because I was so tired and hungry, and also because the teacher spent most of his time dealing with unruly students and paid us little attention. There were only three classrooms in the building and Wei-Ming had at first been separated from us, until she cried so hard they put her in with Leuk and me.

At the end of the day, Yee-Lin returned to walk us home. It was almost a straight line from the school down the main street that led past the courthouse. A large crowd milled or sat idly around the courthouse steps. They didn't look like people with much to do. Some were women who sat on the cold stone steps with full bags of shopping from the market; others just looked bored. As we were leaving the square, the courthouse doors opened and a man came out and posted a large notice sheet on a board. Immediately, all the idlers hustled up the steps to look at it, though we kept walking.

We spent another evening by the brazier. It ought to have bored me, but I was so tired that I was happy just to sit still before bed. My uncle listened to the radio on the table next to his chair, his head tilted as he absorbed a stream of static-strewn news about the war. The maid, who had had the day off yesterday, came in with a fresh pot of tea and retreated quickly into the kitchen. I watched her leave and thought about Ah-Tseng, and then our kitchen, and the staircase to the cellar, and the orchard in front of the house. It didn't seem real. In my memory it was like an image preserved in ice, and in this stillness my thoughts returned constantly to my mother. I wondered how she was doing without us. Without the sound of trucks in the streets, or screams from distant apartments and alleys, the evening silence of the village became like the walled silence of our old house, and in the centre of this silence sat the memory of my mother.

My aunt seemed uninterested in the radio. Leuk and I were intensely curious to hear the news, but we had to suffer through an evening musical show instead. I asked my uncle if there had been any news earlier about the war and Hong Kong. For a second I thought he was asleep, but then he opened his eyes and shook his head, reaching over to turn the radio off. "Nothing," he said.

"How can there be nothing?" said Leuk. "Didn't they say anything about Hong Kong?"

My uncle waved indifferently. "No, nothing at all. Just the usual about the Japanese. It was mostly about them being in northern China." He spoke as if this were somewhere in Europe.

"We saw a crowd on the courthouse steps today," I said. My aunt dozed on the divan, her head propped uncomfortably against the ornate wooden back. "What was that?"

"Ah," said my uncle. "A trial concluded today. And I was the presiding magistrate." He straightened in his seat as though he were in court, but everything around him — the dim lighting, the cramped provincial parlour, the low droning from my aunt's nose — diminished him to a silhouette in an old chair.

Leuk leaned forward. "Did someone commit a murder?" he asked eagerly.

"No no," my uncle replied, regretting his small effort to gain attention. "Some silly grown-up matters. Nothing you need to worry about. Tai Fo is very safe. Even the Japanese aren't interested in us."

My aunt started awake in her chair and looked dopily around and then sent us to bed. Yee-Lin stayed up with them a little longer, and as I got into my pyjamas I heard muffled bits of conversation through the bedroom door.

Leuk and I moved our mattresses around so that our heads came together at right angles in the corner under the window. Yee-Lin returned and lay down on a cot with Wei-Ming, and they were both asleep quickly. In the dark, with only a little moonlight coming through the small window, Leuk and I talked. It was a long whispering conversation, as though we were in hiding. We talked about the movies, about school, the classmates we missed and the ones we didn't. As we talked, a thin bar of moonlight crawled across the wall opposite, like a snake.

We talked about the occupation: the soldiers everywhere, the rations, the water. I told Leuk about Shun-Yau and the snakes, and we wondered how he and his family were doing and if they had reached Guangdong safely.

Then Leuk turned on his back and said, "I wonder how Mother's doing."

Instantly, a terrible ache spread outward from my ribs. My limbs burned and my stomach tightened, I pressed my lips together, and before the sadness overcame me, I grew angry at Leuk for mentioning her. Since the evening we left the house, I had tried to keep my thoughts of our mother for only the most private spaces, when I was alone and masked by darkness, like the first night on the boat.

I told him bluntly that I didn't care, but the words came out half choked and wetted. I turned onto my side and faced the wall, away from the fading bar of moonlight, protected by the darkness and my anger.

FOURTEEN

One morning on the way to school, we stopped at a pond by the road. We passed it every day, and in the week since our arrival in Tai Fo we had become fascinated with the sudden appearance of flowers at the pond's edge and a group of turtles that lived in it. We left our school books on the road and crouched at the edge, with our shoes right at the limit of the earth before it became muddy, and peered into the water. Wei-Ming threw some vegetable scraps in, taken from the midden in our aunt's house, and within seconds a turtle appeared. With his long snakelike head and jaws, he snapped up the rotten leaves and stems, and small beetles fled from the concentric rings of his motion.

When the water calmed, I looked at our reflections. We were still as thin as when we had left Hong Kong, despite the relative abundance that our aunt and uncle enjoyed in the countryside. I didn't obsess over food as I had back in the city, but my belt still tied at the same spot it had before, and I noticed the thinness in my sister's face, who should still have had a little of her childhood plumpness.

"I don't want to go to school," she said into the mirror of the pond. "I hate the teacher." Wei-Ming had been moved back to the other classroom after her first day of accommodation. Now she endured the boredom of a class that was a year behind what she had been learning at St. Mary's. She found a stick and traced its tip over the water, trying to entice the beetles up the shaft.

"We have to show up," said Leuk. "If you don't, the teachers will tell Uncle."

I tried to guess what our uncle would do. I couldn't imagine him beating us. We saw him in the evenings only, lounging in his chair with tea and a newspaper, his left eyelid drooping in anticipation of sleep.

School was a bore and there was little for us to do in the village. There was no cinema, no theatre club, no organized sports, and the local kids kept their distance. We sat together at lunch and walked home together every day. We did our homework quickly, usually finishing it before the end of the school day. When this became known, the few kids who had talked to us cut us out completely.

We left the pond and got back on the road, speeding up to get to school on time. In the village, a couple of policemen were blocking off a large part of the town square, and some labourers were building a platform in the middle as though for a performance. Women swept the steps of the courthouse, and a man was preparing to unfurl some banners from its eaves. I guessed there would be a festival starting soon. Wei-Ming asked me if I knew what it was, but we were in too much of a hurry to stop, and in any case the policemen were urging everyone along.

I thought about the square during the school day to relieve my boredom. On a piece of foolscap during a history lesson, I sketched out the platform in a corner of the page and decorated it with lanterns and drew fireworks in the air. Leuk, who was made to sit three rows away so that we wouldn't talk to each other, kept stealing quick glances over at me to see what I was doing. I covered the sheet carefully with my hand. At the end of the day, I snapped my books shut and we were the first out the classroom door.

By then the notion of something exciting happening in the square had become a small obsession. It would be fun, it would relieve our boredom in this village, it would be like the parties in Hong Kong. Wei-Ming ran beside us until she dropped her tiffin boxes. We stopped and reassembled them quickly, and I wiped my greasy hands on my pants. People walked past us and glared in disapproval. Most also seemed to be heading to the square. I took Wei-Ming by the hand and we walked quickly.

The platform was up, but there were no lanterns, and the banners were illegible as they snapped in the wind. All that had changed since the morning was that a simple wooden arch like a picture frame had been put up. There were people everywhere, and hawkers had gathered at the fringes of the crowd. We had managed to worm our way close to the front of the audience when the smell of grilled snacks reached us. I lost a brief argument with my siblings and had to go back through the crowd to buy them.

They were nothing like the snacks back home before the war — some simple rice cakes with shallots and peanuts. But I got one for each of us. As I waited for the hawker to wrap them up, I looked over the crowd and saw my uncle standing in the doorway of the courthouse, flanked by a policeman. The courthouse doors were open wide. My uncle looked very different in his formal robes, which I assumed he changed into at his office — not the drowsy old man I knew from the parlour. This was one of those events where public officials are called on to declare the start of the celebrations.

I held the snacks close as I pushed back through the crowd, and handed them out to Leuk and Wei-Ming. We devoured them quickly, peering between the adults around us. I didn't see any other children there.

The policeman stepped onto the platform. Then he just stood there. He stared far over our heads towards some distant point, and I began to sense I should not follow his gaze to see what it was. In parts of the crowd a silence — like breath being held — rolled over until I could hear Wei-Ming breathing next to me. In other parts people's chatter grew louder and more rapid, and the few bits I could make out sounded like gibberish. From far off, outside the crowd, a voice broke through. A large bell rang three times.

"Make way! Make way!" a man shouted. I sensed the crowd breaking up on one side, and people shuffled to clear a path. I couldn't see anything, and Leuk and Wei-Ming had no hope of seeing either. The crowd opened up near us. A policeman stepped forward. Behind him, a man and a woman stumbled, and behind them were two more officers. As the procession mounted the steps to the platform, I saw the couple had their legs shackled, and they bowed forward as if bearing an unseen weight. Their wrists were bound behind them. Strapped to their backs were long bamboo poles that rose at least three feet over their heads, and hanging from these were large paper banners with the words *adulterer* and *murderess.*

I heard a man near me say that the woman and man were lovers, and that she had paid someone to kill her husband. They were haggard and drawn, not with hunger like me, but as if from the exhaustion of some inner torment. The other policemen positioned the couple directly beneath the wooden arch facing the courthouse. Both officers took their own places beside the prisoners. Standing with the courthouse to our side, I saw all their faces in profile—the policemen, the man, the woman—and in each of them a waxen heaviness weighed their features down. I felt an oppressive weight spread across the whole square, as though we too should stare downward.

Our uncle now emerged from the courthouse. Through the open doors flanked by rippling banners, he walked slowly down the stairs accompanied by a young clerk holding a scroll. He stepped through the crowd towards the platform, his black robes fluttering like wings. His face was placid, undisturbed, in contrast to the figures on the structure. As my uncle stepped onto the platform, the chained man began to shake and sob in a high-pitched voice. A policeman's face shone with sweat. But my uncle remained aloof, his plump jowls hanging comfortably beneath a look of ceremonial boredom.

His clerk handed him the scroll and my uncle read it

out—the full indictment, the confessions, the high price of shame, the poor example set for the young, on and on. I watched the man and woman as they bowed deeper into their grief, restrained from collapsing only by the shackles at their backs.

I remember this event as embodying so much of the adult world that I was learning to detest: the love of obedience and ceremony, the overbearing sternness, the slowness—and the strange agonies of love that seemed to bring nothing but torment, as they had for Mrs. Yee. And around it all, like an old and crumbling wall against the world, curled the shadow of regret.

In the faces of the man and woman I now saw this pain—as they equated their past to this moment and all their shame. For the first time in my life I grasped the meaning of these grieved expressions, of torment coming not from soldiers or emperors, but from inner weakness, from failure. The woman swung her head from side to side as she wept, and her tears fell onto the platform.

I lost track of what happened next. Wei-Ming seized my hand and pulled hard on it, shouting at me and trying to draw me away. She began to scream. Either Leuk was silent or I couldn't hear him. The droning pronouncements stopped abruptly up on the platform, and then the prisoners' heads were bagged like livestock and ropes were swung over the arch. With a nod from my uncle, the lovers rose slowly into the heavy air, turning and twisting like broken twigs. They swung crazily at first, and then more slowly as they succumbed to the dwindling rocking of their bodies under the arch. At last the woman kicked and briefly entwined one leg around the man's, and he seemed to cling to it with his. In my confusion I thought I felt the panicked tugging of her limb, but it was Wei-Ming yanking my arm and shouting my name.

"I want to go!" she shouted again. Leuk already held her other hand and was starting to lead her away through the crowd, who were stupefied by the spectacle. I heard them all exhaling, open-mouthed, a damp and foul atmosphere choking the square. Unable to look away, I let Leuk and Wei-Ming pull me through the inert mass of the villagers. I ran home behind them, stumbling from the lightness that seemed to fill my skull.

We slowed as we got near the house. Leuk was sweating in the cool breeze. His shirt stuck to his back even through the undershirt, and Wei-Ming hung on my arm and dragged her feet over the gravel. I caught up with Leuk before we reached the door and touched his arm.

"Don't tell anyone about this," I said. He frowned and pulled his arm away.

Our aunt and Yee-Lin were at the market, so the three of us had the house to ourselves. Inside, we took off our shoes and put our school bags down, and it was as though my weight had been cut by half. Leuk and I stood in the middle of the parlour for a moment. Wei-Ming dropped down onto the sofa with a pillow and fell asleep. Her hair hung lank across her face as though she had been drowned. Leuk and I sat down in our usual chairs, but as soon as I sat down I felt queasy, thinking of our evenings with my aunt and uncle. I stood up again and leaned against a wall, staring sideways at the kitchen door.

Leuk rubbed his eyes. "Do you think those people are really dead?"

It took me a moment to understand what he'd said. I thought I recognized death: the shaking and the stillness, the strange humidity that hovers over it. I realized that today was the first time I had witnessed people dying. I'd heard it happening, standing in my bedroom looking over the darkened skyline of Hong Kong, where there was nothing to see but buildings on fire.

I wondered about the man and woman on the platform. Had they been cut down unconscious? Had they been further humiliated before the crowd? I wanted to believe this, not because I longed for the cruelty, but because I didn't want them to be dead, whatever they had done. And yet, in the faces of the crowd, even as I ran confused among them, I had seen the acceptance in their eyes that came with witnessing destruction and somehow taking part in it.

Wei-Ming gave a low groan, like an old woman, and shook herself awake. She sat up abruptly, her hair still over her face, and began to ramble incoherently.

"Where's Mama?" she shouted. "Where are all my things?"

My shoulders and back tightened. "What do you mean?" I shouted back at her. "Are you stupid? Don't you know where we are?"

Wei-Ming looked as if she had been drugged. She tried to brush the hair away from her eyes but couldn't manage it. She rose awkwardly from the sofa, took a second to regain her balance, and with a sob ran into the bedroom.

I looked at my brother. "Don't stare at me," he snapped. Then he rubbed his eyes again, harder. His words sounded like nonsense, and he looked as though he wanted to hit me.

I walked into the kitchen and took a glass off the shelf. I filled it with water and drank, and as soon as I tasted it, I realized I was dying of thirst. I refilled the glass and drank more. I drank again and again, working the pump handle so violently it creaked and the water poured over the lip of the glass and my hand. My throat ached and I felt I might vomit. Thinking I was sick, I went to the bathroom and looked in the mirror. My eyes were bloodshot as if they'd been scratched, and my lids sagged as though I hadn't slept in days.

Despite what the three of us had seen, we didn't start to fear or mistrust my uncle. We kept up our evening routine in the parlour with him and my aunt. But where he had once struck me as bland and ordinary, I saw him now as two different people: an idle conversationalist, and a stern executioner. I reflected on my uncle's sense of ceremony, on Shun-Lai's disappearance, on the cart loaded with corpses. I could explain none of these things, yet I began to see them not as chance events but as revelations about the limits of my understanding. My uncle's little routines, his evenings sitting by the brazier, head tilted towards the radio, his floral teacup—these things still fit with my earlier view of him, though a side of him was now unknowable to me.

I replayed trivial details from the day in the square that helped distract me from the moment at the heart of the event: the crowd talking over my uncle, the shabbiness of the officers' uniforms, the crude wooden arch, so inferior to the great architecture of Hong Kong. In my thoughts I diminished and mocked everything under my uncle's command, even those puppets that dangled over his stage. And when we sat down to eat each night and I thought of the dark world outside, I was still glad he had taken us in.

I keep a small garden that has been shrinking over time. When I first brought it into the world, in our backyard in Chicago, rough-sided and oppressed by weeds, it was a walkable square. I made it large enough to stride through, so I could enjoy exploring it. I formed it into provinces: squashes and melons here, chilies in one corner, a patch of foundering taro, unfailing cabbages everywhere else. On warm spring mornings the scent of compost rose from it like incense.

I put a lot of time into the garden, though mostly it did its own invisible work: the roots mined the softened history in the soil, the long-decayed plants and insects having degenerated into that warm, unsensing pulp that covers the whole earth.

Time is arching downward. The garden now is a set of four square pots that I arranged inside a larger square on the balcony off the flat, but the contents are simpler. Two of the pots have some edible greenery that someone else planted there, though I can't recall what it is. That would be my granddaughter's handiwork. The scent of the garden is exotic: Kuala Lumpur doesn't have the cool seasons of Hong Kong. Even after seventy years, the start of November suggests to me that a chill must be coming, but that change of weather never comes to pass. The memory of cold just pricks at my skin, reminding me of what was.

Now here, hanging over the edge of a pot, there's a half-dead sprig of the stuff I can't identify. It smells like mint. I can reach over and pinch it off. Someone will see me leaning forward in the chair and come running, worried I will fall. I might as well crush the leaves, smell it, this mystery, a little thing that makes my mouth water.

FIFTEEN

Over the following week, I fell asleep later and later each night. During the day, when I was out walking or sitting in school, bored, I thought of all the usual things: Hong Kong, food, my old school, my mother and family. But during those sleepless nights, all I could think of was the execution.

I don't think I was alone. Wei-Ming talked a lot in her sleep and often woke in the night. Leuk talked, too, and I think he woke often but pretended to sleep, because his breathing sounded tense even though his eyes were closed.

Each morning, I woke at the same moment. It was when my uncle got up to leave for the courthouse. I would start to wake when I heard him getting up and dressed, and by the time his door opened and he went to the kitchen for his breakfast, I was fully awake. He and my aunt spoke little. What I heard was the gentle clink of his spoon each time he set it down in the porridge bowl. I lay in bed and was fixated on the sound and image of the spoon: up, down, up, down, striking the edge of his bowl with gentle certainty, like a bell.

The morning after the hangings, we stopped at the pond again to look for the turtles, but both Leuk and I thought the water smelled odd, and we decided not to stop by it anymore. Wei-Ming just stayed on the road. She said she didn't want to be late, even though she hated school. Once in the village centre, we walked quickly through the square. There were no traces of what had taken place there.

Yee-Lin knew something was wrong with us. She asked us what it was, but at first we wouldn't tell her. Finally, one evening when our aunt and uncle were out visiting, Wei-Ming blurted out the whole story. We were sitting at the kitchen table, picking at our dinner, when she started to cry. When she got to the description of the platform, I grew afraid and told her to stop. But she wouldn't listen. Then she described the hanging itself, though all she could say, over and over again, was, "And Chung-Man wouldn't leave!"

My dinner rose back up my throat, and I covered my mouth. I ran out the kitchen door and vomited. I leaned against the wall and took deep breaths, turning my face into the breeze. When I went back inside, Leuk had taken over and was recounting the event again, in more detail. Wei-Ming repeated that she wanted to go home.

Yee-Lin sat silently for a while. She looked down at her plate and then uncomfortably at each of us. Finally she said we should clean up and go sit in the parlour. She lit the coals in the brazier and made tea, and then we all sat on the sofa together even though we barely fit on it. None of us spoke. I heard a low buzzing sound and a muffled voice. My aunt had left the radio on with the volume turned down. The voice, though incomprehensible, sounded agitated. Yee-Lin got up and shut the radio off. She sat back down and Wei-Ming put her head in her lap.

Yee-Lin said, "I think we should leave."

Leuk and I took a few books from the school. Strictly speaking it was theft, though we had every intention of returning them someday. I felt badly only for Wei-Ming, who said everything at the school was boring and stupid; I was unable to find any books I thought she would like to keep her company.

Yee-Lin made sure that our clothes were all clean. I think she was glad we were going, away from our aunt, who had begun to bicker with her, and from the tedium of her days. I know that she missed Sheung terribly.

When we agreed that we should run away, the idea ought to have been shocking—disloyal, unappreciative, dangerous. But broken off from our true family, those little ceremonies of feeling fell away. I stood in the parlour doorway one evening and watched Wei-Ming read on the floor, Yee-Lin in a chair beside her. Opposite were my aunt and uncle, whom I barely knew. I envisioned them dead and shrouded, a voice intoning over their pallid forms beneath the flapping of funeral banners, and I felt nothing. And I thought to myself, *I feel nothing.*

Our bags were packed. Leuk had bought a map from a bookstore and we located a village nearby called Lau Kwan. I was certain our aunt and uncle wouldn't care. What would happen to the school fees? I assumed my uncle would keep them. It occurred to me that he might write to Sheung to say his wife was missing, and then what? It seemed I was the only one who thought of that. When Yee-Lin talked to us about leaving and what would happen next, life in Hong Kong seemed far from her thoughts. She said she knew it might be a while before she saw her husband again, and that she would rather be free than stuck with our aunt.

It was one in the morning, March 4, 1942. After Yee-Lin checked that our aunt and uncle were sleeping, she woke Wei-Ming. We stood in the room in our socks while Yee-Lin did a final check.

"I put our shoes outside the front door," she whispered.

As I passed my aunt and uncle's bedroom, I stopped to listen. I heard snoring and the creak of bedsprings echoing against the hard floor and walls.

We just walked away from Tai Fo. There was no immediate danger, no calamity impelling us onto the road, and we didn't run. It was a warm spring night, no rain falling, a soft breeze blowing, the plants around us hissing a single note as though in preparation for the dawn. Our shoes sounded light on the well-packed gravel, and the bag slung across my back felt lifted up by the darkness. Our plan was to reach Kukong, the wartime capital of Guangdong province. We couldn't tell from Leuk's map how far it was, and we hoped there would be a train.

The moon was very bright and almost full. The land on either side of the road was clear, with no trees encumbering the light. I held Wei-Ming's hand as we walked behind Leuk and Yee-Lin. From time to time Yee-Lin asked Leuk how he was doing, and every time he answered, "I'm fine."

Since our arrival in Tai Fo, I hadn't thought much about the Japanese, and I worried now that they might be close. But there were no planes or tanks, and the sound of boots seemed unlikely on the open road that night.

After an hour, we were tired. There was a hint of dawn over the hills, a slight greying of the sky. I had been keeping myself awake by listening to the constant calls of insects in the woods, and as the light changed, I noticed that their music grew quieter. We found a spot under a cluster of trees and made a small camp, improvising a tent out of two sheets taken from our aunt's linen chest. Leuk tried to set it up using sticks and some twine he had brought, but we couldn't do it in the dark, so we just draped the sheets over a low branch. Leuk and Wei-Ming lay down to sleep while Yee-Lin and I stayed up to keep watch, though for what I didn't know. The air was free of menace and I felt more relaxed than I had since we left Hong Kong.

Everything I knew seemed far away. My memory of the city was flattening, as if into the pages of a photo album; it seemed a colder place, cracking under the thunder of war, where the air was stricken by smoke and disembodied cries. I didn't miss it, if I didn't think too much about my family. I thought of Chow and the gun he had tucked into the back of his pants those last weeks in the house, and as I sat against the tree, watching over my siblings with nothing to keep me dry, I imagined he would be proud of me. I dwelled on that thought, the memory of his voice coming to me down the river and past the menace of the village: *Well done*, I heard him say, *you did the right thing.* It gave me a little solace, and I believed that it was true.

In the morning, we ate. Yee-Lin had filled a tin with a kind of biscuit she made by grinding toasted rice and mixing it with sugar, pork fat, and dried soybeans. They were very good. We washed our hands and faces in a stream and continued down the road. The sunlight lifted the veil of secrecy we'd moved in. Wei-Ming asked how far we were from the next village.

Leuk pulled out the map and looked at it. "Not far," he replied, though I don't know how he knew that. Soon we saw an old sign that read *Lau Kwan.* The paint around it was faded and the posts leaned to one side. Beyond it, in the middle of a field off the road, sat the remains of several old houses, with squatting heaps of eroded stone and brick and broken roof tiles strewn around them.

"Is this the village?" said Leuk, looking up from the map.

"It isn't a village anymore," said Yee-Lin. We looked at the ruins, and I retraced the image of the fallen houses from the outlines of the broken walls. I imagined the simple dirt roads running between them to the collapsed well at the centre of the heaps. It seemed too overgrown and forgotten to have been a real place any time recently.

"Let's keep going," said Wei-Ming. "Maybe the real town is after this."

Leuk pointed to another road that curved around a low hill.

We walked faster as the day brightened. A donkey cart came around the bend in the road. A crouching figure sat in the cart while a man walked beside the animal. The early morning dust hung low in the humid air, and as the cart drove near us, the soft creak of the axles groaned in time with the animal's shuffle. An old woman crouched in the back, concealed under a broad hat against the sun, and her stooped husband walked ahead. He had a long walking stick in one hand and the other loosely held the donkey's harness.

We stopped and said good morning. The woman didn't speak. The man nodded and looked at us curiously. Despite the curve in his back, he held his head and neck upright, as though to tighten his tanned, unwrinkled skin. His hair was cropped short and his white eyebrows bristled like straw.

"Where are you going?" he said. He looked us over carefully and then addressed Yee-Lin. "Are you lost?"

"We're going to Lau Kwan," said Yee-Lin. "We saw the old sign back there. Is it close?"

Leuk stepped forward and held out his map. The old man looked at it for a moment and made a thoughtful hum.

"We are leaving Lau Kwan," he answered. "Why are you going there?"

"We came from Tai Fo," said Yee-Lin. "We want to get to Kukong eventually."

Leuk was still holding the map up for him. The old man reached over it slowly, his eyes fixed on my brother's face, and touched his shoulders with the tips of his bony fingers.

"Fold it up," he said. He repeated the words, and Leuk put the map back in his bag.

The old woman leaned forward and asked what was

happening. I could tell from her question and the way she moved her head around that she was blind.

"We'll go soon," he called back to her.

She put her hand to her ear for a moment and shook her head in irritation.

"We're leaving Lau Kwan," he repeated. "My brother is in a village just outside Tai Fo, where you came from. You should go back."

"What happened?" I asked him.

He looked over Yee-Lin's shoulder at me, then raised his hand to her face and waved it slowly in warning. "The Japanese," he said. "Someone said they were coming. First from the north and, now that they've taken Hong Kong, from the south. Did you know they were there?"

"We came from Hong Kong," Yee-Lin said.

"I thought so," he said. "You sound like it. I don't know why you want to go to Lau Kwan."

Yee-Lin glanced nervously at us. "We can't go back," she answered. "We want to go to Kukong."

The old man looked at her for a second. "Then avoid Lau Kwan. Take the ferry north if you can. Now, I need to hurry up."

We thanked him and he climbed into the cart. His wife was badgering him about the delay and I could tell she was nervous. Her husband picked up the reins and the donkey shuffled forward, no faster than a walking pace. As they pulled past us, I caught sight of the old woman's clouded eyes. Most of their belongings were bundled up and piled at her knees, and she crouched forward and passed her hands lightly over them as though to make sure they were still there. Her bony hands ran and trembled over the packages like mice. I looked back a moment later and saw her still leaning forward in the cart.

Though it was late morning and the sun shone, the road now felt colder. Wei-Ming took my wrist with her left hand. Her right hand was already in Yee-Lin's.

"Where are we going now?" she asked. "Where's the ferry?"

Yee-Lin told Leuk to get the map back out. He took it out of his bag and unfolded it slowly, as though the old man had cast a spell on it.

"Where are we now?" asked Yee-Lin. She leaned over the map opposite Leuk and their index fingers ran over the creased paper until they agreed on a spot. We still knew nothing about the ferry's route. The old man's warning had unsettled us. We debated about the ferry but had no idea where it would take us.

Wei-Ming pulled nervously on my hand and began to cry. "Don't we know where we are? Are we lost? Maybe we should go home. I want to go home." I tried to console her while Yee-Lin and Leuk started bickering about the road to the ferry. Wei-Ming stared at them fearfully and then asked me again if we were lost.

I shouted at Yee-Lin and Leuk to stop. "Hey!" I shouted again when they didn't listen. My sister-in-law scowled at me. "Just stop," I said.

She told me to be quiet and resumed arguing with Leuk, both of them pointing hopelessly at different points on the map, running their fingers up and down the river line to see where a ferry might go. Wei-Ming started to wail and Leuk took his eyes off the map long enough to tell her to be quiet.

A noise from far off made us stop, a low droning sound that we all knew, a single plane flying low. I looked for a place to hide, and seeing the fields on one side and the sparse woods on the other, and the light colour of the gravel road against the greenery, I knew we could be seen. We looked up as the dull-grey wings soared overhead, pale against the sky but for the red symbol of the sun.

I grabbed Wei-Ming by the hand and we headed for the trees to our right. We stood around the trunk of a large tree and looked into the canopy. I remember the fullness of its leaves that day, the silence the tree itself seemed to impose, as though the heavy wood beneath the bark could soak up every sound we made.

Another five planes followed the first in formation. They ignored us and soared northward, towards Lau Kwan.

We hid under the tree for several minutes after the planes had passed. I took the map from Leuk's hand and tried to smooth the creases. I found the fork in the road towards the river. The water angled gently northwest and reached Kukong at the upper corner of the map.

"This road can't be far," I said. "Look how far it is from Tai Fo. We should be there within an hour. We should do what the old man said."

"I don't think we have any other choice," Yee-Lin said.

We picked up our bags, and Leuk strapped Wei-Ming's things onto her back so she could hold Yee-Lin's hand while we walked. The side road came up sooner than we thought it would, and at the corner was an old sign indicating the way to the dock and ferry.

Walking got easier as the road sloped down towards the water. The gravel was coarser here and our shoes sang loudly over the stones. Leuk stopped and put his hand to his ear.

"Stop making so much noise!" he said. "Listen."

We halted and looked at him. A rumble came from far away, not of engines or thunder but something deeper. The sound rose and fell. I couldn't tell if it was a single wavering sound or a sequence of rumbles. The noise stopped and then resumed.

"Bombs," he said, and he took his hand away from his ear. "Is that what it is? It's hard to tell. If it is, it's far away."

I didn't doubt what it was. Only minutes ago the planes had flown over us towards the town. I didn't want Wei-Ming to worry.

"It sounds like bombing," Leuk repeated.

I glared at him. Wei-Ming clung to Yee-Lin and whimpered again, and there was nothing to gain by terrifying her. I was frightened too, and Leuk's casual tone made me want to punch him.

"Don't be stupid," I said loudly. "Those are trucks on the main road, that's all. Bombs are a lot louder. Weren't you paying attention when we heard them in Hong Kong? Come on." I stomped ahead and took Wei-Ming's other hand, and the three of us kept going without Leuk. He caught up, but I ignored him still and smiled at Wei-Ming. I told her we were going on another boat ride.

Leuk started to speak, but Yee-Lin told him to be quiet. Finally he seemed to get it.

The road turned and we caught our first sight of the water and a large dock below. Wei-Ming's face brightened and I felt better. Lau Kwan was a large town with lots of people, and I didn't care about any of them.

SIXTEEN

No, I didn't care about the people in Lau Kwan, a town I'd never seen before and that might at any moment be strafed by Japanese bullets. All I had to think about was myself and three members of my family, and the packs we carried, and the map, and the cookie tin, and my tarnished belt buckle.

The road to the river was all dried mud carved by cartwheels and hooves, and our shoes scuffed over the ridges. Wei-Ming held my hand and stumbled over the ruts, so I took her backpack and carried it along with my own. She stepped carefully into the patches of sunlight that filtered through the heavy vegetation, and I played along with her until we reached the water.

Back at Tai Fo, the docks were large and built of stone, with deep steps rising up from the water to the town. The dock here was of stained timber slung here and there with oily ropes. It leaned into the river and was the colour of earth where the river darkened the soil. It extended from the water onto a simple platform, where we put our bags down. We got out our water bottles and snacks, sat on the outer side of the dock, and took our shoes off. Wei-Ming sat between Leuk and me and nibbled a rice cookie. A small cluster of the sugary dried grains fell from her snack, and a fish came up and ate them.

Wei-Ming reached out with her cookie and pointed. Another crumb fell, and another fish came up as she stood. "There's the ferry!"

The ferryman stood at the stern of a long skiff, leaning into a bamboo pole while the motor laboured behind him. The only movement was the flutter of his loose black shirt in the wind and the slow descent of the pole into the mud. We all waved at him, and the boat drifted towards the dock.

The ferryman leaned sideways and pushed the pole at an angle to turn the skiff. He turned with a gentle motion, thickset legs and arms moving slowly like seaweed, and I had the impression of a man who went days without speaking. He angled the boat into the current with his eyes set on the dock. The motor ran harder and I watched him shift against the pole that yoked him to the riverbed.

When he was near the dock he tossed a rope out, and I caught it and started clumsily tying it to an iron ring on one of the posts. Already I wanted to impress him. He drew the boat up quietly to the dock and took the rope from me as he stepped out.

"You want to cross?"

"We want to go to Kukong," I stammered.

"That's too far," he said. "This is just a ferry, and getting there on this boat would take days."

Leuk stepped up with the map and handed it to the ferryman. He took it with his thumb over the front and fingers splayed out across the back so that it stayed flat. He looked at it upside down while he held it out to us, as if he had just drawn it.

"Wah Ying," he said. "See it? I can get you there in a day if you pay my way back."

The map slowly gave in to all the creases Leuk had made in it and hung limp in the ferryman's large hand. All this walking and planning, and then all we had ahead was a town we didn't know existed, and the only route open to us was the water. I glanced back at the road, hoping we might just get back to our original route. Yee-Lin's face tightened, and I felt something cave in my chest. Leuk reached over and took the map back with his eyes fixed on the ground.

The ferry bumped gently against the dock as the mud-coloured water lapped its sides. The ferryman stood quietly to the side, almost silhouetted now in the falling afternoon sun.

While we hung in our indecision, a man and woman came down the road with a small cart drawn by a donkey. They moved quickly, staring at us as they approached. The woman had a baby bundled on her back and the cart was piled with their belongings. They stopped and looked us up and down before speaking.

"Did you just arrive?" the farmer asked us.

Yee-Lin and I nodded.

"We just want to cross," the man said. He pointed at the far side of the river. I turned to look across as if to confirm it, but the river was wide and in the sunlight I saw only the broken sparkle of its reflection.

"I won't be long," the ferryman said to us. He stepped forward to look at the cart, sizing it up for his boat and the condition of the water. He gripped the side of the cart and tested its solidity through his arm and shoulder, maybe estimating its roll over the current, the motor's force, the probability of cargo upsetting his boat. I imagined the family crossing with their cart, and the ferry tipping over, leaving them to the river's mercy. My head hurt, and I sat down on the ground. My shoes were pale with dust.

The ferryman helped the farmer get the cart onto the skiff. The donkey was nervous, so they wrapped a cloth over its eyes. When everything was balanced in the middle, the ferryman started the motor again and pushed off. The woman sat on the boat's deck with the baby in her lap.

"Five yuan to get you to Wah Ying," he said as he left the riverbank. "That's all. I'll be back soon."

In the end, it took him over two hours to get the farmer and his wife across and come back, and by then it was early evening. The ferryman said it was now too dark and he wouldn't leave until sunrise. We would have to sleep outside again. I thought Wei-Ming would be frightened, so we rigged up the blankets we had rolled up into a kind of bird's nest for her, and Leuk and I found a spot near the girls where the ground was comfortable, and we covered ourselves with our jackets.

I watched the ferryman in the moonlight. He rolled out a heavy blanket onto the bottom of the boat and then tested the ropes to make sure he wouldn't drift away during the night. I was worried about thieves and animals, but before settling down, the ferryman walked the length of the path a few times with his bamboo pole and a lantern, listening carefully to the woods.

"Nothing here, kids." And instead of climbing into his boat, he took a small brazier from it and lit a coal fire on the ground near the dock. He sat up and kept watch, and I fell asleep to the sounds of the hissing brazier and the river.

The fear of drowning must be born with us, but it must arrive incomplete at our birth, needing time to form. Once, when I was twenty-three and studying in California, I fell into a lake. I was at university and spending the afternoon with a girl I wanted to impress, a Chinese girl from Singapore, Yvonne. The French name appealed to me, though she was pretty, too. I first met her at a church function and invited her out at the end of it. The event was meant to show off the domestic skills of the young women taking part, by having them make lunch for everyone after the service. Yvonne was at a large table making noodles by hand, something she'd surely never done growing up and wouldn't be expected to do in marriage. But she was managing it well. I watched her mound the flour and make a well, and then add the water from a Thermos while she gathered the wet dough with her right hand. The ball of dough built quickly, and she heaped more flour onto the board to roll it out. She pushed the rolling pin over the dough to stretch it out, her pale arms gliding over the soft white mixture like a boat over water.

I asked her out on a date, and a few days later we went to the park for a picnic. I rented a rowboat and suffered a fit of nervous laughter as I paid for it, because I suddenly remembered the stupid term *pleasure craft* from an old English lesson. Yvonne sat across from me. Her dress was aglow in the October sun. I rowed out to the middle of the little lake and pulled the oars in to let us drift. She had left her white hat on the shore with the picnic basket, and when she raised her arm to shield her eyes, I saw the underside of her arm. The skin tone was the same as on her upper breasts. I grew painfully erect.

I had a very expensive camera, a Rolleiflex that Sheung had given me as a going-away gift. I kept it safe in its brown leather case, and now I put it in my lap to hide my erection, and told Yvonne I'd like to take a picture of her. She was thrilled, and I started fiddling with the settings to impress her.

Let me turn the boat a little, I said, to get the light right.

This made her glow. She put her hands together.

I put the Rolleiflex down carefully and picked up an oar. I moved to get up and set the oar in the water to turn the boat, but my erection touched the inside of my pants and I crouched to hide it. The boat rocked a little and Yvonne gasped. I looked down and thought I saw the camera tipping, and then worried I'd knock it with my shoe. I stumbled to one side to avoid it, and in a second I was in the water.

I knew how to swim, but something else had taken over. I thought of the camera and Yvonne inside the little boat, neither of which could get wet. I thought of grabbing the side of the boat but saw water fly from my hands onto the camera. My pants ballooned and turned me around before quickly sucking up the water and pulling me down. I'd been nervously holding my breath in the boat; my lungs were empty.

The lake water burned in my nostrils and throat. I was cold. I scrambled upward but went nowhere until the handle of the oar appeared, dipping into the water, and I seized it. Once my head was above the water, I grabbed the edge of the boat with my right hand, and Yvonne helped me back in.

SEVENTEEN

I hunched over on my seat in the boat, gripping the edge and getting angrier by the minute at Leuk.

"I'm sure those are planes," he repeated.

I looked at Wei-Ming, who was lying on a makeshift bed on the bottom of the boat. She didn't hear the rumbling, either because she was asleep or because the sound of the water under her drowned it out.

"If they're bombing, why don't we see any planes?" I whispered to him.

"They fly low, really low," he said. "And they could be using the hills for cover."

"You don't know that," I said.

"I do," he answered. "I heard it on the radio in Tai Fo one evening, someone talking about how the Japs fly their planes."

"That doesn't mean it's happening here," I said.

"It could," Leuk said. It was as though he wished for there to be imperial bombers crouching over us at any minute.

My anger contracted to a leaden ache, and I told Leuk to be quiet.

"What do you know?" he said.

I put my bag in my lap and slid over to the edge of the boat. "Leave me alone," I said, too quietly for anyone to hear.

Leuk moved to his side of the boat and turned away to watch the water. I heard him sniffle. Even if he was crying, I wanted nothing to do with him. Twigs drifted past and I thought of the gutters in front of our house. My memory of Hong Kong was of a place perpetually cloudy, doors and windows shuddering in the wind, of streets either filled with silent people or empty under its long imperial watch. And here too there must be eyes, along the riverbank and in the water, and in the skies, scouring a world stripped bare by sunlight, looking for the defiant, the lost, the unexploited, the unsuspecting.

In the evening, I sat quietly in the boat. The motor ran noisily as it had since we left, but it receded into the background and I heard the splashing of fish in the water and snippets of birdsong. Yee-Lin was telling Wei-Ming a story. It was getting dark and the ferryman hadn't said anything for hours. I felt that we would never stop, that we would drift on and on, beyond the sight first of our enemies, to a point of no return.

But after a long bend in the river, the village emerged. At first I saw nothing, just lanterns strung like pale emissaries among trees that seemed to rise from the middle of the water. I rubbed my eyes and squinted into the twilight.

It was an island. That was how wide the river had spread since Lau Kwan, broad and deep enough to hold an island midstream, a dark, forested mass in the water. As we drew closer, twin stone bridges appeared like long arms reaching over the water to the riverbanks. They too were hung with lights. But the centre of the island was mostly dark.

Against the dark green of the thick bamboo grove along the island's banks, the grey masonry of the docks emerged. Lanterns hung in the still air and a few people walked along the docks. The ferryman stopped the motor and dropped the pole back into the water, guiding us slowly to a small landing on the far side of the dock.

He brought the boat up to the dock and a boy ran down the steps towards us, one hand extended, shouting at the ferryman to throw him the rope. He was in peasant clothes and bare feet, and three other boys like him stood nearby and watched. The ferryman waved him off and said he'd do it himself.

"I'll keep my money," he said and waved the boy off again, this time with the end of the pole. The ferryman climbed out and tied the boat to a mooring, and one by one we disembarked.

He leaned on the pole and nodded at us. "You have all your things?"

I looked around quickly at the small heap of bags at our feet. All our things.

"Five yuan, then," he said.

He took the money from Yee-Lin and laid the coins out thoughtfully over his palm as though to read rather than count them. They stretched from the bottom of his palm to the very tip of his middle finger.

"Do you know where to go?" he said. "There's an inn here."

"Thank you, we'll find it," said Yee-Lin. Leuk and I picked up the girls' bags and carried them up the steps.

To get to the village, we first had to walk through a thick bamboo grove. We walked down the road in the twilight. I imagined the ferryman walking behind us, his pole thudding lightly on the ground like a giant walking stick, his hand extended outward like the Buddha with his open palm.

The inn was very small and simple. The couple who ran it were serving white liquor to clusters of men at wicker tables, and when Yee-Lin approached the wife to ask about rooms, she paused and looked Yee-Lin up and down while balancing a tray of little wine cups stacked in a tower.

"We're full," she said. "But there's a family who can take you in." She called her daughter out of the back room and ordered her to take us there. She was about my height, thin, with her hair tied untidily in the back.

As she walked us down the village road, she took out a cleaning rag that was tucked into her belt and worried it between her hands. She ignored most of our questions.

"The family is Lee," she said without turning. "Their son has a new wife and the mother is sick."

The inn and the other buildings near it were rundown, broken shutters hanging off the windows and all the paint worn off the exteriors. The Lee house was newer. The man who greeted us was the husband. He looked younger than Sheung and Tang, but his face was grimy and his hands and arms were scraped from hard work. The girl from the inn explained what we wanted, and he nodded in the lantern light.

"I'm Kei," he said to Leuk. When Yee-Lin spoke, he

avoided looking at her and replied to Leuk. We told him where we'd come from and why we were on the road. Leuk even told him that we didn't want to stay with our uncle. Maybe it was Kei's youth, or our desire to be taken in, or the ferryman's long silence that made us want to talk. Kei looked distractedly at the ground while we rambled before interrupting us to say, "I'll show you the rooms."

Yee-Lin negotiated a fee with him, which turned out to be for a single room in their house. It had two beds and there was room for Leuk and me to sleep on the floor. Kei brought us mattresses. We stacked our bags in the corner and cleaned up, and once Wei-Ming had eaten and lain down in her bed, the rest of us fell asleep.

The house was very quiet. In the morning I found a young woman at the stove making breakfast. When I walked in, she glanced quickly over her shoulder at me. The steam and the water clinging to the vegetable leaves made the room feel very damp and chilly. Kei, still buttoning up his shirt as he stepped out of his bedroom, introduced the woman to me as his wife, Ming. She turned again and smiled. Looking at this girl, I thought of Shun-Lai, of her nightgown and her hairbrush, and her silhouette in the window the last night I saw her. But Ming was in a plain white blouse and grey skirt, and her arms were flecked with bits of cabbage, and there was none of Shun-Lai's glow about her.

At first, Kei and Ming kept their distance from us. Kei's father, Mr. Lee, lived in a larger house nearby and had given this one to the couple as a wedding gift. He came over often to check on them. He was a small but fierce man who puffed almost continuously on handmade cigarettes that perched between the index and middle fingers of his right hand. His right arm moved in a seemingly permanent crook from smoking. He had a barking voice that he used to good effect, ordering his son and daughter-in-law around the house. He kept a shop in the village but often dropped by unannounced.

We signed up for the local school, where the three teachers alternated between mumbling their lessons and enforcing harsh discipline. After attending for two days, Leuk and I started played hooky, and after no one came to look for us, we brought Wei-Ming out of school, too. There was a small river near Kei's house, and we took to swimming there daily. Yee-Lin knew we were skipping school, but she didn't seem to care, and on the third day she sat on the riverbank and watched us play. I noticed Kei and Ming watching us from the front window.

They were a very quiet couple. The morning was always rushed as Kei got ready to go to his father's shop and Ming began her housework. The house was spotless, but every morning at some unpredictable hour Mr. Lee would appear and start criticizing Ming for its condition. During these tirades she stared downward, at the floor where there might be dirt, at shoes that might be unpolished, over at the cutting block, the stove. One morning I got up late and walked into the kitchen just as Mr. Lee was yelling at Ming. She stood before him holding a senseless combination of a broom in one hand and a pot lid in the other, her head bowed in shame. Mr. Lee sharpened the humiliation by raising his voice as I entered, reminding Ming how public her failure was.

In the afternoons she did laundry from both houses. Mr. Lee had three pairs of pants and insisted on having two pairs pressed daily. Mrs. Lee was an invalid and we never saw her. I knew her only as baskets of soiled cloth. Her clothes and sheets were always washed separately, covered in grimy streaks of brown, yellow, and lurid green. She had no skirts or blouses, only loose gowns and wraps, and Ming boiled them each day in a large outdoor pot before hanging them to dry. Mrs. Lee's sheets and garments billowed and sank like trapped eels in a tank, first in the roiling water, then in the wind on the drying line. When they were dry, Ming folded them so that the stains were on the inside.

One day, after we'd been in Wah Ying for nearly two weeks, Ming moved the clothesline from the side of the house to the front. There she could watch Leuk and me swim as she hung the wash up to dry. We splashed and yelled when she appeared. I caught her smiling, then laughing a little. She took her time hanging the laundry, letting the damp cotton and linen hide her as the sheets flapped in the wind.

I ran out of the water and up to the clothesline wearing only my soaking underwear. I grabbed a bedsheet on the line to steady myself and let the water drip from my arm onto the freshly laundered cloth.

"Can you swim?" I asked her.

"I don't know how," she said. She glanced quickly over my shoulder at the river, her eyes shifting between the water and the laundry.

"I could teach you how," I said. "It's easy."

Mr. Lee was away in another village for a few days, so once Ming was done her morning chores, she met us down by the river wearing an old white cotton dress. I helped her in and showed her how to tread water. She got the hang of it quickly, even though that was all she could do. Leuk dislodged a piece of driftwood from some rocks, and once she was able to float with it in the sluggish river, she didn't want to get out.

In the afternoon, when Kei returned from work, he discovered us and joined in. He was thrilled to see Ming learning to swim. Kei was already a decent swimmer and he loved being in the water with his wife for the first time. He got out and ran around the riverbank looking for more driftwood, and Ming was pleased having two pieces to float on. When Leuk and I went back up to the house, Ming and Kei were still splashing around in the water, and she was laughing as I had never heard her laugh before.

Yee-Lin took the three of us into the town for a late afternoon snack and we walked around the little square, but in the evening I was bored and wandered home. Kei and Ming were usually inside in the evenings; now the front room was empty. I wandered down to the river. It would be dark soon and too cool to swim, so I picked up a switch lying on the grass and zigzagged down the slope to the riverbank, whipping the grass and sending the clipped leaves into the air ahead of me.

As I walked through a little stand of trees, I heard a splash. I thought it might be a bird fishing, so I crept closer to the river to get a look. Kei and Ming were standing close together in the water, and though she was facing me, her eyes were half closed. Her dress billowed around her in the slow current.

He was moving up against her in the water and she clung to him with her mouth parted. Her lips, and her fingertips gripping his shoulders, were blue with cold. Blue like pale marble, like the veins beneath my wrist in the grey weeks of winter. Kei still wore his shirt, but it was open, and their white garments floated and bobbed like jellyfish around her. In the red sunset light they were an islet of pallor in the cold water. I watched until they were still.

EIGHTEEN

The following afternoon, Leuk and I again skipped school and decided to go swimming. Walking down the road back to the house, I noticed the laundry had been thrown loosely over the drying line and a few pieces had been blown onto the ground. I heard Kei and Ming laughing and splashing in the river, but as we approached, their voices were cut short by a man yelling.

Mr. Lee was home a day early from his trip. He must have been angered to find the house empty. He stood on the riverbank, a cigarette ensnared in his right hand as he cursed. In his other hand he clutched a sheet that had fallen from the line, and he shook it. Leuk and I hid in the same trees where I had watched Kei and Ming the night before.

Ming screamed an apology to her father-in-law. She smoothed her dress down against her legs as she stumbled up the bank. Kei leapt out of the water beside her. His shirt and pants were hanging over a branch, and he reached for them as his father turned on him.

"What the hell is this? Who gave you permission?" He was shaking and his face turned dark with rage. Kei stumbled on the grass and tried to put his pants on, but he was soaking wet and slow to dress.

Ming stammered a few more words of apology. Mr. Lee strode over and struck her on the face with his free hand and told her to shut up. She fell to the ground, and Kei, still shirtless, dropped to his knees with clasped hands and kowtowed to his father, begging forgiveness. A sudden gust shook the trees. Two of the sheets on the line billowed wildly in the air, and the yellow tarnish at their centres blazed like the banners of a diseased army. One smaller sheet came loose and blew towards the riverbank, sailing over the grass. It collapsed, one corner snagging on an exposed tree root while the rest sank into the water. The current drew it up along the river's edge while the root held it fast. With a cry of rage, Mr. Lee ran down and seized his wife's laundry from the water. He let it drag over the ground and then held it up in disbelief as he turned on his son.

"Who did this? Who ruined your mother's clothing?" Ming sobbed on the ground while Kei crouched like a dog. When he saw the sheet in his father's hand, he got up on his knees with his clasped hands before him, and in a high-pitched, wailing voice he begged his father for mercy. He was only a few feet away from me.

Mr. Lee threw the wet sheet on the ground. He went over to the garden and reached across to the trellis at the back where the beans ran up a slender framework. He pulled one of the long bamboo staves out of the ground, tearing most of the vines out in the process. Trampling the garden, he stomped back to his son and started thrashing his naked back with the bamboo.

"Idiot! Disloyal son!" he shouted, and after a moment

the welts on Kei's back opened and his blood began to flow. The bamboo switch soaked it up like a paintbrush. Kei knelt face down on the grass and begged for mercy, screaming the same apologies over and over. Ming got up and ran over to her husband, her hands outstretched and mouth open in horror, though she managed nothing more than a wail.

Mr. Lee stopped for a moment, holding the bloody stick inches from his son's skin. He looked at her, and on his face there was a look of discovery and triumph, as though being surrounded by offenders could only increase the rightness of his grievance. He turned and grabbed Ming's wet hair and dragged her forward until she fell face down. As she fell, her arms flew out and she pulled down one of Mrs. Lee's stained sheets. Mr. Lee lowered the stick onto Ming's back and legs, and she screamed louder than Kei as she clawed the brownish bedsheet beneath her. Kei begged his father to stop.

After Wei-Ming had gone to bed that night, we told Yee-Lin what we had seen, and she sat at the kitchen table and cried. I told her I felt bad for Kei and Ming, too, but she looked at me and said she was only crying because the story made her feel alone.

The next day, Leuk and I were kicking rocks along a street near Mr. Lee's shop. We stayed clear of it until we saw him leave the shop for home, where Ming would serve him lunch after cleaning up his wife. We walked into the shop and found Kei in the storeroom. He was lifting boxes from the floor up onto the shelves, moving slowly and wincing as he raised his arms. He wore a dark striped shirt to mask the blood still seeping through. Leuk approached him.

"Kei, are you all right?"

He turned around to look at us. His face was grey and tight, and his eyes were sunken beneath dark circles. "Please go," he said quietly. "I need to move these boxes."

I looked at the boxes. The storeroom was half empty, and I wondered if he'd been told to move them because of the pain it would cause. I pointed to his back.

"You're still bleeding a little. Did you bandage your back?"

"He said not to. Please go."

It was very quiet in the shop and the street outside. Other children were in school and most adults would be eating lunch. Leuk shuffled uneasily on the sawdust-strewn floor and it was like the roar of a rock slide.

"We—When you get better, maybe we can swim again," said Leuk.

Kei closed his eyes hard for a moment and shook. He put one arm out to lean against a wall, and then grimaced and put it back down to his side. I felt embarrassed for him, but I also wondered if he wanted to be watched, however shameful it might be.

In October 2003, I travelled to Seattle to meet Leuk. We planned to spend a few days there before driving down the coast together. It took a while to arrange, because he was never much of a traveller, and there was a long exchange of letters before I convinced him to come. When he finally agreed to go, he wrote that he would also like to see the coast and the famous forests along the Pacific. In one of his letters he reminded me that once, in 1963, he had taken a ship all the way from Hong Kong to Italy through the Suez Canal and back. Despite having enjoyed it, he'd taken no trips longer than an hour or two since, usually by land or sea.

I booked a hotel in Seattle with a view of the harbour, and we settled into a routine of breakfasting in the hotel before taking walks along the water and down some of the nearby streets. He seemed to be enjoying himself. We went to a museum and took a bus tour of the city, and while he was interested and even took a few pictures with his old camera, he seemed content to let all kinds of sights go by while we conversed. After two days of this, I also preferred just to talk.

One Saturday afternoon, after a morning touring the old military base at Magnuson Park, we had a late lunch at a restaurant near the hotel. It was warm for October, and we sat at one of the last outdoor tables in our windbreakers. We both found the options on the menu baffling and unappealing, and while the diners at other tables tucked into huge and overly garnished platters, we ordered the same nursing-home lunch of soup and sandwich. There we sat, munching and slurping, each of us tugging on our windbreaker as we noticed the day was not as warm as it had seemed when we were walking. We retreated into this slight discomfort and disappointment before paying the bill and heading for the public walkway along the pier. There were many people out.

Leuk was very pensive; maybe it was the hint of fall odours in the air, or the effect of a dull meal. He leaned over the railing and looked into the water. He adjusted his sunglasses and looked at me.

So different here, the harbour. Very peaceful. Do you miss Hong Kong?

Always and never, I suppose.

This harbour's quieter, like it used to be back home. Do you remember? All that time we used to spend down there. We used to run past the old hospital on Village Road, near the club.

Yes, I sure do, I said, I remember those places. My throat felt dry.

And then something wasn't right. Something in Leuk's last words stuck in my ear, a jumbled fragment recomposing itself into a cruel jab — remember, home, time, hospital. The ground swayed and I thought at first it was an earthquake, but when I looked at my brother I knew I was alone in feeling it. My heart knocked violently inside my chest and my skin burned in extremes of heat and cold. I watched the expression on my brother's face change with a terrifying slowness. I broke into a sweat and stumbled against the railing, reaching out in confusion to grab it. My left hand missed, but my right hand caught it, though I still stumbled and fell to the ground. I was aware of looking ridiculous as I let out a shout and my hand slipped from the railing. A tropical dampness, a shock of hot, cadaverous stench, stung my nostrils, and my stomach heaved.

A young man ran over to help and knelt down to lift me up. He called me sir. I felt his hands on my arm and shoulder, but as his grip tightened to lift me, my vision blurred and I saw only a dark-haired figure coming down towards me. I reached up and struck him on the face and shouted at him in Cantonese, and I felt his glasses fly off his face. They clattered over the concrete walk. I yelled at him again to go away.

I remember shouting something else, something about leaving, and two other people came and helped me over to a bench. All I remember next is Leuk sitting beside me with one hand on my back. He was telling me to sit still. I pieced the last few moments together and put my head in my hands. Pedestrians on the pier stared at me and I heard an ambulance approaching. A waitress from the restaurant ran over with the medics and, thinking I couldn't speak English, translated their questions to me into Cantonese. I told them I didn't know what had happened, though it would have been more honest to say that I didn't understand.

Standing by the railing with her mother, a little girl, maybe about seven, looked at me gravely while holding a gold balloon. She wasn't concerned for me, I felt, but I imagined that behind the downward turn of her mouth and her knitted brow was her dismay at being exposed to such a thing, to my shameful decline and humiliation. I tried to smile at her. My face was wet and I wiped it with a handkerchief, and then I reassured the medics one more time and waved them off. Leuk thanked the waitress for me.

I sat with my brother while the gawkers moved on. From the bench I watched a cluster of young birch trees sway and rustle in the October air, and I calmed myself by timing my breath to match their motion, until I imagined my exhalations echoed their dry and leafy murmur. I got back on my feet.

Let's go on that drive, I said to Leuk, and we made our way back to the car. That evening and the next day, I would show him the old Pacific forests, and we would drive in silence inside those primitive monuments that bristled darkly against the fortress of the ocean.

NINETEEN

Most of the men in Wah Ying seemed violent like Mr. Lee. Fights were common. One day there was a traditional festival in the town centre, which meant a little music with plenty of firecrackers and lots of alcohol. The women of the village had prepared huge open tables of food—mostly noodles, vegetables, and some fish. The men who could escape from work lined up on benches at the tables, where they ate and drank greedily. It wasn't like any festival I'd ever been to in Hong Kong. Within a couple of hours the musicians and the children's snack tables disappeared, and the festival was just a ramble of men drinking rice or millet liquor from earthenware jars. A large pile of these sat under some trees in the square, but before long most of the men couldn't walk there to restock their tables.

There were two large families who made up most of Wah Ying—Lee and Cheung—and when they were drunk, it was easier to see how they were related. The Cheung men in particular turned a frightening shade of deep ruby, and their faces bloated from the alcohol, as though their heads were giant, engorged tics. The Lee men's faces turned blotchy, and they got sick faster. The gravel paths of the square and the tables where they sat quickly became smeared with vomit that stank in the island's warm spring air.

Leuk and I stayed away from the men at the tables. We had no interest in most of the festival, except for some coloured paper flags that had been hung around the square between the trees. Leuk had found a box of matches by one of the extinguished cooking stations, so we decided to burn the flags. Our first thought was to pull them down and set them alight in the middle of the square, but then we decided it would be more fun to set fire to them while they hung in the trees.

Leuk knelt down and I climbed on his shoulders with the matchbox between my teeth. As I crouched to stay balanced, I lit a match and held it near the flags, but the flame wouldn't catch. I lit a second match but dropped it, and the stick landed next to Leuk's foot, where it continued burning. He carefully put one foot out to step on it, and I wobbled on his shoulders and gripped the tree.

"Stop it," I shouted.

"It's okay," he said, "I just don't want to cause a fire." He seemed to have forgotten why we were doing this in the first place. He stuck his foot out again and brought it down hard on the matchstick.

I fell. My hands skimmed the smooth bark of the tree as I went down, right next to the jars of liquor. I landed on the ground, and as I tried to right myself, my knee caught the handle of a jug, and a pyramid of four vessels collapsed and smashed on the gravel. The liquor sprayed my clothes and face. For a moment the scent of vomit that hugged the ground dissipated and I could smell only alcohol. My eyes burned.

One of the men, a Cheung by the look of him, thrust a

wavering finger at me. He shouted at me in a hoarse voice, but none of the other men paid him any attention. He rose with difficulty from the bench and came towards us. I was still getting up and reeling from the sting of alcohol. He pointed at me and struggled to say something, his lips curling as he grunted hoarsely like an old dog. Leuk took me by the arm and pulled me away. I looked back at the man staring at the broken jars, swaying on bowed legs. He put one arm against the tree and released a stream of vomit down its trunk.

We started to run towards home, but I knew I wasn't done. We stopped at a street corner.

"Let's go back," I said. I wanted to see the flags burn.

Leuk's face ran with sweat and his shirt clung to his chest. I showed him I still had the matches, and he laughed. Then he put his arms out and started staggering around like a drunk. He leaned over and pretended to throw up on the grass. He was very loud and disgusting, and I laughed hysterically. When I could breathe again, I did the same, and soon we were trying to outdo each other with our impressions of the worst vomiting sounds we could make. We settled on the version we thought best and rehearsed it for several minutes.

A door swung open and an old woman shouted at us to shut the hell up. She had a big piece of firewood in one hand and threatened to beat us with it. When we didn't stop, she took a few steps forward and waved the wood in the air. It was still smoking at one end. We snorted and waved at her and ran back to the square.

When we returned, it was a different scene from the one we'd left. Many of the men were gone and some of the remaining ones were passed out on the tables or ground. Several others were fighting, though they seemed too drunk to really harm each other. They swung wide punches at each other's heads or stomachs while a couple grappled on the ground.

Gunfire erupted behind us. I hadn't heard shots fired since Hong Kong, and Leuk and I dropped to the ground, expecting to hear the roar of trucks and tanks coming down the road. A few of the men ran in zigzags between the houses. As the shots continued, I noticed rifle barrels sticking out through narrow slots cut in the houses' walls. The men took shots at each other through these, though I don't know how they could distinguish who was who or even aim properly.

We hid behind a tree and waited and watched. The men fighting in the street separated quickly when the first shots sounded and retreated to their houses, where I assumed they too would start shooting each other. One of the men, drunk and now limping after a fight, took a bullet in the neck as he searched for his house. He clutched his neck and staggered sideways as the blood coursed through his fingers and down his forearm. From one of the houses came uproarious laughter, followed by more shots.

One of the last men in the street staggered over to us. "You little bastards," he shouted, "you broke the wine jars." He pushed his sleeves up his arms and said he would beat us. He could barely walk straight but kept coming.

I grabbed Leuk by the arm and shouted at him to run. Instead, Leuk shouted back at the man and told him to get lost.

"Little bastards," he repeated. "I'll skin you both alive."

Leuk crouched down and picked up a large rock. He drew his arm back and took aim, and as the man came closer, my brother swung around and hurled it at him. The rock struck him right beneath his left eye, and I heard a terrible crack. The man screamed and fell backward, clawing his face as though he thought the rock was embedded in his skull. There was blood everywhere.

Leuk shouted that we should go. But I wasn't ready to leave. I took the matches from my pocket and clambered up a low branch. One of the strings of flags had come loose and was within my reach. It took only a moment for the flame to catch, and as I landed back on the ground, the fire was spreading quickly through the tree. The fire ran through the string and flags to the next tree, which was diseased. Its dead leaves sparked to life with an angry crackle, and just as we turned to run home, a pair of swallows sailed from the branches and out over the ruins of the festival.

Two days later, I was by myself in the little Wah Ying market. Ming had sent me out to get some vegetables, though I hadn't really paid attention to her instructions. I stood at the meagre vegetable stall trying to decide what I should buy, while the vendor glared at me in annoyance. The girl next to me knew what she was doing. She was about my age and dressed in servant's clothes. I thought she was very thin, but I rarely saw myself in a mirror and easily forgot how thin I was, too. I had a rash on my legs that wouldn't go away, and a small sore on my hand that was healing very slowly.

I asked the girl what she was getting and which one was water spinach. She pointed to a small heap of greens and asked me if I knew how to cook them. I laughed and said of course not, but then immediately felt stupid. She looked contemptuously at me and said it wasn't hard, and I nodded in embarrassment.

She spoke with an accent I'd never heard before. After paying, she hoisted a shopping basket over her shoulder, and I realized I'd seen her many times before in the market. She was always in a rush. I asked her if I could walk with her. I found her very pretty despite the scowl on her face. She looked at me nervously for a moment and then agreed but said she had to get back.

She was from Shantou and her name was Ling. Despite her small size, she was actually sixteen, and she seemed relieved to hear I was only twelve. I asked her a couple of times why she was so far from home, but she only said she was here to work. She was a servant in the home of one of the richer merchants in town, a Cheung patriarch I had seen around and who was very old. She was quiet and a little sullen after that, but when I said I came from Hong Kong, she became excited and asked me all about the city. I described it as it was before the invasion, and her face lit up when I talked about the Jockey Club, the harbour, and the food stalls.

When we turned a corner and the Cheung house came into view, she stopped and said she would go on her own now. I asked if I could walk her all the way home, but she shook her head and became quiet. So I asked her if we could meet again, and she said she went to the market at the same time almost every day. She said she could meet me there again if I didn't delay her and if I would tell her more about Hong Kong.

I met Ling at the market three days in a row, always mid-morning. I enjoyed being with her and told her all the stories about Hong Kong I could think of. She especially liked hearing about Western things and the British, so I talked about the church my father had built, my school, Christmas dinners, and still more about the Jockey Club.

These stories filled our walks to her house. She said her employer knew when she left and watched the clock while she was out, so she had to keep shopping while we talked. On the first day, when I asked her about her family, she gave a vague answer. When she reached out to pick through the goods in the stalls, I noticed she had bruises on her arms. She didn't strike me as a typical maid, because she could read and spoke well. She took a lot of care in selecting the food she bought, and talked a lot about which ones were good for a person's health and why. I started to tease her a little about these ideas and made her laugh.

On the fourth of our morning meetings—by which time Leuk had given up on having someone to spend the first half of the day with—she told me I could come into Mr. Cheung's house with her.

"Is that safe?"

"Yes, the old man's away visiting his son. There's just the old woman and the gardener at home now."

"I don't want to bother you."

She said not to worry. She paid for the last of her vegetables and put the rest of her coins back into a small cloth bag that she wore around her neck, and we left the market together.

At the end of the market, a woman had laid out some pottery for sale. Ling noticed a large serving plate painted with chrysanthemums in red and blue. She pointed at it and said, "I like that." A swallow flew from the eaves of a nearby building, and she looked up and watched it for a moment. "Tell me again about the garden in your house," she said.

I knew that she meant the rooftop, so I described it again.

"Chickens on the roof," she said. "That's funny."

We were about halfway to the Cheung house. The basket looked heavy, so I offered to carry it. "I have a lot to do," she said.

"I could come in and help you. Or would the old woman come down?"

"No, she can't walk and stays in bed all day. I have to carry the food up to her room." We came up to the front gate.

"Can I go inside with you?" I asked again.

She looked at me and pushed the gate open. We went in through the servants' door at the back, and as we entered, I noticed the gardener tending a small garden with a fish pond. He looked up and watched as we went into the kitchen.

Ling got to work immediately. She laid out the vegetables and started to wash and chop them after putting a large pot of water on the fire. She scowled as she did this, and when she rolled up her sleeves to chop, the full extent of the markings on her forearms was visible. She made this motion quickly, probably out of habit, and the minute she did so, she looked up, saw that I was looking, and pushed her sleeves back down.

For a minute she stared down at the counter. Then she started sniffling over the vegetables and wiped her eyes.

Like an idiot, I said nothing. She paused, resting her palms on the chopping block, and cried harder. Finally, without looking up, she spoke to me.

"Please go home."

"What's wrong?" I asked her.

Then she really began to weep, a deep, gasping sob that she struggled to repress as she held her apron over her mouth, as though through long practice she had learned that the depth of her breathing was the only thing she could control. I walked over to her and put one hand on her back as I guided her to a chair, the way I had seen Kei do with Ming. I brought her a cup of water while the soup bubbled on the stove.

After a few minutes, she told me who she was. Her father had been a merchant in Shantou, and she had been born in a large house near the port. She and her brother went to school and worked in their father's business from time to time, a store that sold traditional medicines in bulk.

But when she was thirteen, her mother died, and her father began to gamble and drink. He fell heavily into debt to members of a criminal gang, who then auctioned his debt off to their cronies, one of whom was an associate of Mr. Cheung's. Finally, Mr. Cheung was the next in line, but he didn't assume the debt. Instead, Mr. Cheung offered to absolve it if Ling's father would grant him the children in perpetual servitude. By then the father was a permanent drunkard and the business was closed. The children rarely saw him and had to fend for themselves. Two years after her mother's death, gang members came to their school one morning and dragged Ling and her brother through the street to their headquarters. Her brother was sold to yet another family, and Ling was brought to the countryside to be a bondsmaid in Wah Ying. She had no idea where her brother was.

Ling wept during parts of the story, while other parts she told plainly. She said Mr. Cheung beat her regularly, as did his wife when she came within reach of the old woman's chair. The old woman was always wrapped in silk robes and shawls to keep her warm, and Ling dreaded the swishing sound the old woman made as she lashed out at her, even as Ling tried to feed her.

She rolled her sleeves back up to show me her arms. The Cheungs had weakened in the two years since she arrived. Age and infirmity were degrading their bodies, which at first was good for Ling. But with their infirmity a new fear had arisen, namely that they would die and she would be inherited by Mr. Cheung's son, whose able-bodied violence she had experienced once, when he came to visit.

She coped with her terror of the future by obsessing over the quality of the food she prepared for the old couple. She had learned a little about traditional medicine from her father's business, and in the market she was constantly asking vendors which foods and vegetables were the most sustaining. From this she had put together her own beliefs about what to serve the old couple, at what time of day, how best to prepare it, what to make when either seemed ill or tired or reported some new complaint.

She straightened herself, wiped her face, and went back to making Mrs. Cheung's lunch. As she talked, she calmed herself by telling me her theories about how the food she made would cure or sustain them, or at least keep them on a slow but steady decline until they became near invalids with only the ability to eat. She talked about pickled mustard root, steamed bamboo shoots, rice cooked with salted pomelo skin. I knew a little about these old medicines from my mother, but none of what Ling said made sense. My mother used to visit the pharmacist and herbalist and return with their compounds. Everything Ling said was her own invention. Later, I watched her climb the stairs to Mrs. Cheung's room, inhaling the steam from some thin broth of who knew what, convinced that she was drawing out her captors' lives when her efforts may well have been useless.

Everything she did seemed to come from the unsettling serenity of someone sealed up in her own world, in a secret, deeper prison invisible even to her owners. She was making a small batch of noodles for the soup, and as she worked the soft dough over the floured board with a rolling pin, she stared into its blankness. The flour clouded the air around the board and settled on her arms like a mask to conceal the bruises.

She looked up for a moment and smiled to herself as

she stretched the dough out as long as possible. Long life, of course, because everything must stand for something else. I saw that Ling, like me, had seen things she wanted to forget, and—as with her ideas about medicine—she worked constantly to transform her memories into something else. The story of her mother's death echoed in my thoughts. I thought of how alone and lost we were, and I yearned to hear a different voice, a solid, adult voice, that could speak to me across the distance of space or from a different time and reassure me. From her expression Ling looked as though she was deep in some well-rehearsed daydream of comfort. Her arms stretched out gently over the floured board. The loose flour rose up as she worked it, and it seemed as though she would disappear into that cloud.

At that moment, it seemed like a mistake to have touched her earlier. I opened the hand I had laid on her back and suddenly my palm felt dry and dirty. She looked at me again and I believed she read my thoughts about her. She smiled all the same. Somewhere under my ribs, I felt a subtle crack.

A harsh metallic clang woke me the next morning. I ran out of the house wearing only my underwear. A man was running through the streets striking a gong and shouting at everyone to get up. Many people were already out, and I ran back to the house to wake Leuk, Wei-Ming, and Yee-Lin. A half-dozen planes flew overhead.

The Japanese had been spotted on the road just before dawn by a civil defence volunteer. The townspeople were unprepared and panic erupted. A man from the neighbouring house said he would fight and shook an old rifle in the air to the cheers of other men.

Yee-Lin was already up and packing our belongings. I got dressed, found my belt, and made sure Leuk had his too. Only Yee-Lin knew about the gold we carried, and we never talked about it. Wei-Ming would be certain to say something if she knew.

"Chung-Man, get Kei and Ming and tell them to come with us," said Yee-Lin.

"Where to?"

"I don't know. Into the woods. To a river if we can find a boat. There must be a way out. They may know how."

I went to the kitchen and found them already up and strangely calm.

"It's the Japanese, isn't it?" said Kei. "What should we do?"

"Run. We're going to try to make it out. Come with us and tell us where to go. Is there a place to hide in the woods, or a boat?"

Kei looked at Ming. "I have to get my parents first. I can't leave without them."

Ming looked stricken. She froze for a moment, one hand tying a string around a small bag of rice. She stared at Kei. "Your mother can't walk. How can we bring them?"

"I can't leave my parents, Ming."

Yee-Lin came into the kitchen, laden with our bags and holding Wei-Ming's hand. She gave me my bag and reached over and seized Ming by the arm.

"Don't wait for him," she told her. "Come with us." She stared hard at Ming, and then she put her hands over Wei-Ming's ears and turned to Kei. "They won't want your parents," she said in a low voice. "They'll butcher them and take their house. They may even force you to kill them. They'll take Ming for themselves. Forget your parents, and help us out of here."

Kei put his hands on his wife's shoulders and looked at Yee-Lin. It took him a moment to understand what she had said.

"All right."

We took everything we could and ignored the panic in the village. People were arming themselves with hoes, rakes, and hunting rifles, and hiding their children in cellars and sheds. I watched them scurry around and I thought of the streets and skies in Hong Kong: the constant hum of trucks and planes, the empty faces, people beaten and left on the pavement, the ration stations. I thought, *You haven't seen their flag.*

Kei led us to the edge of the village. We avoided the main entrance to Wah Ying since we assumed the Japanese would come through it. When we were far from the town centre, it was almost quiet. We were approaching the river, and when I heard it rushing, I thought of how we used to swim in it.

"Kei! What are you doing?" Mr. Lee was stumbling up the road, cigarette in one hand and his shirt half buttoned. "Where are you going?"

Kei and Ming could easily have outrun the old man but instead turned around, and Kei tried to answer him.

"Father, it's the Japanese. The Leung children have seen them before. They said we should all leave the village now."

"Leave?" screamed Mr. Lee. "How can you leave us? Your mother is in bed. She needs help. There's nowhere to go. Stay here, you coward. Let these filthy kids rot in the woods." When Kei didn't respond, Mr. Lee struck him on the face. He fell to the ground and Ming screamed for him to stop. She knelt down to help him and Mr. Lee started to kick them both, screaming at them to come home.

Kei covered his face as his father kicked him. I thought the old man would kill him this time. Though Mr. Lee tottered and missed twice, he landed another kick straight to his son's head, and in his blind rage he drew his foot back to strike again. Then Kei reached out and seized his father's ankle. Mr. Lee stumbled, and his shoe came loose and struck Kei in the face, and Mr. Lee hit the ground hard, striking his head against a dried rut in the road.

He lay gasping on his back and Kei sobbed and apologized. Yee-Lin and I shouted at him and Ming to come with us now. Mr. Lee rolled onto his side, clutching his head as blood ran from his scalp and down his neck. I grabbed Kei by the shoulder and forced him to look at me.

"Show us where to go," I said. He came to his senses and led us away.

Behind us, Mr. Lee propped himself up on the gravel and shouted after his son. "You dog! Don't run away from your mother! You'll rot in hell!"

Kei took Ming by the hand and pushed forward, aiming for the forest at the village edge.

What made us think they would come by the main road? Of course, they came from everywhere: the roads, the sky, the trees. I heard the planes again just as we reached the woods. *Maybe Tai Fo is burning now*, I thought. I saw my aunt and uncle in their home, the roof blown open by artillery and the walls ablaze. My aunt ran in circles in her slippers and my uncle, ensnared by his long magistrate's robes, whirled with flame.

We weren't far into the woods when I spotted them. Maybe twenty soldiers in khaki uniforms, but so drenched in sweat they seemed to be swimming through the trees, bayonets in hand.

They saw us too, and two soldiers in front pointed their rifles at us. Ming screamed and Kei shouted at us to turn around. But Yee-Lin, Leuk, and I were long past the shock. There was only one thing for me to do if I was to live. I dropped my bag, grabbed Wei-Ming with both my arms, and dragged her quickly back towards the village.

TWENTY

The soldier who spoke Cantonese was in charge. He barked the words out, spittle flying from his lips, and he seemed about to burst out of his uniform as he forcibly enounced each syllable. In the late afternoon heat he marched slowly up and down before village men who'd been made to kneel in long lines while his commanding officer sat behind him on a folding stool, drinking tea beneath a tree. The soldier who poured the tea wore white gloves and looked about Kei's age. In the distance, I heard a house collapse as the last of its supporting beams burned away.

"Any household found concealing valuables will see its family members shot, one by one, starting with the youngest. As long as there is compliance, no one else will be harmed." He made this promise as he looked out over the bleeding heads of the Chinese men who knelt before him on the ground. But they weren't kneeling to him, or even to his commander behind him. They were kneeling to the emperor, who sat far away across the sea, serene in his cool palace, his divinity preserved by our capture.

"China is a province of Japan," he went on, echoing the posters I had seen back home. "Your property belongs to us now, and you will be taken to a camp."

He didn't say where because he didn't care if we understood. Leuk, Yee-Lin, Wei-Ming, and I stood together. Their bags were on the ground behind us. Mine was still somewhere in the woods, and I was thinking about how I could retrieve it. I couldn't see Kei or Ming anywhere. Soldiers strolled around us with their rifles cocked, and I loosened my shirt from my pants to conceal my belt buckle. Leuk did the same.

I believed that retreating to the village, rather than trying to run, saved us from getting shot. By the time we were caught in the woods and driven back into the village, only minutes after the Japanese reached Wah Ying, the resistance was over. I doubt it ever really started. Every man seen carrying a gun or even a rake had been quickly shot, and their bodies lay like stepping stones in the streets.

They put us under guard with about twenty women and children, ordering us to gather by a well at the end of the street. This was the same street that led to Mr. Cheung's house, and I craned my neck to see what was happening there. Four Japanese soldiers broke open the gate and entered through the front doors; it was a desirable house, and the commander would want it for himself for the night. I heard the soldiers yelling from within, and then Mr. Cheung was dragged by his collar from the house onto the gravel walk. Blood flowed down his chin, and when a young soldier aimed a pistol at the back of his skull and fired, more erupted from his mouth. A moment later there came more shouting from an upstairs window and a large set of shutters opened. Two soldiers appeared in the window. They seemed to be struggling with ornate curtains that fluttered in the wind, made of a heavy cloth brocaded in gold, jade green, and sky blue. Then a pale hand thrust out from the fabric, and I realized it was Mrs. Cheung in her robes. The shutters flew back in the wind, and a soldier pushed them out again and held them open. The old woman's hand waved madly and clawed the air as though addressing us. Now Mrs. Cheung, her long grey hair unbound and intertwining with her robes against the wind, rose into the frame as the soldiers threw her from the window. Her mouth gaped, a dark hole inside the whirl of silk and hair. She fell headfirst onto the paving stones below.

The front door opened again. Ling and the gardener ran out, a soldier aiming his rifle at their heads. Ling turned to look at Mrs. Cheung's body on the ground, but she showed no emotion. The soldier marched them through the gates to join another group of villagers clustered by a fountain, mostly young people. The fountain was in the middle of a small square, visible from the main bedroom window in Mr. Cheung's house. It wasn't working now, and Ling and the others stood by its empty basin while the sun beat down on them.

We walked in a long convoy between army trucks spewing exhaust into the woods. It was very hot on the road and I was thirsty. Wei-Ming complained that she was thirsty, too; fortunately, Leuk had a water bottle and gave her some. She cried the first couple of hours and asked repeatedly where we were going. Yee-Lin kept telling her we didn't know. Of course, not knowing our destination wasn't why Wei-Ming cried.

I thought about Ling and wondered what had happened to her after the fountain. I hoped she was still alive, because I wanted to see her again. I felt bad for her. Her story was far sadder than my own, and thinking about it distracted me a little from dwelling on my own circumstances.

The Japanese divided us up into groups of twenty, and each group was separated by a truck full of soldiers. How many of us there were in total I didn't know, because so many had been killed or left behind in Wah Ying to succumb to their injuries. Some of the soldiers marched alongside us, the rest rode in the trucks. After the first couple of hours they began to jeer and taunt us, especially when captives started failing in the heat. A few people had animals with them, ponies and water buffalo, and had managed to strap their belongings to the animals' backs. The Japanese must have considered our possessions worthless if they let us keep them.

We rested regularly, but the marching between rests felt long in the heat, and not knowing where we were being taken made it much harder. We marched until just after sunset. Then the Japanese halted and said we would sleep on the road for the night. There was a stream by the road where everyone ran to get water. I knelt and drank. Near me, dozens of Chinese stooped over the stream, lapping like animals or scooping it with their hands or into whatever vessel they had managed to bring with them. I looked around for Ling. We tried to settle as best we could on the roadside. Wei-Ming had fallen asleep long ago as we carried her, and the three of us slept around her.

The next morning, the Japanese reorganized us into different groups, and the four of us ended up marching with a family of five who had a water buffalo. In the morning shuffle I looked around but didn't see Kei and Ming, and there was still no sight of Ling.

The family we walked with had three sons, one of whom was my age. The other two were in their late teens, and I feared their stupidity. The biggest one muttered repeatedly about fighting back, saying he would stick it to the Japs at night or grab their guns. His mother kept whispering harshly at him to stop, but he wouldn't. Finally, during one of our rests, his father took him off into the bushes and beat him with a stick. Then he stopped bragging.

The Japanese were watching and called to the father as they returned to the convoy. These idiots had drawn attention to us. I placed my hand over my belt buckle beneath my shirt. It was hot and I feared that the mercury would melt away in the humidity and expose the gold. I looked down very carefully through the top of my shirt and saw it was still tarnished. Leuk watched me and whispered that his was safe.

The Japanese seemed amused and annoyed by the father loudly beating his son and were eager to exploit the rift. The family had strapped baskets with their belongings over the buffalo's back. The soldiers rifled through the baskets as they walked alongside and removed a few things for themselves, tossing the rest aside. The soldiers then brought out some ropes from the truck, and loaded the animal with an unwieldy mountain of their own packs, which they tied across its sides and back.

For the rest of the day, the family walked beside the animal, and the parents took turns leading it by the rope around its neck. As the animal struggled under the heavy and imbalanced load, so that its legs trembled at times, they slowly distanced themselves from the creature they had probably owned since its birth. The father held the rope indifferently in one hand, while the boys and their mother walked ahead with their few remaining goods. When the animal began to slow, the Japanese gave the father a bamboo switch to strike its flanks.

By the third day of the march, the buffalo was stumbling along the track and its breathing was loud. Unwatched by the Japanese, the father let the switch drag on the ground beside him, and he pulled harder on the rope without looking back at the buffalo. Its flanks and cheeks gleamed with sweat, and long webs of thickened spittle descended from its lips.

We were walking a few yards behind the buffalo later that day when I noticed the stench. The buffalo's bulk rocked ahead of us, and I told Leuk and Yee-Lin to take Wei-Ming farther ahead so they wouldn't be near it.

After they moved up, I approached the animal with my sleeve over my nose. The Japanese packs leaned heavily to one side and forward, pressing against the animal's right shoulder. The guide rope dragged along the ground and the farmer walked idly beside it. A cloud of flies hung over the animal.

Under the weight of the packs, the rope tied by the Japanese had slowly sawn through the thin hide over the buffalo's spine. Right before me a piece of bone, the tip of the animal's sacrum, rose through the abraded flesh. The spinal bone was the colour of dull grey marble, and the hide around it was receding farther, like the gums of a diseased mouth. A small bird alighted on the buffalo's back and pecked diligently at the maggots emerging from the wound.

I picked up my pace to get ahead of it. The farmer saw me with my nose covered, and this seemed to upset him more than his animal's misery.

Later that night, I lay on the grass unable to sleep. I touched my cheeks and chest to feel how prominent the bones were becoming. In the dark and not wanting to be noticed, I carefully assessed the integrity of my skin for any flaws or openings, especially the spots with little muscle or fat: my elbows, clavicle, skull, and hips. These and not my mouth and eyes were the real doorways to my body, where the injurious world would strike and enter.

In old age, grief is the only thing that seems to slow time down. For two years after Alice died, I was nearly always at home. Travel meant the grocery store, the pharmacy, the gas station, and coffee shops I knew our friends would never visit. Evelyn invited me to spend time with her, and I always declined. In the first year my excuse was the pile of legal affairs after Alice's death, as if being a homemaker involved some immense regulatory burden. In the second year I claimed to be enjoying the discovery of a new routine. Whenever my daughter called, I always commented on how busy she seemed to be.

I immersed myself in false beginnings. For the first time in my life I discovered a taste for cold breakfast cereal and bought four boxes of it. I examined the nutritional labels, mouthing out *riboflavin* and *beta-glucan* over the kitchen table as though pondering a diseased organ. I read about oat bran, psyllium fibre, and ground flaxseed. Standing in the cereal aisle of the twenty-four-hour grocery store, I huffed disdainfully at the health claims on every box. I did so aloud, because I only went there late at night and there was never anyone to hear me.

In a small notebook that Alice had used for shopping lists, I began a daily record of the exact times of sunrise and sunset, checking these against the predicted times in the *Tribune*. I circled the errors in red. Round and round. Round in anger, round in disarray, in a muddy groove without direction. Obviously I just wanted to be dead. But what is the point of admitting that? It is easier at times to be a pallid vessel of events and memories, rather than the bearer of a life. And in grief, I felt I must now bear the weight of two lives if hers was not to disappear completely, but never felt competent to do it.

The park near our house had a duck pond I used to take Evelyn and Chris to when they were little. I got back into walking there every day, to the point where people on the street knew when I'd pass and would come out to wave or chat with me. I'd sit on a bench by the willows, throwing stale bread to the ducks. When I finally admitted that I hated cereal, I began to throw that too. I had a lot of it, and the ducks were tolerable company.

One fall evening, I was on the bench and a group of boys, mostly about eight years old, were playing on a hill nearby. A disagreement broke out, and one of them, after exchanging insults with another, ran off and stood by the pond. I heard him crying while the other boys resumed playing. After a moment I called him over.

What's wrong? I asked him. He didn't reply, and I asked him again. Then he told me his friends wouldn't play with him.

That's because you're all the way over here, I said. Just get back in there, it'll be fine. He shook his head and stayed by the pond.

I held up a box of Raisin Bran and offered him some to give to the ducks. He took a fistful, digging his hand all the way in so that his jacket sleeve bunched up his arm. He stayed with me by the bench and faced the pond.

He extended his arm, and with the sleeve pushed up I saw it was streaked in mud from playing on the damp ground. He brushed it clean with his free hand. He dropped a flake of cereal into the water. At once two ducks swam over, and the boy crouched down. He opened his hand and the ducks drew nearer, so close he could almost have touched their beaks. Piece by piece he dropped the cereal into the pond. When he was done, he gave me a funny look.

Yes, it's boring, isn't it, hanging out with an old man, I said. Go back and see your friends.

He dropped the last of the cereal in and ran back, and

it was as though the fight had never happened. How easy that was. I sat and watched them for a while, then sprinkled a little more cereal over the edge of the pond and walked home.

There's another boy I always wish I could console, although I've failed to. Strange to feel so powerless, like Mrs. Yee at our old dinner table. It's the boy I was then. He shouldn't exist anymore. He should have faded away with my teens, as my teenaged self should have faded into adulthood, leaving me unburdened, with just my eighty-six-year-old self to worry over.

But the boy I was still feels real and separate. He's there still, always near me but just out of reach. He waits, wanting to be taken home. And I have to sit and watch him, knowing there's nothing I can do.

Sometime in the countryside during those years came the moment when I was divided, twinned, and separated by blast waves or the wind from burning fields, or by the sound of boots on dark roads.

TWENTY-ONE

We arrived in a town called Tung Koo Chow. It was much larger and older than Tai Fo. As we marched through it, we passed two large temples, a school, and, sitting on large grounds and built in a European style, a Methodist hospital. The words over the gate reminded me of my school: *St. Paul's Hospital*, in iron letters inside the arch. Far back from its entrance, the stately white building with its rows of windows gleamed coolly in the sunlight. A small ambulance was parked outside, and I caught a brief glimpse of a nursing sister in a white-and-blue uniform.

People who asked questions were hit with a rifle butt or ordered to be silent, but we did learn from some of the prisoners that the Japanese had taken the town in the last month. In some places it appeared untouched, in others we marched by damaged buildings and signs of shelling. We shuffled through the town, watched here and there by lean, half-hidden faces in windows or behind crumbling walls.

We stopped at the far end of the town. There, in a large field, sat six simple, long bamboo buildings. A wooden guard tower stood at one end, and some soldiers were building a heavy fence of wooden posts and barbed wire around the field. The last truck in the convoy pulled up behind us, and when its engine shut off, the air around us seemed to collapse into emptiness. We lined up for water from two large, dirty-looking cisterns with rubber hoses attached. Even in my thirst I winced at the stale, pungent taste of the water, and I prayed that Wei-Ming wouldn't spit it out. But when it was her turn, she grabbed the hose tightly in her fist and took in all the water she could, and I felt embarrassed for having disliked it. Then we were ordered into a second lineup. Two villagers with bandaged heads handed out small metal bowls, and at the end of the line two women dished out a weak gruel of millet and unhusked rice.

My family sat on the ground together. Next to me, Leuk quietly counted out the spoonfuls from his bowl. "I want to remember how many make up a bowl." He reached fifteen. Yee-Lin watched him as he did this. She watched her own bowl carefully and ate a little, then gave the rest to Wei-Ming.

We sat in the sun and slurped our gruel. None of the farm animals had survived the last day of walking. The Japanese threw them onto the trucks to butcher later. Flies harassed us everywhere. They swarmed over our faces and arms and landed on our bowls and swarmed around a soldiers' latrine just outside the fence. I imagined they must be thick around the trucks where two dead water buffaloes and some ponies were lying.

Then we sat and waited. A few soldiers watched over us while the rest disappeared. Soon the smell of roasting meat drifted through the village, and we heard the occasional crack of gunfire.

Later, the Cantonese-speaking soldier reappeared. He

called himself Sergeant Akamatsu. After wiping his greasy lips on his sleeve, he laid out our fate: we would help build the rest of this camp, all of us without exception for age or health, and here we would wait. Nothing else. Immediately, more soldiers appeared. They tipped a large wheelbarrow full of shovels onto the ground and the men and boys were ordered to line up for them, while a few other men were marshalled to collect bamboo from the grove at the town's edge.

The soldiers separated the women from the men and then divided the women into two groups. Those in their thirties or older, or who were sick, were put into one group, and the younger ones were put in the other. Many mothers were taken from their daughters, and the Japanese seemed to enjoy shouting at them to be quiet and stop their wailing. When they started to hit the older women, the younger ones learned to be quiet. Standing next to Leuk in the line for shovels, I glanced repeatedly at Wei-Ming and Yee-Lin and tried to catch Wei-Ming's eye.

I was very hot and thirsty. The soldiers ordered us to dig and showed us where, because none of us knew what we were building. It didn't take long for the soldiers to start lashing out. Next to me was an older man I recognized from the vegetable stalls in Wah Ying. He had a large sore on the side of his head that looked very raw. He winced as the sweat from his bald scalp ran down into the sore, and when he dabbed or covered it with his dirty sleeve, he gasped and shivered. He was very slow and the soldiers took a special interest in him. A lieutenant approached him, kicking dust up into his face. He shouted,

"*Baka!*" repeatedly. The old man stumbled, blinking in the sun and shielding the sore with his arm. He turned to them, and when he saw the rifle, he collapsed in despair, sobbing and bowing to the soldier with the shovel in one hand.

The soldier shouted back at him, with the explosive syllables and bobbing head that the Japanese often used. The old man muttered back and turned and tried to dig a little more, as if to propitiate the soldier. The shovel head scraped the dry earth and twisted in his hands, achieving nothing. The soldier raised his boot and kicked the old man to the ground. He was rolling onto his side to get up when the soldier raised his leg again and put the sole of his boot on the man's neck. He shouted something else as he braced his boot against the man's throat, and then he lunged forward.

I heard a crunch. The man's tongue protruded and he flailed on the ground, eyes wide in terror. His hands flew up to the boot on his throat and he clutched feebly at it. His lips and face darkened to a bluish shade, and then he was still. The soldier turned and ordered two other prisoners to haul his body away.

Most of us had stopped to stare at this, but as soon as the man was dead, we were ordered to resume our work. I stared at the sun-baked soil and pushed hard with the shovel, thinking of it as a knife, a spike, a deadly instrument to outdo every other shovel nearby. The hunger in my stomach disappeared and I felt as though I'd been injected with a potion that gave me immense strength. The ground crumbled under the shovel's tip, and I heaved the dirt away in quick snapping motions. I looked carefully at the others near me, checking to see how fast they dug and making sure I brought my shovel down harder and faster.

Leuk was in the next row, dragging stacks of bamboo over to another site. I wanted him to look at me, but he was squinting in the sunlight and his hair was sticking to his face. I worried that he wasn't working hard enough. One of the other boys carrying bamboo was older and very strong, carrying twice as much as my brother. I wanted to hit that boy with my shovel, break his arm to weaken him and get him into trouble. It was the farmer's son, the braggart who still bore the bruises on his face and arms from his father's beating.

In the evening, Sergeant Akamatsu reappeared as we lined up for water and gruel. He picked meat from his teeth ostentatiously, and then he flicked the scraps onto the earth and ground them with his boot. He told us the camp still needed work and that we would sleep in the huts tonight. Anyone seen leaving would be shot, no matter the reason.

Leuk and I ended up in the same building, and I prayed that Wei-Ming and Yee-Lin were still together. The floor was hard, with a few straw mats over it, and the building was crowded and stank of unwashed bodies. It had been three days since the Japanese attacked Wah Ying, and since then I'd slept on the ground. It was very dark and the windows were shut, but air worked its way between the slats and a cool breeze soon blew away the stench. The soldiers closed the door and fixed it shut with a chain, and under the light shining through the door jamb I saw the shadow of a guard. I heard a cough and thought it was Leuk. I closed my eyes and filtered through the sounds around me to locate where he was.

That night, I slept and woke a dozen times, maybe more. I doubt if more than half an hour went by before I woke again, hearing sounds around me or dreaming them. Each time, my eyes went to the same spot: the thin stroke of moonlight beneath the door. I tried to count the number of times I woke up but lost track.

I watched the light closely. Twice the shadows broke it when boots shuffled lightly over the planks.

The third time I woke — which I guessed was before midnight — I began to wonder if everyone else was also waking up. I sat up very carefully and tried to see in the dark. I was confused and thought Yee-Lin and Wei-Ming were in our building. I worried that Wei-Ming would awake and make a noise or cry. And then what? I doubted Yee-Lin could quiet her fast enough. I ran through it in my head a hundred times, and the scenario changed each time. At first I imagined Yee-Lin and I leaning over her, hushing her to sleep before anyone else awoke. But the story took over. As the night wore on and I woke up again and again, it became a scene of stifled riot. The others around us would wake up when they heard her. They'd be angry. The farmer's wife would sit up and reach around with clawing hands, looking for something to hit with. We'd be pressed in a corner, kicking out at the attackers. I felt someone try to pull my shoes from me and a dusty hand clawed my belt buckle.

My heart raced in the dark, and I rubbed my face to rouse myself from the fantasy. My head cleared and I heard only the others breathing dryly. I slowed my breathing down, timing each breath with the hush of the wind in the trees outside the fence. I was the only person awake. When I realized this, I was thrilled to have privacy. I sat straight up with my palms pressed on the floor beside me. No one could see me. The light from the door jamb lit nothing.

I loved the strange freedom of this moment, and I kept turning my head to listen for the sound of another person moving. I made wild faces in the dark, stretched my jaw and stuck out my tongue, rolled my eyes around, and when my eyes began to ache, I rolled my head around in the dark, flicking my tongue out like a snake.

I moved my jaw up and down while making no sound. I turned to a man and mouthed *wa-wa-wa* at him, stretching my jaw wider with every syllable. Then I mouthed silent words. I held my breath deep in my lungs as I sounded out phrases and clicked my tongue against my teeth, directing my lips at everyone in turn: *idiot, fatty, loudmouth, frog-face, lumpy.*

Then I mouthed sentences. Over the slumbering bodies I thrilled to the dry clicking in my mouth as I hurled insults at the other prisoners: *you snore too loud, you drink nun's piss, you love Japs, you love farts, you eat chicken shit.* I avenged myself against the attackers in my dream. And when they failed to reply, I redoubled my abuse.

Then I felt dizzy and shivered with exhaustion. It felt like deep night, maybe three in the morning. My head swam until I couldn't stay awake anymore. It was the last time for months that I'd feel the pleasure of solitude.

. . .

More prisoners arrived over the next few days, and the Japanese ordered us to keep building. We lashed bamboo poles together while the women and girls wove mats out of leaves and grass. The soldiers clustered near where the younger women such as Yee-Lin knelt and wove, talking loudly to each other and leering at them.

We had eight large huts for the prisoners, who now seemed to number at least a hundred and fifty. A few times I helped put up a wall or helped a woman with some mats, and I'd feel a brief flash of achievement. But I knew these were cages.

No one had enough to eat and the Japanese worked us relentlessly. Each day our pace slowed and we struggled to complete the work they gave us. I was tired all the time and often dizzy, and even at mealtimes I found it hard to stay awake. By the second week in the camp, the older people started dying. I came across an old woman one afternoon whom I recognized from the village. Her clothes and skin were so permeated with dust that I almost didn't notice her on the ground. She had lost all her hair, and flies trafficked in and out of her toothless mouth. I thought of an old woman who used to sell candies at a stall near our house in Hong Kong, who used to call me a handsome boy. The old woman's eyes were still open. I reached down to close them with my fingertips. That was all I could manage.

When children began to die, the Japanese changed their ways. Most people tried to give an extra share of gruel to their children, as we did with Wei-Ming, but sharing became harder with time. One morning the four of us sat together with our bowls, all of us very thin. Wei-Ming could barely keep her eyes open and was too tired to chase the flies off a sore on her lips. I still remember how I thought, *She's too tired now, she can't eat anyway.*

Sergeant Akamatsu appeared one afternoon to announce that the rations would be increased. We all knew this was because his supply of workers was dying off, but he made a point of telling us it was because so many villages had been captured that they had more food. He almost smiled as he said this. Vegetable scraps and even beans started appearing in the gruel, and everyone was now allotted a boiled sweet potato with each meal.

That evening, we stood in one of the lineups for food. It was a very hot evening, my shirt clinging to my back and chest, and the smell of burnt food made me feel slightly sick. A constant murmur of worn voices drifted through the prisoners' ranks, until an argument broke out between two people in the next line. I wouldn't have noticed it had I not caught Ling's voice. I peered through the crowd and saw her standing with her bowl, shouting back at an older woman who'd accused her of trying to push ahead in the line.

I called to her. She turned, and at first she looked afraid—as though someone were joining in attacking her—but then she saw me and called back. I pointed the way to where we ate and she promised to meet us there. I had convinced myself she was dead.

By the third week, most of us felt a little stronger and had stopped losing weight. With careful washing, the sore on Wei-Ming's lip slowly disappeared. Each of us made a point of giving her a small portion of our sweet potato. When we sat down after lining up for food, Leuk, Yee-Lin, Ling, and I would compare the quantities of food we had and try to ensure they were equal. One evening Leuk suggested we start saying grace again. Yee-Lin didn't care and at first I didn't, either.

"Don't you remember the grace we said at our school every evening before supper?"

I shook my head. "I don't want to start saying that."

"I'd feel better if we did." His voice was dreamlike and he seemed to be looking at something in the distance.

Wei-Ming didn't join in because our mother didn't enforce grace, and Yee-Lin just went ahead and ate. Ling found it very strange. But my brother and I bowed our heads over the greyish liquid in our bowls and recited our school grace. The sound of the words in my mouth, our mutual mumbling of them, brought me back in an instant, and in my mind I saw briefly what Leuk had seen: the blank white walls of the school, the old banyan tree where we used to meet, the muted green of the lawns. We prayed for peace and consolation.

The next day, we finished building our camp.

TWENTY-TWO

Sometime in the spring — one of the newer prisoners told me it was the middle of April — we started wondering if the fortunes of the Japanese were changing. They seemed very gloomy. Sergeant Akamatsu and the other officers gave regular speeches to the troops in which they all cheered defiantly and shouted *banzai*, but the officers' faces were grim and there was a misery in their demeanour that I hadn't seen before. They meted out harsh discipline against their own. The newer prisoners whispered about what they'd heard in the news before their capture. They said the war was turning against Japan, and whenever planes flew overhead, it was to reinforce the eastern front, where the Allies were striking hard.

Akamatsu gathered all the younger male prisoners together one morning. He announced he had an urgent task for some of us. He prefaced this with a long speech about the emperor, his divinity, his descent from the primordial sun god, and, above all, the unbreakable devotion of his subjects. In a small clearing outside the camp, revived drills by the Japanese troops underscored his point.

"A large number of our heroic injured soldiers will arrive tomorrow morning by train from the north," he said. "The hospital in Tung Koo Chow will be their new home, and the existing patients must be relocated. The staff will co-operate."

It would be our job to help move the patients from this hospital. These were mostly locals and a small number of foreigners—Western missionaries and teachers—and Akamatsu said they would go to a nearby farmhouse.

The Japanese piled into four trucks while the dozen of us they picked to help marched in the middle of the convoy. I was with Leuk, the farmer's sons, and a few others prisoners all about our age. A breeze blew over the road, but we still choked on the fumes from the trucks and I walked with my hands cupped over my mouth and nose. Along the road, a burned-out farmhouse gave off its last wisps of smoke, and clusters of crows fought loudly over dark forms on the ground. I thought I heard a child screaming in the distance, so I took my hands from my mouth and covered my ears and coughed until the farm was out of sight.

Tung Koo Chow was very quiet. If the townspeople had been out earlier in the day, the sound of the trucks must have sent most of them inside. I looked back, and as the trucks passed, people crept out of their houses and the front doors of shops reopened.

We stopped at the entrance to the grounds of St. Paul's Hospital. Outside the gates, an officer waited in his car while his driver briskly ran a cloth over the hood and windshield. Three trucks and two ambulances were lined up behind it. As our convoy pulled up, curious faces emerged in the hospital windows. A senior Japanese officer spoke harshly to Sergeant Akamatsu and pointed repeatedly at the hospital's main door and then went back to his car and was driven off, the ambulances following him.

Sergeant Akamatsu opened the gates and marched ostentatiously down the path with ten soldiers behind him. He ordered us to follow them, and we shuffled behind the neat clip of their boots. As we approached, a doctor in a white coat and a nursing sister came out and stood on the front steps of the hospital. The doctor left one hand resting on the large iron door handle. Akamatsu walked up to him and asked if he was in charge.

"I am," he said stiffly. Like the nurse, he looked past the sergeant at us. Maybe he thought we were patients.

"Many of our soldiers are coming by train this evening. You need to empty the hospital for them. Move your patients out to the village or discharge them, but we need this place emptied out within four hours."

"We can't do that," said the doctor. "Everyone here is very sick; there's nowhere else for them to go."

Akamatsu's jaw flexed. The rest of his body was rigid. Only because I stood close to him was I able to see one index finger drop slowly along the length of his riding crop.

"I said move them," he answered.

The nurse fingered the small metal cross that hung from her neck, and the doctor looked at us again. I realized I had been standing with my mouth open and felt stupid. I closed it and my tongue scraped against the dry inside of my mouth.

"We can't," the doctor repeated. "Where on earth could I put them?"

Akamatsu's neck and scalp flushed. "You think you can't? Then we'll move them," he answered.

The doctor's demeanour broke and he swallowed hard. "I said—I said there is nowhere else they can —"

Akamatsu turned and shouted orders at the other soldiers. His voice raked the air like gunfire, spittle flying from his lips. I understood none of it, of course, but the meaning was in his body—the fists, the blood vessels on his face, the torrent of words.

When he was done, the soldiers shouted "*Hai!*" and marched up the hospital steps. Akamatsu told us to get off the path and wait on the front lawn. Nurses and some patients had been watching the scene from the windows on all three floors, and they retreated when Akamatsu started shouting.

The doctor and nurse ran after the soldiers, but the last soldier up the steps turned and shoved them back with his rifle and then slammed the door. The doctor got up and turned to Akamatsu, saying they weren't allowed in. Akamatsu put his right hand on his pistol and shouted at the doctor to step aside. The doctor hesitated when he saw Akamatsu touch his gun. His expression changed and he started to say something. Akamatsu didn't care. He drew his gun and shot the doctor in the head, and when the nurse turned to run, he shot her twice in the back. He kicked their bodies off the steps into the bushes and went inside.

Through the windows, I saw and heard the staff and patients trying to keep the soldiers away. One orderly shouted at another to help him block the doors of their ward, and an older nurse pulled a patient from a window. I felt a drumming in my head as though I had been struck from behind. I rested my hand on my burning stomach. Watching the swirling forms of soldiers, staff, and patients through the windows, I felt time slow. Already the months of my exile had felt long and the changing of the seasons delayed, and now the day itself slowed to an inhuman crawl.

Leuk, the farmer's sons, the other men and boys, we all stared at the white facade and the three neat rows of windows. The sounds were very clear: the screams, the doors breaking apart, the collision of bodies with solid objects. Two white-clad nurses wheeled patients away from the doors and struggled to stop one patient, who looked as though he was deranged, from leaving. But they were on the first floor. The soldiers were starting at the top.

They began shooting the patients. Despite all the gunfire we'd heard over the past several months, Leuk and I started at the first shot. On the top floor a window opened, and the shouting became much clearer as all the windows banged violently open. It was like the rising of a curtain at the theatre.

An old man with a bandaged head appeared suddenly in a window in a tall-backed wheelchair. One of his hands was raised and waving strangely. He lunged forward as the soldier behind him tipped his chair. The old man plummeted to the gravel below. Another man, much younger, followed from the same window. The soldiers disgorged the sick and mutilated into the air, as though unloading bags off a truck. One soldier, a burly man I'd noticed earlier, dragged an injured woman towards a window. The uniformed hands of a nurse seized him by the arm and tried to break his grasp. The patient gripped the window frame with one hand, but her other was pressed over a bloody bandage across her abdomen. The soldier shot the nurse and pushed the woman through the window with his boot. The nurse was the next to fall.

When she landed, I thought her eyes looked into mine. She had fallen on her back, on top of the others. The bullet had passed through her neck, but her face was untouched. She was pale, young, and wide-eyed, gazing far away as only the newly dead can do. She looked almost alive, but in the staring white of her uniform she seemed already dressed for burial.

The Japanese started clearing the lower floors. When one man tried to climb through a window, Akamatsu shot him and he fell into the bushes. Behind him, a nurse laughed hysterically. Two soldiers, seeing no one left to deal with, holstered their guns and tore her uniform from her before throwing her to the floor.

Many survived their falls, even some who had been shot. With the upper floors cleared, the Japanese turned their fury on the survivors outside. They dragged a man from the heap who was smeared with feces from a corpse that had fallen on him. All the while the man cursed them loudly. A soldier took a garden hose off the wall and put the nozzle up between his legs. They turned the water on and he swelled until his belly gleamed and his cursing blazed into a wordless scream. They dragged the last few nurses through the hospital doors and laid them on the ground, and then used them into a despairing silence and shot them all when they were done. When I saw the expression in the nurses' eyes before they died, I stopped believing that this could ever end.

I felt each blow, each fall, every gunshot exploded in my ears and every scream stretched my jaw. I lost all sensation of myself — the hunger in my stomach, my soaking cheeks, the grass pricking my naked ankles. I felt only what I saw and heard in the glacial crawl of this moment. Beside me, my brother heaved dryly and struggled to stand. I felt the bile burning his throat. I was utterly empty, nothing more. Then, as Leuk retched and the farmer's son sobbed loudly behind me, I wiped my eyes until I saw clearly that all the victims were finally dead.

Their stillness cleared my mind. For a moment I heard nothing of the soldiers' laughter and shouts, or the sobs of those around me. The scene before me disappeared. I wanted only to be gone, to be home, and never hear screaming or gunfire again. I wanted to sit in the garden beside my mother, or run up the cool stairways of my school, smelling its camphor and old paper, and the wild aroma of its orange trees in blossom. But those things were very far away and very old now, memories from another person's life, and they were fitted to a world I'd left behind.

Akamatsu stepped forward as some of his soldiers dropped shovels and jerry cans on the ground beside him. He jerked his head to the lawns on our right and looked at us with a mocking smile.

"Now clean this up."

. . .

We staggered over the road back to camp. Open calluses bled on my hands from the shovel, and my clothes and hair stank of gasoline and smoke and scorched flesh. We still had to walk between the trucks. They let us stop at a stream on the way, where I sucked in the murky water like a lamprey. I held my brother's hand, and we were silent all the way back.

As we returned to the camp, it began to rain. Leuk went inside, but I stood away from the shelter and let the drops land on me. I hung my head and the rain fell over the nape of my neck, and I tried to let its lightness and slow trickle displace the pounding in my brain. Soon I was soaked. The dirt ran from my skin into my clothes. Grey water dripped from my fingertips, and the water stung my calluses. I stared vacantly at my shoes, which had torn open at the toes, though the laces were strangely intact. The lower buttons on my shirt were gone, and when I saw the tarnished belt buckle exposed, I raised a trembling hand to conceal it. Someone called me. Three times I ignored it and stayed standing in the rain.

"Chung-Man, are you sick?"

I couldn't answer Ling. She was as soaked as I was, and yet seemed cleaner, so clean that when she reached out to touch me, I recoiled and moved away, fearing I would destroy her.

"Come inside," she said. Her hand was open and her arm clear of its old bruises. I backed away.

"No, I want to stay out here. I feel hot. The rain, the rain is—" I gasped as though I'd been hit. I looked up to make sure the rain covered my face so that no one, especially Ling, could see the tears pouring down it. I screwed my eyes shut tight and covered them with my hands, but behind them there burned images that I couldn't look away from. I inhaled hard through my nose, trying to smell something that was real and in front of me, anything but the stench of gasoline. I clutched the buckle and let the pin dig into my palm.

It rained until long past dark that night. I didn't line up for the meal, but Ling brought me some food. We sat together outside the shelter and ate, saying nothing to each other.

TWENTY-THREE

More and more people were brought into the camp. I tried to guess from their appearance and behaviour what was happening in the war. One afternoon, a Japanese convoy arrived with about two dozen people, and because they were healthier-looking and better dressed than we'd first been, and seemed to be in shock, I guessed that they had been taken from a newly captured town. Other people looked as worn as we had when we were brought here. From one of the newer arrivals, a teacher from a nearby village, I learned it was now the middle of June 1942.

The hut where Leuk and I slept was badly overcrowded. It now slept forty men and boys. After evening curfew, some of the younger men bossed the other boys around. They forced them to sleep in the far corners of the building, where it was hotter and stuffier. Most of the boys were afraid of being trapped there. The younger men fought to sleep nearer the door, though twice soldiers intervened and beat a few of them for delaying the curfew. Leuk and I had trouble sleeping at night, and we often tried to nap during the day. The skin around Leuk's eyes was turning grey, and in the evenings there were long periods when he just stared into the distance. At night, he always volunteered to take the corner, partly out of pity for the younger boys, and partly because he found sitting in the corner allowed him to stay awake longer. I think he had a lot of nightmares, and he said he liked listening to the insects at night.

At mealtimes, I sat with Yee-Lin, Wei-Ming, Leuk, and Ling. We had our spot, as other groups did. It worked out to twenty paces from the north wall of one of the women's compounds where Yee-Lin and Wei-Ming slept. We sat in a circle with our wooden dishes and learned to manage our hunger by eating as slowly as we could, so that we finished just as the guards shouted at everyone that mealtime was over. I remembered my mother's old edict, "Chew your rice twenty times before you swallow it." I'd watched her at the dinner table many times and noted that she never followed this rule herself. But here her wisdom made sense.

Our habit was to take the bowl of gruel, made from a barely edible unhusked reddish rice and sometimes millet, and put some of the cooked sweet potato into it. This displaced the gruel and made the bowl look fuller. We then sipped it very slowly. At first it was hard to get Wei-Ming to eat more slowly. She was so hungry all the time that we just let her eat as she wanted. When she was done, she'd stare enviously at the rest of us eating and ask us for a share. We always gave her a little, but giving up food was hard, and I sometimes resented doing it. Eventually she learned to slow down with us.

After slurping the last of the gruel, we'd eat the rest of the potato by breaking it up into small pieces. The first pieces we used to wipe down the sides of the bowl so as to catch every bit of liquid and grain. The charred potato skin stuck between my teeth, along with bits of hard rice bran.

Together they formed a bitter, fibrous grit that I ground distractedly between my molars before swallowing. I was always digging fragments of it out of the spaces between my teeth, and the burnt skin was so hard I sometimes cut the tip of my tongue against it.

Because our clothes were slowly turning to rags, Leuk and I thought constantly of our belt buckles, and worked out a plan to keep them concealed. We saved bits of loose thread, and used these to repair our shirts. Most boys had lost the buttons on their shirts, but we were careful to keep ours and tie them back on if they came off. If I could button up my shirt, then I could cover my buckle. When we had to remove our shirts, because of the heat or because they were being washed, we flipped the tops of our shorts over to hide the belts. We were so thin that even with the belts our shorts didn't fit, and we had to tighten them around our waists with strips of torn cloth.

In several corners of the camp, hardy plants crept through the barbed-wire barricades. During the day I would take Wei-Ming to one of these corners, and there we played make-believe games about the thickly growing plants, though we were careful never to sit too close to the fence. I feared the barbs that hung in the wire, and also the Japanese, who had shot people for touching the posts.

Wei-Ming and I would lie on the ground facing the little plants and pretend we were watching a forest. There were tigers and monkeys in the forest: the dark beetles that roamed the ground were tigers, and the aphids and ants that lived mostly on the stalks were monkeys. We didn't pick them up or move them around; all we did was lie on our bellies and watch them and make up stories about what they were doing. The monkeys always outsmarted the tigers. Sometimes we took a sprig of weed and poked the beetles or ants away, but they always came back. If Wei-Ming asked me to play this game with her, I never said no, and as the days passed, it saddened me that it distracted her so well. She asked less and less when we would go home, and over time she became quieter. During the game, she often gazed silently into the spindly stems and leaves, murmuring to herself some story about the animals. Once I lay quietly on the ground beside her with my ear near her mouth, and tried to make out one of these stories, but it was whispered and broken and made little sense to me.

Games like this filled our time, and the days went by. Without school we had to build a routine for ourselves. We cleaned our bowls; mended, washed, and hung our clothes; stood in line for food; and groomed ourselves as best we could. And we had not just our corner in the yard but corners everywhere: by the fence to play, in the buildings to sit and talk, corners of time when we met, and in our conversations there were corners where we went and others we avoided.

The natural world around the camp appeared to change. Outside the barbed wire, the bamboo seemed to grow higher and denser each day. I guessed that the animals that normally ate it had been scared away or killed off by the Japanese. Abandoned by predators, the grass grew wild, thick, and dark, and over the weeks I believed I could detect, while lying awake deep in the night, a subtle change in how the wind sounded through its stalks and leaves, from the gentle hushing of younger grass to a deeper sound like that of people sleeping. The grass was the first thing I noticed each morning when I stepped outside, as the world around the camp drew so much nearer and became so much quieter.

I woke very suddenly from a dream one night. I was confused by the sound of the wind, and for a second I thought there were Chinese soldiers hiding in the grass, waiting to kill the Japanese. Then my mind cleared. I blinked and looked through the cracks in the walls, and outside there was just wind and grass, insects snapping their wings against the lamps, and miles of empty road.

After the violence at the hospital, I woke often in the night. It seemed as though every sound in the dark was magnified through a speaker. When I lay down, I felt that I was drifting, losing control of my thoughts. I could only fall asleep if I kept my eyes open as long as possible, and stared at the stars through the openings in the walls or the moonlight coming through the thatch. When I awoke with a start from dreams, as I often did, I learned to listen first for the sound of the grass. It masked the heavy sound of my breathing and at times the shouts of others around me as they dreamed. The farmer's sons often muttered in their sleep about things I tried to forget.

One morning, Akamatsu summoned all the prisoners to the main yard. It was the first time we had been gathered all together, and there were so many that our ranks spilled over into the spaces between the buildings. Wei-Ming was asleep. Yee-Lin tried to hold her over her shoulder, but she no longer had the strength to lift her. I sat Wei-Ming on the ground and she leaned against my shins and dozed while Akamatsu spoke.

The idle weeks of governing the camp hadn't worn his swagger down. He strode out before the crowd with a bamboo switch clutched in one hand, and he beat the air repeatedly in small gestures as though to some music audible only to him. He and the soldiers behind him all looked thinner and dirtier.

"The progress of the Imperial Army," he said, "has led to the capture of many more prisoners. This camp will now be used only for prisoners from this area. The rest of you will be moved this afternoon to a new camp. Those of you not from the following villages must be ready by noon." He then read out the names of several villages, including Wah Ying and Tung Koo Chow. I was surprised at how long the list had grown, though Hong Kong wasn't on it. I was frightened that we would be singled out for extra mistreatment if it was discovered we were from the city.

A group of guards moved through the camp accompanied by a trio of Chinese men carrying folders full of documents. I recognized one of them from the market in Wah Ying, a tall man who still had his glasses while most of the prisoners had lost theirs, and who looked well-fed and clean by comparison. The three men all had recent haircuts. The one from Wah Ying marched around the camp with two Japanese soldiers, who handled him roughly to show he was beneath them. They left him alone with long lists on crisp yellowish paper. He pored over these with theatrical care, calling out names and pointing them out to the soldiers when prisoners responded. When he turned his head to point at an elderly couple in one corner of the yard, I noticed that a large part of one of his ears was missing, taken off in a clean vertical slice that looked recent.

He told the old couple to wait by a section of the fence, and then read out more names. As they moved to the fence, he announced they would all go to the new camp. I checked my belt, as did Leuk.

The soldiers started spreading throughout the camp, brandishing their rifles and harassing people at random. Something in this moment, in this disruption of our routine, filled me with sudden terror, and sweat poured down my face and neck. I ran my hand over my shirt again to check for the buckle. I started to think that it was visible, the tarnished shadow beneath the thin white cotton, like a mark or wound in my centre. The soldiers butted a few prisoners with their rifles. The Chinese collaborators walked behind them and shouted at more prisoners to move to the fence. I thought I heard our family name being called. My hand felt heavy. I looked down at the ground as my head swam, and my right leg trembled violently against the dust.

Leuk moved beside me. "Chung-Man, what's wrong?"

I couldn't look at him. I put both hands over my buckle and vomited. An orangey puddle of sweet potato flecked with greyish bits of grain lay on the ground between my feet. I heaved again, but nothing came out, and I felt an odd relief at no longer being hungry. Flies gathered quickly over the mass and I stepped back, bumping into Yee-Lin. My stomach settled and I looked up, afraid that I had drawn the soldiers' attention. I held my hands steady over my buckle. It didn't seem any of the soldiers had noticed. Yee-Lin took me by the arm, and we joined the others by the fence.

Only an old woman, wrapped in a tattered flowery gown, stared at me from a few steps away. Her mouth hung open, a toothless hole, and her eyes were sunken so that I couldn't tell if she even saw me. I stared back, exhausted from the strain of throwing up. Her lips moved slowly, mouthing indeterminate words, while she gestured with her hands. A young woman sat on the ground beside her, resting her forehead on her knees. From time to time she looked over at the old woman, and reached out and touched her arm. This calmed the old woman a little and her hand would sink to her lap before she became agitated again. She seemed to have no sense of why she was moving, or what she was trying to say, or even of where she was.

The Chinese collaborator awakened me from the strange hypnosis induced by her movements. He finished calling out the prisoners on his list, and the moment he was done, the guards seized him roughly and dragged him away. Akamatsu stood before us. He told us quickly that we would now be moved to the new camp. His speech stayed with me, not because of what it meant for us but because at that moment an ashen veil of clouds had begun to draw across the sky. It made the camp not gloomy but cooler, tempering the light as if to promise we would be sheltered on our walk.

We had little time to get ready to leave. Yee-Lin took my sister and ran back to their quarters with Ling, while Leuk and I ran back to ours. We grabbed our belongings and met the others at the gate, where a wavering, distorted voice blared out orders through a megaphone.

In early 1994, I was finding any domestic routine, or any part of life outside my work, chaotic and riddled with errors. Alice had been in and out of hospital for over a month, and it was only after our son Chris flew in to help me that I was free to deal with other pressing family issues.

My trip to Hong Kong at the end of January seemed doomed from the start. In my rush to leave, I forgot my passport at the house — one of those details Alice always took care of — and at the airport I learned my flight was delayed. As we approached Hong Kong, after I'd spent sixteen sleepless hours in my seat, we had to circle the airport for thirty minutes because of the air traffic, and I found myself feeling resentful about the whole journey. Of course I was ashamed of this feeling. I was healthy then, still working, and I had no business griping when my brother was dying. Sheung's son, Tat-Choy, had phoned me a week earlier to say the cancer had become more aggressive. I expected this to be my last visit with my brother.

Of course, there are times like this — overnight flights, long waits in hospitals, sleepless nights — when you are, if not captive, at least bound by some prolonged obligation, with no way out. Then the mind will wander like a spider crawling over the floor of a lightless cellar, heading into every corner imaginable in search of an exit or a home. Sitting in my seat in between two other passengers, my mind ran through a hundred things and in such a disorganized way that at times I felt I was thinking total nonsense. I thought of Sheung, now seventy-five years old, and how little our lives had crossed as adults. I was sixty-four at the time, still feeling that I had much ahead of me, and my brother's condition made me feel not older, but more distant from him.

We landed late, and there were delays at customs, and huge lines for taxis, and traffic jams. I decided to delay checking into the hotel and went straight to the hospital with my luggage, hoping to call the hotel from there to hold my room. Something about hauling my luggage around, lifting it, being able to manage last-minute changes to my plans, made me feel even more alive and younger, and thus more distant from the infirmity around me.

These thoughts disappeared when I got to Sheung's room. Tat-Choy was waiting for me in the hallway outside.

Uncle, my father died a few hours ago. My wife and son just left, but Mother is still with him.

Yee-Lin was sitting beside the bed where her husband lay. Her hair was tied back simply, coming loose around her face in a girlish way, and she seemed thinner than I remembered. She leaned over him, one hand resting on his hands, which were folded over his abdomen. She got up and briefly took my hand before we both sat down at the bed. She put her left hand back over his and carefully slid her right hand under his shoulders and neck.

He's still a little warm. I keep checking. You know, just

after he died, when the nurse finally took the mask off his face, that was the first thing I did.

I put my arm around her shoulder and briefly reached over to touch Sheung's forearm.

I'm sorry I didn't make it.

No, don't apologize. He'd been unconscious since yesterday. They started giving him more morphine then, and after that he stopped fidgeting. You must be tired. Have you eaten?

Tat-Choy sat down on the other side of the bed.

Mother, I spoke to the doctor. Now that Uncle's been here, they're going to move Father to the morgue soon.

Yee-Lin's lips trembled and she slid her hand farther down her husband's back.

You know, Chung-Man, all the arrangements have been made. He made them all years ago. He always took care of things. He was so good at that. He knew everything. I don't know anything. What will I do? I can't drive, I don't know the lawyer's number or how to pay the bills.

Sister-in-law, I began.

She fell forward and put her head on his chest, burying her arm beneath his back, all the way to her bony shoulder.

After the funeral I flew back to Chicago. My program had just relocated to a new hospital near Northwestern and it seemed the ribbon-cutting would never end. The hallway chatter and official memos were studded with platitudes about how this facility had the latest of everything and with clichés about the hospital of the future and the miracles of science. The constant stream of these bromides drove me to a kind of hypnotic dullness, and in idle moments I found myself gazing stupidly at the banks of new computer screens, the automated equipment in the labs, and oversized photographs of grimacing philanthropists that loomed in every hallway. None of it interested me. Both novelty and routine seemed to peel away to disclose the underlying emptiness. Then there was a fire at my favourite lunch spot down the street from the hospital. It wasn't a big fire, but when the restaurant reopened a month later, I didn't return to it. My habits seemed more easily broken.

I went back to Hong Kong four months later. Tat-Choy picked me up at the airport and warned me Yee-Lin wasn't doing well. In his car, he turned to me with a desperate look.

Uncle, I haven't been able to tell anyone in the family. But you're a doctor. You need to see her.

In nervous and rapid speech, which he punctuated by either clearing his throat or squeezing his hands over the steering wheel, he told me of his mother's sudden decline after his father's death. He said the maid began to call him at odd hours in a panic. The first time Tat-Choy went over, he found his mother in the bathtub wearing a cotton dress, soaked and half buried in a mass of soap foam, shouting nonsense. Then she complained of foul odours in the flat, and if it happened during or after meals, she would vomit on the spot no matter where she was, even the building elevator. She said the flat smelled like sewage and she drove the maid to tears with her cleaning orders. She washed herself constantly, burning herself with hot water and scrubbing pads. One night she said the stench of sewage was so unbearable that she ran out onto her balcony on the twentieth floor. Tat-Choy and the maid had to pull her back inside. He sobbed at a traffic light as he told me how he and a nurse had to drag her into an ambulance.

We arrived at the hospital. Of course, it was all beyond me. I had seen much as a doctor, bodies tormented with disease. But in that role I stood apart from the suffering and was bound to my patients by abstractions such as duty and decorum. When I saw Yee-Lin at the hospital—and I admit with shame that my visit was brief—the illness, the injury, the damage, whatever it was, wasn't hers alone. It was something that I shared intimately with her, that I recognized like the sound of my own heart in my ears, and I recoiled. Knowing that Tat-Choy couldn't possibly understand this, and maybe shouldn't, I stammered that only the doctors at the hospital could help her. I couldn't say anything else. He looked straight at me, my nephew, my flesh and blood. My turgid words fell flat and my throat seemed to close, and I knew that I had only gazed blankly at the wall above her head rather than look at her. My banality was a facade. He stared at me as I revealed the depth of his mother's suffering, and her distance from the world to which he always thought she had belonged.

TWENTY-FOUR

We were quickly marched out of the camp, only to be made to wait for hours outside the fence. Most of the Japanese trucks were idle, their hoods open and spare parts spread over the ground on large oilcloths. Some were up on jacks at dangerous-looking angles while soldiers crouched under them with their tools. One soldier worked with this shirt off. His ribs stood out as starkly as mine did. At the front of one truck, a sunburnt driver stood before the open hood with an armful of cables and hoses, looking dazed and uncertain. Akamatsu moved between them, his uniform undisturbed and his voice full, barking at them to finish up. He seemed the only machine that could not fail.

Earlier, I had heard we would be driven to the new camp to save time, but now Akamatsu said we would walk. I looked around and counted about sixty prisoners. Each one had a meagre collection of belongings. The Japanese ordered us to carry the food supplies as well, even those reserved for the soldiers. There were large bags of rice weighing about twenty pounds each, sacks of mouldering sweet potatoes and millet, and bamboo cages with live chickens that the soldiers had taken from the villages. Women and some of the smaller children, including Wei-Ming, were given bags of millet to carry. Some of the men were made to carry bamboo poles across their shoulders with baskets holding sacks of rice at either end.

One man, a merchant called Mr. Yuen, was fitted with one of these as he knelt on the ground on legs covered in ulcers. When he tried to get up, his legs shook so badly that it took him a while just to get one foot back on the ground, so two soldiers kicked him in the back and kidneys. Then he was up on both feet, though he still bent forward because he couldn't lift the rice. After more blows, he straightened his back, but as soon as he rose, he shook terribly. The loads were unbalanced and I knew he would end up on the ground again, so I ran over and removed one of the sacks from the heavier side. After that, he straightened up, though he was pale and covered in in sweat. One of the soldiers pointed angrily at the bag and gestured for me to carry it. I put it over my shoulder opposite my own bag.

It had been a cool morning and clouds still hung across the sky, but now in the forest it felt hot and suffocating. I walked with Leuk and couldn't see Yee-Lin, Wei-Ming, or Ling. Yet I was strangely unafraid. Maybe the load on my back gave me a sense of purpose again, or my sudden act in aid of Mr. Yuen had lifted my spirits. I could see him walking ahead, shaking. I shifted the load on my back as I watched him so that I felt its weight all the more and imagined that I was diminishing his trouble. As we walked, I focused intently on him, so that aside from Leuk huffing next to me and the occasional sounds of the forest, my mind was absorbed in the struggling motions of Mr. Yuen. I marked when he passed a tree and counted the number of steps until I reached the same mark. The count dropped as I caught up with him. These games were all I had in the moment, and not knowing where the girls were, and fearing that any word to Leuk would get me beaten, I retreated into these exercises.

The one truck the Japanese had brought with them rumbled noisily at the front of the convoy. The soldiers bringing up the rear on foot were getting impatient with the stragglers, and I heard prisoners shouting as they were hit. Akamatsu allowed short breaks for water and food. Each time, we found it harder to get going again. I looked for the girls whenever we stopped, but because we were ordered to remain in line, I never saw them. By midday, Mr. Yuen had fallen far behind me so that I could no longer count my distance from him and needed other games to occupy me.

It was the middle of the afternoon and becoming un-bearably hot. I was so tired and thirsty that even thinking seemed to wear me out, and all I could do was walk. Then I heard familiar voices and turned to see Ling and Wei-Ming, and Yee-Lin holding her hand. They were being led up the edge of the road by a soldier and were fol-lowed by two girls and two boys who looked to be between eight and ten. They put all the children together and the soldier walked beside us. Leuk and I talked briefly to Wei-Ming, but we were breathing hard under our loads. I was glad to see that Yee-Lin, Ling, and the children had less to carry.

The forest thinned to a shrubby field of sparse palms, with hills ascending in the distance. The road turned to take us alongside a river. The sound of rushing water distracted me while I plodded heavily beside Leuk. I leaned to the side where I carried the sack, as though I might topple into him. Next to us, a field of midsummer grain shook in the wind and birds gorged themselves on the unripe seed, swarming in dense clouds as they must have been doing all over the country, feeding on crops whose harvesters had fled or died. At the edge of the field a collapsed house smouldered, dissolving into ash and smoke against the downdrafts off the hillsides. Wei-Ming and Yee-Lin walked on the outer edge of the line, and when a low-hanging branch appeared, the soldier who walked with us paused and held it up until the girls had passed, leaving the prisoners behind to deal with it themselves.

In the early evening, we halted. I had thought we would be driven on like cattle into the night, but the soldiers too looked exhausted. Wei-Ming hung asleep over Yee-Lin's shoulders, and Leuk was almost delirious, muttering under his breath about going home to bed. Then I realized that at some point he had taken the sack of rice off my shoulder and carried it himself. Ling was behind us. Because she had no possessions, she had nothing to carry and was the most alert among us. Her face shone with sweat and was scratched up by branches.

Most of the prisoners were too tired to eat, but some ate the stinking rations the Japanese gave out—cooked sweet potatoes that had been carried all day, knocked to a pulpy mess. They put sacks of these down and people crouched around the open burlap bags, scooping the mash up with their hands and licking it off their fingers and wrists. Wei-Ming woke up and complained that she was hungry. That made me angry. I was hoping she would sleep through the night, and though I was hungry too, I dreaded having to share food from those sacks. I would have eaten even worse food, but my fear was that the other prisoners would knock me away to keep me from getting anything.

The soldier who had walked beside us during the day called to all the children. He walked slowly and looked us over as though doing an inspection. The adults watched him warily. Finally, he spoke to Leuk in hesitant Cantonese, asking if we were hungry.

At first I thought he was taunting us, until he reached into his pocket and pulled out a crumpled mass of waxed paper. He unwrapped it carefully and held it in his palm for a moment. Inside the paper were several large brown lumps of cane sugar. He broke the sugar into pieces and distributed all of it among the eight children and Yee-Lin. When his hand came near me, I hesitated to reach out because I didn't believe what he held was real. I took a jagged piece from his palm, and as I brought the sugar to my mouth, a thick stream of saliva poured from my lips onto my wrist. I put the whole thing on my tongue and slowly closed my mouth. The edges of the crystal scraped the skin inside my cheeks. I closed my eyes. I let the crystal rest on my tongue. Despite my thirst, my mouth became awash in saliva, which dissolved the sugar to form a syrup. The saliva ran out from under my tongue, and I could taste where the syrup ran out beside it like two streams colliding. I swallowed it as slowly as I could. When the crystal had shrunk to a little ball, I opened my eyes. The others were all doing the same. No one had thought to bite down on their sugar or swallow it in an instant.

Then the soldier told us to come to the soldiers' campfire for some food. Leuk and I got up at once, and Wei-Ming, hearing of food and seeing us rise, got up too. Ling took her hand and told her not to go and then looked at me and said we shouldn't go with him.

"If he has food, I want it," I said, and even in my fallen state I could hear the lonely animality of those words. Ling didn't move, but when Leuk and I started down the path behind the soldier, the other four children came too, and then Wei-Ming, and finally Ling and Yee-Lin followed. We hurried down the line, passing the adult prisoners who had fallen or lay exhausted on the hard, trampled earth. The sugar had sharpened my senses; a small, diamond-like piece of it sat delicately under my tongue as we walked. The odour of the prisoners stood out sharply in the forest air.

Akamatsu was nowhere to be seen. Six soldiers had set a grate over a small fire. On it sat a thin metal pot, which one of them stirred with care. They had broken open one of the bamboo chicken cages. Two chickens hung, still living, from a branch and another was in the pot in pieces, swirling in the opaque broth of rice starch. One of the soldiers shredded some salted fish with his hands and threw the pieces in. On the ground behind them lay an exploded mass of feathers and chicken guts, already aswarm with little black beetles, so that the mass still seemed to be a living creature.

The soldier who had given out the sugar told us to sit down. We sat in a half-circle just behind the soldiers. We were silent, partly because we were afraid, partly because a breeze kept sending the odour of the stew our way. The last bit of sugar had just dissolved in my mouth, and with that and the smell of food, I felt revived.

A soldier gave the pot a final stir and picked up a pile of wooden bowls. He and another soldier dished out the stew and began handing the bowls to us. There were only five bowls, so we let the other four children and Wei-Ming eat first. The soldiers were already eating, and when it was my turn to have some, I was afraid there would be nothing left. But the bowl I received was full. It had been filled right to the edge, and for all my hunger, I moved it towards myself slowly for fear of spilling even a drop. Little mirrors of fat floated over the stew, and when I took my first sip, a piece of fish slipped between my teeth. I remembered my mother's rules and ground it slowly between my molars before washing it down with the broth. Like those who'd used it before me, I wiped the bowl out with my finger before handing it back with thanks. I didn't ask for more.

The soldier walked us back to our place in the line. He offered his water bottle to Yee-Lin and she drank. Then he passed it around. The adults sitting on the ground, their mouths streaked with sweet potato and dirt, stared at us. A man extended his hand to ask for some water too, and the soldier pointed to the muddy stream. The man turned like a dog and crept down the bank, where he lowered his lips to drink. He came back when the soldier was gone and asked us if we had eaten anything. I told him chicken and rice, and he laughed bitterly. I couldn't tell what he meant by it.

In the morning, we marched. The soldier who had given us the sugar told me to carry the rice sack again, and it felt even heavier now. The terrain became more uneven, and as we were climbing a muddy slope I slipped and the sack fell off. The soldier walked over and slapped me three times on the back of my head until I got up. It didn't really hurt, and as I was picking the sack up I found a small hole in the corner of the fabric. I worked it open with my finger and let the rice seep slowly out. By midday it was much easier to bear.

Around noon, when the sun was directly over us, the road widened and the forest thinned, leaving us more exposed. The heat, the openness, and the sudden drop in the breeze unsettled both the soldiers and the prisoners. Twice, small flocks of birds burst suddenly from trees, and the soldiers took aim but didn't fire. They shouted back and forth. The truck braked abruptly three times, and each time the soldiers behind us ran ahead to talk to the others. While the truck was idle, the engine laboured noisily, and the noise seemed to unnerve the Japanese. After the third stop, the truck resumed driving very slowly.

It had crept along for less than a minute when gunfire and shouts erupted ahead. The soldiers ran forward with their weapons out. We fell to the ground. The shooting was erratic and the truck engine, far ahead and out of sight, revved loudly. I shook against the ground, pressed my hands over my ears, and felt my belt buckle scratching against the dry, sandy earth. The soldiers shouted and gunfire seemed to be everywhere, but I also heard shouting in Chinese, and prisoners screaming. My heart pounded so hard I could feel my skin pulse against the hard soil. I called to my siblings and reached out over the ground. I found Yee-Lin's hand, and Wei-Ming was next to her. Then I heard planes flying overhead, very low.

The soil beneath my face stank. It didn't have an earthy smell or the dry mineral odour of sand. A stench emanated from it, as though the earth itself were putrefying. Feeling as though I might vomit, I turned my head sideways and caught sight of the planes just as they vanished over the canopy. Moments later I heard something like thunder, the sound of bombs falling on what I prayed were Japanese soldiers.

It was over quickly. No one moved. I heard terrible screaming, far up the line. In the winter, when I had heard such screams through the windows in Hong Kong, I could usually discern something about them — young or old, man or woman, injured or just frightened. But in these screams there was an indistinctness that revealed nothing of age or sex. Some stopped or faded quickly, others rose and fell. Soon the Japanese ordered us to get up and resume our march down the road.

A few minutes later, an old cemetery appeared on our right, between the river and our path. People in civilian clothes lay in its grounds and by the road. I guessed they were locals who had tried to ambush the Japanese with hunting rifles and stolen handguns. Crows were already descending.

Near the road, one man staggered towards one of the large curved tombstones. He stumbled forward, turning his head back to look at us. I didn't understand where he was headed until he stopped abruptly and fell down next to a stone. A moment later we were just a few feet from where he sat. He had propped himself into a sitting position facing the road. He looked straight at me.

His intestines were spilling into his lap and open hands, and he clawed through the entrails as though trying to grasp moving water. He shivered violently. I stopped, unable to look away.

"This is my family tomb," he said in a hoarse voice. "What are you doing with the Japanese, boy? You must run. Run away."

His mouth fell open. His last word was flat and lifeless like a dry breeze, yet all over he was soaked in sweat and blood. The whiteness of his face and eyes was like cold fire, as was my own skin, and all the air around me, and my blood, and the sun that went on burning us as we walked the final hours of this road.

TWENTY-FIVE

As the sun set, the air cooled rapidly, and just before dark we approached a gravel drive that turned off from the road. At the entrance, a large iron gate, which must have been very imposing once, lay in twisted ruins in the grass, its concrete support pillars knocked over and crumbling. In a ditch running beside the drive lay a blackened, windowless car, stinking of gasoline and burned flesh. The truck rumbled ahead, sounding as though it might break down completely at any moment.

The drive ended at the opening of a rectangular wooden fence that enclosed a large, well-kept lawn about the size of a city block. We were ordered to walk along a muddy area that ran just outside the fence, beside a forest.

Along its other three sides stood a barn, a farmhouse directly opposite us, and a bank of trees that looked as though they led down to a river. In the middle of the field, grazing freely in the cool air, stood a group of horses.

The Japanese directed us to simple tents set up along the fence. A large bamboo latrine sat at the far end of the tents, and from its stench I guessed we were not the first captives to be brought here. The soldiers' quarters were at the other side of the field, in and around the house. We set up in two tents, one for Leuk, Ling, and me, the other for Yee-Lin and Wei-Ming. We wanted to be as far from the latrine as possible, but other people had quickly pushed and fought to take the farthest ones, and we wanted to avoid any fighting. In the tent next to us was a man, his wife, and her sister. He was very tall, and one of the women reminded me of Ming.

The soldiers had rushed to their own quarters on the other side, and they seemed not to care what we did. Over the field I saw them setting up cooking fires and going in and out of the house with big pots. I sat on the ground and watched them.

A quarter of the way around the field, midway between us and the soldiers, stood the barn. Its doors were wide open, and of all the buildings on the property it seemed the best kept, or maybe the most untouched. On the field I counted five horses, two black, two brown, and one grey. I heard more whinnying inside the barn. An older boy was tending to one of the black ones, adjusting a saddle and stroking its neck. He seemed to have come from another place, ignorant of the war burning up the land and air outside the farm. He was clean, dressed in good clothes, even well-fed, and the instant I saw him caring for the horse, it struck me that no one in our group was in a state of mind to concern themselves so easily with the welfare of another animal. It was beautiful and mysterious, as though I were watching a film about the life I had once lived.

An officer in riding clothes approached the boy, who bowed to him. The officer mounted the horse and began to ride in a wide circle, and the boy watched him briefly before heading over to one of the other horses. I could have watched this for hours. I called Wei-Ming over and she sat beside me, and there was no need for me to point and say, "Look at the horses," because it seemed so clear that they were there for our enjoyment. When had I last seen something move that way, free and careless, living an untroubled life? I thought of Ming swaying in the river water, her hair moving behind her like the horse's mane.

I looked down at Wei-Ming and brushed some dirt off her cheek. She didn't blink when I touched her face.

The prisoners in charge of food set up our outdoor kitchen quickly. We lined up and I shuffled forward with a bowl in my hand, looking sideways at the two horses grazing in the field. The memory of rice porridge with chicken was still fresh, and that strange reprieve seemed to belong to the same world as the horses. We crouched on the ground outside our tents as I scooped the food from my bowl the way I had back in the camp, although I now paid more attention to my teeth. The old woman I had seen staring at me back in the camp now had a bad tooth infection. Her granddaughter struggled to help feed the old woman, who was starving but hissed and scratched the girl every time she moved food near her mouth. The old woman held her hand lightly over her jaw.

Four soldiers were carrying something heavy over the field towards us. They opened a gate in the fence and two of them set down a large wooden tub half full of water. The other two poured three buckets of hot water into it and put another bucket beside the tub. They shouted and gestured for us to line up, and a soldier reached into the last bucket and took out a bar of soap.

They pointed at the younger women and the children to go first, so that by the time Leuk and I got to the water it was already cloudy and flecked in soap scum. I still managed to get cleaner than I'd been in a long time. I hadn't had a bath for weeks, and even though the water was murky, it still ran almost black with the filth I'd built up.

When everyone was done, Leuk and I dragged the tub over to the fence at the edge of the field and tilted it onto the grass. The soap scum clung to the leaves, making me think of the greyish foam on seaweed I'd seen on the beach long ago. There were two horses still grazing in the field. When the water gushed out from the tub, the horses raised their heads from the grass and sniffed the air. I raised my forearm to my nose and smelled it, expecting a trace of camphor from my bath. The smell was faintly resinous, as of something put away for years in old wooden crates. I liked it and hoped the horses could smell it too. Leuk walked up to me and asked me what I was doing.

"Smelling the soap," I said, and he did likewise.

"It smells old. Clean but old." He rubbed his forearm and looked at his skin.

We leaned against the fence and stared at the field in silence. An argument was breaking out between a few prisoners, but I ignored them. One of the horses looked at us for a moment and tasted the air again before lowering its head to the grass. I had a brief daydream of it looking up again and coming over to see us, shaking its mane and lowering its head as I extended my hand through the wooden slats. I remembered the stalls near our house that Leuk and I had walked past that day, and the cart, and the strange man drawing on his cigarette in the darkness, and the silence otherwise. The bathwater had soaked into the ground and softened it, and again I felt the stickiness beneath my shoes as I had by the cart.

The horse didn't move. My brother was looking at me quizzically. I glanced down, shivered, and saw I was extending my hand through the fence. *Come here*, I thought. The horse shook its head, stepped forward, and put its nose against my hand. It was warm and damp, and as I brushed the backs of my fingers against it, I felt its breath pulse slowly over my skin. It was a beautiful pale-grey mare with a white diamond on its forehead. Its mane was the colour of dull steel and hung neatly across its neck. I looked at the horse's large eyes, and its unconcern for anything else seemed to open outward like a door into a vast, airy chamber. For a moment I stepped into that space, and all the burdens that I carried, my fear and loneliness, seemed to fall from me. My hand drifted up its forehead and I caressed the spot between its ears. I looked up. A soldier stood up at the opposite side of the field and stared at us with a rifle in one hand. I watched him for a second before looking back at the horse, and then I reached over and took Leuk's hand and placed it gently on the horse's neck.

. . .

Leuk, Ling, and I had trouble falling asleep that night, so we went outside. Wei-Ming and Yee-Lin were slumbering quietly while the three of us sat outside their tent. Across the field, the soldiers kept up the drinking that had begun in the middle of the day. Their firepit and the moonlight were the only light. It was quiet and cold among the tents, and the latrine stench rolled heavily through the camp whenever the breeze dropped. The soldiers were very loud, and I watched them out of boredom and apprehension as they stumbled around the yard outside the farmhouse. From time to time they wandered over to the fence and urinated. The two women in the tent next to ours bickered quietly; I had seen the man leave earlier to escape them. There was a dense forest behind us and the walk back to the road was impossible to see in the dark. Finally, the three of us climbed back into our tent to sleep.

I would have fallen quickly into a deep sleep if it hadn't been for the horses. In the silence, even across the field, I could hear them faintly in the barn as they bumped against the stalls and rattled the chains hanging from the barn walls. I opened my eyes and heard two or three horses neighing and also some soldiers' voices. They were distorted and raw, and I recognized the sound of drunkenness.

During the day the field had looked very wide to me, a huge gap between us and the feasting soldiers. But the soldiers seemed to have flown across the field in seconds. In my half sleep I couldn't keep pace with anything. I heard them outside, boots splashing in the shallow pool of bathwater by the fence. Beside me, Ling woke quickly, her eyes wide as though she'd been shocked, and her breathing went very shallow and quick. The soldiers' voices were garbled, and they tried to choke back their laughter. I stared at the thin tent wall. The moonlight was behind me and no shadows moved over the canvas, though I continued to hear their boots just outside.

I lay very still and rigid, because I knew what would happen. In Hong Kong I had heard those sounds from my window, when the soldiers found women in the streets. These things always happen in a certain way. The man in the next tent raised his voice, but it was cut short with a crack. That was the only sound that made me jump. The two women screamed as the soldiers pulled the man from their tent. Next to me, Ling shook and pressed both hands over her mouth. I listened for the splash of boots again, knowing these soldiers wouldn't be the only ones.

Yee-Lin appeared at our tent. She didn't even open the flap, she just reached in and grabbed us, pulling on our legs and whispering for us to get out. I crawled out after Ling and Leuk and found my sister-in-law crouching behind the tent. Nearby, two soldiers dragged a woman from a tent. I panicked because Wei-Ming wasn't there.

"Where is she?" I whispered to Yee-Lin, though I wanted to yell.

"I hid her. She's in the trees now." For a moment I imagined her sitting in the interlacing branches of two willows, far above the ground so that everything below was blurred and washed by clouds.

Yee-Lin took Ling by the arm and said they had to hide. She would get Wei-Ming first and they would stay together.

"We'll come too," I said.

We ran to the edge of the camp. Yee-Lin entered the trees and disappeared for a moment. She whispered Wei-Ming's name a few times, and far behind I heard the water splash again as two more soldiers crossed the field. Yee-Lin emerged from the trees with one arm around Wei-Ming, almost dragging her through the undergrowth. She took Ling by the arm and Leuk and I followed her.

My sister-in-law made straight for the latrine. It sat a few feet above the ground on poles, and with every step, the stench grew more horrific. Wei-Ming covered her nose and retched. Yee-Lin took a rag from her pocket and gave it to her to cover her mouth and nose, and with their sleeves covering their faces she and Ling crawled with her under the building's floor into the thick pool lying beneath it.

The air around us swarmed with flies, and in the clouded moonlight they were even thicker where the girls were. The ground itself, right up to the pool's edge, shimmered with beetles and other insects that crawled around the support posts. Leuk and I both vomited.

When they were right under the middle of the latrine, I heard Yee-Lin call out to us. I couldn't see them anymore.

"Go back. Don't let them find the tents empty or they'll come looking for us."

"We'll come back for you," said Leuk. She shouted again for us to go.

We ran back towards our tents. I could smell the sewage on our shoes, so we stopped to wipe them off on the grass. When we got back, I guessed there were now about eight soldiers in the camp. I found two male prisoners lying badly beaten on the ground but didn't recognize them. There was silence in the tent next to ours. We each took a tent so that neither would appear empty. I lay alone in mine and pressed my hands over my ears, counting out time in the long measure of darkness, as in a dream of infinite falling.

The following morning before sunrise, I realized that the only things fenced in here were the horses. Unlike our last camp, there were no wires here.

It had rained heavily the night before. The puddle of bathwater that Leuk and I had made was now a small lake. The rain had begun to fall just after we came back from the latrine, tapping against the canvas walls by my head as I covered my ears. Then it fell more heavily and chased the soldiers back to their farmhouse.

When I'd heard the last soldiers leave, it had still been very dark. Now that there was a little light, Leuk and I crawled out of our tents and ran back to the latrine as fast as we could, and just outside it we found the girls stepping carefully out of the stinking pool, groping in the moonlight for the forest's edge. The rain and wind suppressed the smell. In the dark, we helped the girls wash off in the downpour. Leuk cleaned Wei-Ming off, and I knelt beside Ling and scrubbed her legs down with leftover soap from the bucket and handfuls of leaves. They scratched my hands, but she didn't complain. We crept back to our tents and lay down, and tried to sleep.

Only Wei-Ming was able to fall asleep. The rest of us sat together in the other tent and whispered about what to do. I peeked carefully through the opening into the grey light; there were no soldiers around. There didn't even seem to be a night guard posted. Yee-Lin had also noticed that the camp appeared to be unguarded.

The violence of the night haunted me. Ling sat in the corner with her arms wrapped around her legs, shaking with fear on the thin canvas floor. The weeping of one of the women in the next tent drifted in, a lonely, fractured moan that seemed to filter through the wet soil and up through the bottom of our tent.

"What should we do?" Leuk asked a second time.

Yee-Lin shook her head. "We can't stay here. Tonight it will happen again."

Ling began to sob. Her mouth drew open into a silent wail as she hugged her knees and backed up against the tent walls.

Leuk turned to me. "But if we run, we'll be beaten like those people in the last camp." Tears ran down his face.

"There's no one guarding the exit, I think," said Yee-Lin.

"They'll notice the empty tents. Then they'll come after us down the road."

"I think I know where we are. Not far from Wah Ying. We can trace our way back to Tai Fo from there. No one in the village will remember us. I can take some food with us before the others get up, but that will be soon."

Maybe it was true that we weren't always being watched. After all we had seen, it never occurred to me that the entrance off the road might be left unguarded. And as I listened to Yee-Lin, I understood that we had to break up again. She and the girls couldn't stay here, and there was nothing more to be said. Leuk tried to encourage me.

"It's all right, Chung-Man. You and I can stay here. We need to be quick, because it's getting lighter. Sister-in-law, do you have any money?"

"No, the last of it was stolen in the camp."

Leuk quickly took off his belt, rolled it up with care, and passed it to her with both hands. She knew what it was, though it must have puzzled Ling. It would have been too dangerous to explain it to her. The buckle was even filthier than when Sheung had first stained it with the mercury. It had no lustre and was a dirty, greasy brown. Yee-Lin took it and tied it around her waist under her blouse. I took a quick peek through the tent opening and noted the colour of the sky. The sun would be up any moment.

"Where should we meet, if we manage to escape?" Leuk said.

We discussed this quickly and agreed to meet at the Chung Shan gardens just outside Hong Kong. There was a quilt factory there whose owner had been a business partner of our father's.

Yee-Lin took Ling by the hand and led her out of the tent. The second they were out, I started to cry, and Leuk reached over and held my hand.

I lowered my head and looked out the opening, watching them hurry over the mud. Yee-Lin darted into the other tent and carried out Wei-Ming, who was still asleep. *Remember to take something to eat,* I thought. I looked at Wei-Ming's face leaning against Yee-Lin's neck, thin but still untroubled. I took my hand from Leuk's for a moment, and waved silently at her as the girls ran down the path to the road.

A day comes when things must separate. Fruit falls from the tree and, if uneaten, the seeds work through the melting flesh to find the soil. The fetus leaves the mother, the bride her parents, and the soldier his. Families come apart. Deep inside the cemetery soil, the cadaver's hand detaches from its arm, hastened by blind, almost vegetative vermin. The florid hues of sunrise fall away and leave the sun in all its practical and fading brilliance.

Inside me, a tumour does the work of separation. Over time it has pushed aside organs and fused to parts that used to function normally, forcing new diversions of fluids and nutrients. The doctors can't do anything about it. I'm too old now for surgery or chemotherapy, and besides, it would interrupt my routine. Maybe it looks tedious from the outside, but my everyday habits have become a force of nature in my life. No one else can grasp the bloody-mindedness needed to get out of bed when you feel as though your joints are coming apart, to reach the toilet on time, to bring tea to the lips without spilling or scalding, to endure the manoeuvring of a spoonful of curried chicken into your mouth and make its intense flavour override deep bites of thoracic pain. All of you who nod in agreement, you can only be the dead, the historians of these concluded wars.

Knowing I'll die soon doesn't bother me. There's too much now to be unburdened of, the indignity and pain. The fact is that the long contest against death is relatively easy: you win every day, no matter how, until you lose. You know who holds the prize each night when you hit the pillow.

What troubles me is the struggle to stay continuous, to be a single person over time. How can I be certain it was really me who emerged from that boy in the horse farm, or from the one who carried the buckle? He doesn't feel like the same person sometimes. Part of me is still back there, looking into the future as a mystery instead of the crumbling pile it is to me now. He could appear suddenly in the playground outside with my face and name, thin and dressed in rags, and I'd accept he was a separate person. I think he still wonders whether he won or lost that fight and asks how much longer he'll prevail.

That sound at the door is the nurse letting herself in, using the key my daughter gave her. She has a trove of keys, like a jailer, but I like her all the same. She keeps the laptop for her rounds in a turquoise bag she carries over her shoulder. And inside that is the record of all the old men and women she visits in their homes. Hundreds of people, more or less.

TWENTY-SIX

Leuk and I lay in separate tents in case the soldiers checked, and the loneliness kept me awake all night. A few of the older women got up at dawn to start a fire. I noticed one of them cursing when a sack of sweet potatoes was found lying partly open on the ground, and I guessed the girls had taken some.

People didn't speak to each other here the way they had at the large camp in Tung Koo Chow. It may have been that no one noticed the three girls were missing, or that they didn't care, or perhaps they feared that worse had happened during the night. I didn't go near the tent where the two women lay, though later that day I found the wife sitting up, cradling her husband's swollen face on her lap.

Leuk and I were sitting together beneath an old tree when Akamatsu and another soldier crossed the field into our camp, opening a small gate in the fence I hadn't noticed before. They looked around and made faces of disgust at our conditions, though they too appeared unhealthy and miserable.

"Who can help us?" said Akamatsu with a smile.

Most of the women had already run off at the sight of the soldiers. An old man crouched by the fire and tended it gingerly with a stick, staring at the Japanese with unmasked hate. He scraped the tip of the stick over the embers, keeping the fire discreetly alive beneath the pot hanging over it.

"You boys." Akamatsu pointed at us. "You can help us out. We'll even give you something to eat."

At the mention of food, I stood up. Fearing I would leave him, Leuk stood up with me.

"We need help in the stables. Leave all these sick people and come do some work. You'll enjoy it, and we'll feed you."

We walked through the gate onto the field. It felt good to be standing on something firmer than mud, and I dragged my shoes over the grass to clean them off. Walking behind the Japanese in their uniforms, I felt ashamed of my filth. My hair was long and tickled my ears, and wherever my skin met my clothes, I felt sticky. I carefully touched the buckle under my shirt several times. Leuk was watching me. I briefly lifted the hem of my shirt to show him it was still there.

Before we turned towards the barn, I noticed other soldiers setting up a fire and some pots, and thought longingly of the food we would soon be eating. The barn doors were wide open and the horses stirred in their stalls. Akamatsu and the other soldier stopped outside the doors, gesturing for us to go in.

In the barn, we were met by eight older boys, tall, well-fed, and bigger than Leuk and me. Barn dust and straw clung to their clothes, and they looked as though they had been made to wait for something. In the middle of the floor between them lay coiled ropes.

"Hey you," said one of them. They were Chinese, from Hunan by the sound of it. Leuk and I stopped just inside the barn, until the soldier gave us both a firm shove from behind. We stumbled forward and the Hunan boys folded their arms and stared hard at us.

Akamatsu spoke briefly to one of the boys, who stared dumbly as he listened. He answered back in a few halting words of Japanese, and then Akamatsu and the soldier left. The boy looked at us, gloating.

"You're going to clean this barn. Do it quick or you won't like us."

One of the boys took a couple of brooms off the wall and threw them at us.

It was stiflingly hot. The horses were in their stalls, close to us as we worked, and I remember thinking that the heat seemed to come through their scent. Two of the older boys went outside, returning soon with three other boys from the tents, around my age or younger, whom they also set to work cleaning. One of them, who looked to be about eight, had to shovel up the horse dung. The shovel was too big for his hands and it slipped, scattering a load of dung onto the floor. A Hunan boy struck him on the face so hard he fell, and while he was down, the older boy spat on him and told him he'd be killed if he made any noise. The boy stood back up and retrieved the shovel, crying the whole time, and the Hunan boys laughed and imitated him so that he cried even more.

They told him his mother was probably dead and he would shovel shit for the rest of his life.

The sound of him weeping, of his shovel scraping feebly over the wooden planks and drowning out my broom, of the Hunan boys taunting him — it all made me sick, and I began to shake. During the entire war, I was never more frightened than I was then. Leuk sobbed next to me as he swept, and the cold truth struck me like an iron bar: we would be next. Not to be hit or knocked down, not to be spat on or threatened with death, but to be told our mother was dead. Tears poured down my face and a sob broke from my throat. I tried hard to stop. I couldn't think of anything but the Lord's Prayer, so I whispered it in English while I swept. I focused on trying to say it right — I always stumbled on *hallowed* and *will* — and silently in my head I said, over and over, *She's alive.* But even in my thoughts I didn't dare to name her.

The soldier came back and looked over the barn, and then issued new orders to the Hunan boys. They yelled at us to stop and put away the brooms and shovels. There was a bucket of water on the floor with a wooden ladle, and we were allowed to line up and drink quickly from it. It was sour. Then the Hunan boys made us lie down on the barn floor next to each other. Two of them picked up the rope coils and ordered us to lie with our backs to each other and tied us together at the ankles so we wouldn't escape.

Leuk was next to me. He lifted his head off the ground and said he had to pee. One of the boys shouted, "Go ahead!" and kicked him in the stomach. I felt a horrible, freezing pain in my midsection at the sound. Leuk seemed to be exhaling a whispered cry. Then he gasped loudly and wailed and shook violently, his legs twisting in the rope so that he dragged my feet with it. I screwed my eyes shut as hard as I could and stared into a private darkness while he screamed. I smelled his urine on the floor between us.

Four days later, I was sitting up in our tent with the flap open, watching the horses graze. Leuk was asleep beside me. I needed to get in line for our food but didn't want to wake him.

Lately I had been wondering if my birthday was near. I hadn't seen calendars or newspapers since Tung Koo Chow, and the last time I had even paid attention to the date was at our school in Tai Fo. It felt like July in the air. Back in Hong Kong, birthdays had been big events. Sheung always took a birthday photo; my favourite was the one from the day I turned three. My mother had lately caved in to the Western tradition of birthday cakes, ordering a huge one in the shape of a steam engine for me. The sepia print, which lay fixed in an album with a red cover in our library, showed me and my siblings sitting around the table, along with some children of one of my father's business associates. My mother, Ah-Ming, and Ah-Tseng are standing behind me, all of us staring at the cake. The curtains must have been drawn, maybe to heighten the effect of the candles, for the table and everyone sitting at it have a halo of darkness around them so that Ah-Tseng, standing at the edge, is deeply shaded. I am in a light-coloured shirt sitting up on my knees in the chair, supporting myself with one hand on the table, while my other hand is stretched out and pointing at the cake. Leuk is seated next to me. He looks almost like my twin. We have the same cropped hair, the same nose, the same mouth. Both of Leuk's elbows are on the table, and he's gripping his head between his hands and staring at the cake as though afraid he may not get any. I don't know the names of the other children. They're all grinning and seem to disappear behind their smiles.

I thought of this, sitting on the floor of the tent, because there was a scent in the air I associated with July, a floral smell that I remembered not from our garden but from the park off Stubbs Road where my father used to walk.

Leuk mumbled in his sleep. The night before, when we lay down, he told me he felt better and that his stomach didn't hurt so much. His whole midsection was a bruise of lurid colours. In the four days since we were forced to clean the barn, the Hunan boys had left us alone. So had the Japanese. As Leuk recovered, I thought constantly of the girls. I concocted a story that Yee-Lin and Ling knew exactly where to go, that they had found the road back to Tai Fo, met other Chinese wanderers and got help from them, families maybe, and that the Japanese were now too busy fighting to trouble ordinary people anymore.

I sat with my chin on my knuckles and listened. Every day the camp grew quieter. None of the prisoners had the energy or spirit left to squabble. My shoulders ached, so I sat up straight and rubbed my eyes. I was tired all the time.

. . .

I waited until Leuk was awake to get our breakfast. I stood in line in a light rain with two bowls and shuffled forward with the others. While waiting, I looked at the forest next to us. I heard crows and other birds screaming and rustling in the undergrowth, and occasionally saw them flying up from a spot about fifty paces in, the spot to where, by silent consensus, those who had the strength took the bodies of those who died. I hadn't been there and hoped never to see it.

At the head of the line, a woman sat next to a small brazier with a dented pot of sweet potatoes. I noticed her eyeing me even when I was at the back of the line. When I made it to the front, she picked up a potato with some makeshift wooden tongs and held it up for a moment, and then she leaned forward and looked at me with a concerned face.

"How's your older brother doing?"

"He's much better, ma'am, thank you." I held out my bowl and she gave me the potato and some boiled millet. Then she extended a hand and asked for Leuk's bowl. Her whole hand and arm were horrible to look at, covered in sores and swollen veins that crawled confusedly around her forearm. Her arms were dusted to the elbows with ash and I wondered if she rubbed it on as an attempt at medicine. That made me think of the hospital in Tung Koo Chow. I trembled violently and my vision blurred, and the potato in my bowl dropped to the ground. Before I knew what was happening, the woman was shouting at the man behind me, who had snatched the potato off the ground and hidden it in his pocket. Threatened with a blow from the wooden tongs in the woman's hand, he gave it back to me.

She put food in Leuk's bowl, peered into the pot, and pulled out a third potato. She grimaced comically, then smelled it and pulled another face. "This one's all rotten," she said as she dropped it into the bowl. "Nibble what you can off it." But it was perfectly fine, and I thanked her with a nod as I left the line.

I walked quickly back to the tent and shut the flaps. We broke the extra potato in half as precisely as we could and ate it. The walk had tired me and we didn't speak, and when the food was all gone, we sat and stared drowsily at the bowls for a while before Leuk raised his eyes.

"Do you think they've used it?" he whispered.

"Used what?"

"The gold. Do you think they've sold it or used it for something? I know what I'd get: food. And a ticket home."

I shook my head. "Only Yee-Lin knows what it is, and she's too careful." She understood that she had to keep the buckle a secret from Ling and Wei-Ming. My own pressed warmly against my belly as we ate. It was fitting that Yee-Lin should carry the gold that her husband had tarnished to protect us, and when I looked at my own buckle — always in secret and making sure no one was near who might surprise me — its mottled, dull greenish-brown colour made me feel better about my own derelict condition. The once-white shirt that hung over it was thinning in spots, and the caked dirt kept the dark metal from standing out underneath.

At the time, I imagined that I would carry this buckle forever, until my death, a small, damaged rectangle concealed beneath my soiled clothes, a secret masked by its own stains. If I had redeemed it, I could probably have bought the freedom of all the remaining prisoners in the camp, or so I believed. I had no idea how much gold it really contained. But how would I ever do that? To bring it into the light would only endanger my brother and me more. I knew I had only to scrape it gently with a rock to show the gleam beneath, and most likely I would then be killed or lose it to a thief, and our last hope would be gone.

The bruises on Leuk's stomach grew more garish, and I knew that meant it was healing. He still held his midsection and leaned a little to one side when he walked. He ate very slowly because he believed something was wrong inside him now, saying that the food seemed to move differently through him. He looked better to me, but when I told him that, he got angry and wouldn't listen.

The Hunan boys were gone the next day; I didn't know how or why. One evening I had heard Akamatsu shouting at them in the barn, and one of the older boys crying out as though he were being hit, and then I heard nothing more. The grounds were quiet and two soldiers took over the care of the horses.

That afternoon, Akamatsu crossed the field with another soldier. He looked around and shouted that he was looking for Leuk and me. I was taken aback by Akamatsu's appearance: he was unshaven and his uniform was dirty. The other soldier looked even worse. Even as I detested the Japanese, I had still come to see their propriety and order as both menacing and hopeful, a reminder that not all people were as stricken and miserable as we were. There were rumours in the camp that the war was turning against the Japanese, though I had nothing to confirm this, and the thought of such things grew more exhausting every day. In these last days at this camp, my world had never been so small.

"You boys don't look well," he said. He reached down and scratched his leg. I shrugged my shoulders. Akamatsu smirked at us and pointed at our bellies. "What's wrong with you two? Sore stomachs?"

I looked down and saw that I had automatically raised my left forearm to conceal my buckle, while Leuk was nervously holding his stomach where he had been kicked.

"We're just hungry," I stammered. I tried to lower my forearm, and when I finally brought myself to let it drop, I leaned forward slightly so that my shirt hung loose over the buckle.

"Hungry, yes. Do you remember that time when you had some chicken with my men?" I nodded. "We're cooking some more this evening. I'm sure you'd like some."

My brother and I looked at each other. That meal on the road seemed ages ago, though we'd probably been at the farm less than two weeks.

"This is your only chance," said Akamatsu. "If you want to eat something nice, come with us."

We had learned to read every nuance of his heavily accented speech, and to me, at least, it seemed we had little choice. So we walked through the gate and over the field with them. As the barn came up on our right, Leuk moved to my other side so that he was farther away from it.

Leuk had taken to whispering. It was a habit that had started in the camp in Tung Koo Chow with all its crowding, and he kept it up after that. He was afraid to speak too loud at certain times of day. Then, after the blow to his stomach, he whispered even more, and more quietly, even when we were lying in the tent at night and there was no one near us. I became attuned to his whispers like a bird heeding every rustle in the forest. He whispered to me now, as we walked to the soldiers' house. I didn't answer back aloud because I knew the Japanese would hear me.

"What day is it today?"

I shook my head, still looking at the backs of the two uniforms.

"I'll stay with you while we eat, all right?"

I nodded quickly. I looked at the soldiers' heads to see if they could hear him.

"Do you know why I wondered about the date? I was thinking it must be close to your birthday."

I looked briefly at him, smiled, and shrugged my shoulders.

"Maybe it doesn't matter," he whispered. "I don't know the date. Happy thirteenth birthday, Chung-Man."

I touched his arm, mouthing my thanks. We arrived at the house, and Akamatsu had us walk ahead up to the front door.

TWENTY-SEVEN

The soldiers walked us into the living room, where there were two piles on the table: shorts, a shirt, underwear, socks, and shoes for each of us.

"We found them in one of the rooms upstairs," said Akamatsu. "Nobody needs them now. You put them on."

My belt buckle occupied my thoughts whenever we were within twenty feet of any Japanese. It was like a scar that ached in bad weather. I looked up at him. "Do we have to?"

"Are you mad? Look at your clothes."

I hunched forward and clasped my hands together. "What if the boy they belong to needs them?"

Akamatsu gave me a strange look. "Just put them on. In there." He gestured to a bathroom.

So we went in and shut the door, cleaned ourselves and changed, and I hurriedly put my belt back on. I looked at my old clothes on the floor. I had worn that shirt since Tung Koo Chow and all my other clothes had long since disappeared. It was filthy and yellowed, with black streaks along the seams. I picked it up and looked at the collar. A small tag an inch wide was sewn into it: the name of the tailor who had made my school uniform. I worried that the Japanese would see it and guess that we came from a rich family, so I ripped it out carefully with my teeth and told Leuk to do the same. We flushed the labels down the toilet and went back to the living room.

Akamatsu smirked when he saw us. "Very nice." He put his hand on my shoulder and squeezed it.

In my new clothes, I saw even more how dishevelled the Japanese were starting to look. They were leaner, mostly unshaven, and their uniforms were worn and patchy. The house was not well kept.

"Now, I know you're both hungry." Akamatsu brought us into the kitchen. Two other Japanese were there preparing food. A third sat at the kitchen table with his feet up, drinking from a bottle. I didn't think of the Japanese as being so casual, even though I'd witnessed their easy cruelty. There was something defeated in the soldier's posture and his eyes.

There was hot food on the table. The soldier with the bottle eyed us closely but kept his boots where they were. It didn't disgust me that they were filthy and inches away from the food. My mouth watered. There was a bowl of hot rice, a dish of steamed pork belly, a boiled chicken, and a plate of fried vegetables.

Akamatsu stood between us and put a hand on each of our shoulders. "Wouldn't it be nice to stay in a house like this? Hot food, new clothes. Why don't you sit?"

I sat down at the table and Leuk sat at the other end. The bottle soldier smiled at him and shifted in his chair. Akamatsu remained standing and leaned into the doorway to the living room.

"May we eat?" Leuk said.

Akamatsu smiled and gestured at the food. I went first,

but as soon as I touched the spoon, he reached over and seized my wrist.

I didn't look up at him. I just stared into the table, not even trying to escape his grasp.

"Where are the girls?"

I had no idea what to say. It seemed as if I waited an hour before answering.

"Sir?" I said stupidly.

His grip tightened a little, and then he put his other hand on my head and turned my face towards his. "Where did they go?"

I was cold and sweating. I couldn't see my brother, but I heard him breathing, a rapid, shallow panting like an injured dog. His chair squeaked and I realized he was shaking. The soldier seated beside me tapped his boots together; dry mud flaked onto the table.

"They left," I said.

"We all know that," said Akamatsu. "And for some reason you stayed, maybe thinking we wouldn't notice if you did. That's honourable, I might even call it very Japanese, except you aren't. Where are they? Where are they headed?"

He was badly shaven and there was blood on his collar, which was a greasy black elsewhere along the crease. A few small bits of straw were embedded in the wool of his jacket.

"Which way did they go?" He curled the fingers resting on my head and started to pull my overgrown hair. He squeezed my wrist hard. "Tell us."

The other soldier took his boots off the table, walked

around to Leuk, and put his hands on his shoulders. I finally looked at my brother: he was pale and staring fixedly at me, shaking, his hands folded neatly on the table as if he were waiting for school to begin. The minute the soldier touched him, he jumped.

"They just wanted to go home," Leuk said in a dry voice.

"We know that," said the soldier. We all did, and seeing the truth of it, I began to sob.

Akamatsu forced my arm behind my back and told me to get up. The pain in my shoulder was terrible, but I couldn't move, and the other soldier grabbed Leuk the same way. Akamatsu said something in Japanese and the soldier nodded.

"One more time," he said. "Tell us where they went. Are they bringing someone back here? To try and kill us all?" He pulled hard on my hair and my scalp burned as though he were branding it.

"No, it's true," I said. "They just want to go back to Hong Kong."

Akamatsu didn't believe me, and he snapped at the soldier. They dragged us away from the table. I caught a last glimpse of the food I'd never eat, and it looked different. The vegetables were sodden, the meat was roughly cut and jumbled, and flies scaled its surfaces, dabbing tentatively at the pooled fat and pinkish juices.

They dragged us outside and marched us back towards the barn. The door was ajar and the soldier kicked it wide open. It banged against the wall. The horses shifted nervously in their stalls, rattling the harnesses that hung near them.

To my surprise, one of the Hunan boys was sitting in the barn alone. I knew instantly that he had been alone for a long time because of the look on his face when we came in, an unnerving mix of fear and joy, like a mad animal. He shuffled up against the wall into the light and I saw his lip had recently been split.

"Tomorrow we'll talk again," said Akamatsu. He waited for a moment in the doorway as though he wanted us to take in his silhouette. Then he walked away, the soldier slamming the door shut and pushing the bolt in.

I wasn't happy to see the Hunan boy. I doubt he recognized us, and he didn't speak to us. He rocked backed and forth on the straw and stared at us, emitting something halfway between a moan and a sigh every time he tipped forward. It wasn't his movement that disturbed me, but the fact that he seemed to find it satisfying to make this strange, subhuman noise.

Leuk and I sat next to each other, and we put our arms around each other. My shoulder was very sore from the way Akamatsu had twisted my arm, and it felt better to stretch it out. We were against the wall opposite the Hunan boy, who sometimes closed his eyes while rocking in the partial dark.

Hours passed in silence. The dusty sunset light trickled through the gaps between the planks, and the moon came up. The Hunan boy grew still and Leuk too fell asleep beside me. One of the horses shifted noisily and Leuk started awake in distress.

"Where are we? Did we get out? Chung-Man!" He was

almost shouting and grabbed blindly at me. I took him by the arms and tried to calm him down.

"We're still here," I said as quietly as I could, but Leuk was rambling and couldn't hear me. He kicked his legs out over the straw and the dust flew into the moonlight.

"I want to get out! I want to get out!" I couldn't hold him and didn't realize he was still half asleep. His shouts disturbed the Hunan boy. He started rocking again and moaning loudly, as though he were screaming with his mouth shut tight.

"Leuk, I'm right here," I said. He turned to me as though he were only now waking up. The despair on his face struck me cold.

"Let's get out," he sobbed. Snot and tears ran over his lips. "I don't want to die in a barn, Chung-Man. I don't want to die." I was sobbing too and couldn't get him to be quiet.

It didn't matter. The Hunan boy grabbed his hair and started to scream. I think he was crying too, and he stamped his feet on the ground, his wooden sandals clapping on the hard earth. He pulled on his hair and screamed again.

The horses started kicking in their stalls. Their hooves hit the barn walls and the whole structure shook. I felt the bangs reverberate against my back. They neighed and kicked, some beginning to rear up. The Hunan boy screamed even louder at the sight. I grabbed Leuk, pulled him closer to me, and moved as far from the stalls as I could. Dust flew from the walls like little explosions every time the horses kicked.

The stalls had simple wooden gates held shut with rope. As the horses stamped around, they began to come up against the gates. One of the gates made a loud crack as a horse kicked it. I knew what was going to happen next.

Leuk drew his knees up tightly to his chest and shouted at me to do the same, and we got as close to the walls as we could. The walls were shaking and cracking so much I was afraid the barn would collapse on us. The Hunan boy was sitting right under a stack of wooden shelves that began to rock from side to side. Dust streamed onto his head, turning him a deathly colour in the moonlight, and I felt pity for him even though he had been cruel to us before.

With a deafening crack, a horse burst the gates of its stall, shattering the frame and sending wood flying over the barn floor. The horse stepped forward and screamed. Then the other horses pushed against their gates and kicked their stalls. The weakened gates cracked open in quick succession like a strip of firecrackers.

The horses burst out of their stalls. Right in front of us, they panicked and knocked against each other and the barn doors, until at last the bolt shattered and the doors flew open. The dozen horses felt like a hundred as they broke free just a couple of feet in front of me. The ground shook beneath us and all I could hear was their hooves and the three of us screaming. Hard, pebbly dust struck me in the face and stung my hands.

I watched the horses tear across the field as two soldiers standing guard outside shouted. They ran after the animals in the moonlight.

As soon as the soldiers were gone, Leuk grabbed me and we ran out into the darkness. The Hunan boy sat motionless in the corner, a small dusty figure with a lowered head like a temple figurine.

More soldiers ran from the house after the horses. When we were inside the house earlier, I had noticed a second road behind the farm, and Leuk and I now ran down it.

I couldn't help looking back. The road was very straight and the horse farm stayed in sight for what seemed like a long time. Then it shrank suddenly in the distance. The prisoners we'd left behind quickly became faceless to me, as though they'd vanished down a hole. Leuk said he was worried the Japanese would give up on the horses and come after us, but I told him very confidently that they wouldn't. We found a spot in a clearing and slept for a few hours.

Leuk shook me awake. He had twigs in his hair and the sun was shining behind him. I panicked, thinking the Japanese had found us, but he said there was no one around. It was long past dawn and we were both starving, but we had no food on us and there was nothing to eat in the clearing. We brushed the leaves off our clothes and out of our hair and continued walking away from the farm. We must have looked very odd on that road, thin and dirty and with wild, uncut hair, dressed in new clothes. Yet when I looked at my brother, wearing a shirt almost like a school uniform, I felt for the first time that we would soon see our mother again.

Almost a full day had passed since Akamatsu had questioned us in the house. Sunset was only a few hours away, and we guessed that a village must be near. A few miserable-looking workers were pulling carts of goods down the road by hand. The workers were a deep-brown colour from the sun, and all had shaved heads. I asked one of them where we were and if we were near Chung Shan. He looked at me confusedly, almost like an animal.

"Chung Shan is a couple of days away on foot," he said. "But our village is a short walk from here."

Leuk took me by the arm and we started off down the road again. Then suddenly I was pulled off balance and stumbled backward. My collar tightened and I choked. Leuk was staring at something behind me.

I turned my head. It was one of the older Hunan boys from the farm. He twisted the collar to choke me, but the button popped off. I twisted around and freed myself just as Leuk grabbed the boy by the hair and pulled him off me. The Hunan boy moved away and brought his other arm out from behind his back. He had a heavy iron bar in his hand.

He had a black eye, his nose was bruised and crooked, and his upper lip was still swollen from a recent cut. He licked it gingerly and pointed at my feet as he shuffled from side to side, while the workmen by the cart retreated.

"I like your shoes," he said. "Give them to me. Come on." He swung the bar towards us as a warning.

I knelt down and quickly removed them and stepped back. He reached down and seized them, staring at us all the while, and then swung the bar again a few times in warning. He knelt and quickly put them on.

"Get lost," he shouted. "Or I'll come after you."

I stood my ground and stared at the boy. "I can't walk home like this."

"I said get lost!" He lunged forward and swung the bar.

I knelt quickly and seized a big rock, then took aim and threw it at him. He wasn't expecting it and moved the wrong way, and I hit him straight in the throat. He cried and clutched his neck with his free hand, coughing violently while making a feeble wave with the bar. I found another rock and picked it up and drew my arm back again.

"I can't walk home like this!" I screamed. I was shaking, my heart was pounding, and I gripped the stone so hard I thought my fingers would break. My skull was on fire. I stared at him and let out a long wordless cry as I prepared to throw the second rock. He looked at me, leaning to one side like an old rheumatic.

He turned to two of the workmen who were standing nearby, watching open-mouthed.

"You! Give him your shoes!" the boy said. He tried to intimidate them by shouting, but he couldn't speak properly. He took a few steps towards them and brandished the iron bar. The workmen drew back but stayed with their carts. Then the boy lunged forward and brought the iron down onto the cart handle, just an inch from one man's hand. The workman cried out and stepped away then quickly kicked off his shoes and brought them to me.

He approached me crouching, with his free hand raised protectively to his face. He dropped the shoes in front of me. I still had the rock in my hand. The Hunan boy ran as soon as I picked up the shoes.

. . .

The shoes were too small for me. They were made of cloth that stretched only a little, and my heels stuck out over the backs. Leuk offered me his.

"We can swap every hour," he said, but I said there was no point in both of us having sore feet.

It was late and I didn't think we would get far, so we decided to spend the night in the village. We walked warily through the few streets, looking for someone who might take us in. It began to rain. Leuk wondered if the girls had been here before us. I thought of Wei-Ming and how she used to play in the rain in our courtyard, and I stuck my tongue out to catch a few drops.

We found a kind of inn, though it was shabby and dirty and there seemed to be no one there. We peered around the building. A small yard held a handful of stunted chickens pecking over a pile of kitchen refuse. An old man stuck his head out a window and scolded us, telling us to leave his birds alone.

"I'm sorry, Master," I said. "We're looking for a place to sleep."

He came out a side door and looked at us, trying to make sense of how two unwashed, long-haired boys had been deposited into such neat clothes.

"You didn't steal those from this village," he said watchfully. "Did you steal them from a school?"

I didn't like being accused of stealing, but if I told the truth I was afraid he would give us away to the Japanese if they appeared, so I said yes.

The rain was coming down harder and thunder pealed in the distance. Leuk didn't like storms. I asked the old man again if he had a place for us to stay. He sized us up again.

"One night only, and you leave first thing," he said. "Too many people on the road."

I thought of the girls. I described them and asked if he'd seen them. He searched our faces again and brought us in. Once we crossed the threshold, he told us he was called Mr. Ho.

In the grey-tiled kitchen, he turned to his wife, an old woman whose back curved like a shrub. He asked her about the girls. They muttered back and forth to each other as though disputing an unpleasant task. Then she turned back to the small dome of cabbage she was chopping and he looked at us. He said the girls had passed through and were on their way to the city. He didn't know their names. He said he'd heard something about a quilt factory, next to a temple where people took refuge.

That night, it took me a long time to fall asleep and Leuk tossed next to me. All I could think about was the girls. I thought of getting up to ask Mr. Ho if he could tell me more, but he'd already done more for us than I'd expected. We lay on a straw mat under the kitchen table, covered by an old blanket smelling of barn.

In the middle of the night, I woke to the sound of far-off explosions and gunfire. I heard Mr. and Mrs. Ho shuffling around the house and testing the lock on their door, and after that I lay awake until morning.

Our hosts seemed less forbidding in the morning, even kind. They asked us how we had slept, and we thanked them for taking us in. Then Leuk said we must be going.

"Stay one more night," said Mr. Ho. "There was a lot of fighting close by last night. Nobody knows who or where, but there have been rumours of Chinese guerillas along the river."

My heart swelled at the news. In my head I played a scene like a newsreel, of Chinese men in crisp Nationalist uniforms, leaping up riverbanks and through the forest, meting out death to the soldiers of Japan, crushing them like a stampede of wild horses. I asked Mr. Ho where the river was and if we could see it.

"Don't be crazy," he said. "The Japanese will be all over the place now. Stay here another day. You can help us out, and if it clears tomorrow, I'll show you the way to the ferry. It's the safest way for you."

I didn't want to delay finding Yee-Lin and the girls, but Leuk was very worried. "Listen to him, Chung-Man. I don't want to go out there if the Japanese are searching the village."

So we stayed another day and night. We helped clean out the chicken coop and Mrs. Ho fed us rice porridge with pickled eggs and sour cabbage. Mr. Ho ate very little and sat at the table watching us as we devoured the food. Leuk said we would help some more with the yardwork. Mr. Ho waved him off.

"Don't worry about it. It's late. Have a good sleep, and if it's safer tomorrow, I'll show you out."

We thanked them, and after Mrs. Ho cleaned up, we pulled our mat under the kitchen table again and fell asleep.

. . .

The next morning, Mr. Ho woke us. He said it had been quiet all night.

I rolled up the straw mattress, tied it with a string, and put it away in the corner. Mrs. Ho made tea and reheated some of the porridge for Leuk and me. Again, Mr. Ho sat with us but didn't eat. He had a small cloth bag in one hand.

We ate quickly then got up, bowed deeply, and thanked them both several times.

"You were both very kind to us. We can find our way," Leuk said.

Mr. Ho shook his head. "No, no, I'll take you there. I want to make sure the ferryman knows where to take you."

He got up and pulled a padded jacket over his sweater, and dropped the little bag into his pocket. He muttered something to himself about how sick he was of the fighting. Mrs. Ho stood with her back to us. I looked at her and she seemed to be shaking as she scrubbed an old pot over and over again.

Mr. Ho looked at her for a moment and said, "I'll be back by midday." She didn't reply. He turned and put his hands around both our shoulders, and walked us outside.

The ferry dock was at the end of a winding path through dense trees, and I was glad Mr. Ho had insisted on taking us. Few people were out this soon after daybreak. Mr. Ho shuffled along the road with a slightly unsteady gait. At the docks, a ferryman was already waiting in his boat with a few passengers. Mr. Ho brought out the cloth bag and gave the ferryman three coins.

"Three passengers."

I looked at him in surprise.

"Just get in." He climbed in after us and I helped him over the side into a seat. "You have to get off at another village that's harder to find. I want to make sure you get there. After that, the road to the city is easy to get to."

The ferryman pushed off, and once we were moving, he and Mr. Ho began conversing like old acquaintances. They spoke in a dialect that I understood only in fragments.

As we went around a bend in the river, gunfire started up sporadically nearby. Some of the passengers gasped, and Mr. Ho raised a hand to silence us as he leaned forward and peered ahead. The ferryman stared inexpressively into the trees along the river, steering his boat towards the right bank. He brought us in as close as he could, so close that, as we passed by a thicket of leaning trees, I could smell the reddish spherical flowers that hung low over the water as they brushed over us. I would have picked one, but I was sitting very still and feared that plucking a flower would make the branches rustle.

The other passengers were very quiet. One of the women pulled a scarf tight around her head and leaned forward as if to disappear into the boat. Mr. Ho kept talking to the ferryman in a lowered voice. Then he began to speak more urgently and the ferryman responded with quick, wordless nods while peering intently into the trees.

A huge explosion struck the hill somewhere farther up on our side of the bank. Mr. Ho spun around on his seat and listened after the echo. The effort seemed to draw heavily from him, and he crouched to one side as though in pain and his breath grew wheezy.

"Don't stop at Dong Ma," he hissed to the ferryman. "If that was the Japanese, they'll go after the district police station there. Keep going." He gestured violently at the ferryman as if to push the boat forward faster, yet we drifted on with agonizing slowness.

Mr. Ho's face was flushed. One of the women behind us was crying and he urged her to be quiet. "Don't be afraid," he said to us. "I know the river well." But he sounded worried. He was wheezing and breathed through his mouth.

The ferryman pushed on as two more explosions struck the riverbank, followed by gunfire. All of this was taking place farther upriver, and we were heading straight into it.

"The next docks…are very far from the village," said Mr. Ho. He stared across the water, gripping the side of the boat with the bluish, papery skin of his hand.

"Chung-Man, get down!" said Leuk. He slid off the bench onto the bottom of the boat, squatting in the water pooled at our feet. I looked at Mr. Ho, and he waved at me impatiently with a downward gesture and told me to listen to my brother. Then he spoke rapidly to the ferryman, who responded with a slow shake of his head.

Farther up, on the left bank, another shell exploded and I heard trees being torn apart. This one was close enough that I felt the air shake around me. Smoke rose from the blast, and then a great tree and clumps of earth fell into the water. When the smoke cleared, I saw several Chinese soldiers on the left with mortars and rifles firing over the river. I was thrilled to see them at last, and also terrified. All the other passengers hit the floor and the ferryman crouched as low as he could. The Chinese fired their rifles over the water, and it was then that I realized we were on the Japanese side of the river.

"Keep going, keep going!" Mr. Ho shouted. The Chinese paused for a moment and took cover as the Japanese returned fire right above us. "Just keep to the trees. They're shooting from higher up."

We drifted closer and closer to the gunfire. The quiet between exchanges was eerie, with only the fading cries of birds escaping upward. I stared hard at the opposite bank. Another company of Chinese soldiers descended from higher up, carrying mortars and machine guns. They began firing across the river. They unleashed a volley far more ferocious than before, and I heard tree limbs and rocks flying through the air and into the water. Above us and to our right, where the Japanese were hiding, there was a brief silence followed by the screams of the injured. I cheered and wept. I raised my fist and shouted, "You hit them! Do it again!" Then a single burst of machine-gun fire erupted to our right just above us. We were directly between the soldiers.

I prayed that it was over, but the Chinese returned fire when the Japanese stopped shooting. I could almost see their faces in the trees, at least two dozen Chinese. The boat drifted on. Mr. Ho was right: they were firing mostly upward at the higher land on our side.

Something big splashed in the water nearby. A moment later a dripping hand shot up and gripped the ferry's edge. The boat lurched to one side. A Japanese soldier was struggling in the water, barely keeping his head up. He must have rolled down the bank and fallen in. He gripped the boat and swayed in the current, trying unsuccessfully to raise himself despite the shallowness of the water. The woman behind me screamed. When he managed to get his shoulders above the weeds, I saw that his other arm was blown right off and he was bleeding heavily into the water. He didn't even seem to know what he was doing. He looked about sixteen, and I almost reached over to take his hand. He stared at me with cloudy, half-shut eyes and his slack mouth ran with algae.

Mr. Ho turned in his seat and tried to kick the soldier's hand. He was wearing only plain sandals made of straw, and his first few kicks did nothing. Then he stood and raised his knee, and landed the bottom of a sandal straight on the soldier's fingers. With a faint sob, the soldier let go and drifted into the weeds.

Just then the whiz of rifle shots flew by us. Mr. Ho fell to the floor beside me. There was a bullet hole in his neck and the blood pulsed gently from it into the water in the bottom of the boat. He clawed the air and started plucking at the clothes around his throat, and his wheeze turned to a gurgle. Leuk and I knelt down beside him.

"Old Master! Old Master!" I screamed. I put my hand under his head to lift it from the water, but the blood kept washing into the boat. I called him Master to show respect, thinking it would bring him back.

TWENTY-EIGHT

Just as Mr. Ho had told us, the docks were outside the village. Leuk and I chose not to walk into the village, and instead followed a sign that indicated the way to the main road. We found a bamboo grove that stood apart from the rough forest, and we stumbled into it exhausted.

There was a pinkish wash all over my shorts and the front of my shirt. I tried rubbing the stains off with some dried grass. That didn't work, and I didn't want to go back to the river to wash. I tried not to look at the stain. I rubbed my hands and forearms with some of the grass and leaves, but it gave me a rash, so I stopped.

"Chung-Man, we need to rest," said Leuk. We sat down at the base of a slender tree. I was starving and we had no food or money. I said to Leuk that we should look for a coconut or mango tree, or any other fruit nearby, but the bamboo dominated the grove and there was little else within sight. I had no energy to go searching.

As soon as we sat down, the world grew still. The only sounds were of a light breeze running through the bamboo, and thousands of insects. The river seemed far away, and even the sun was muted by the swaying, bright-green stalks surrounding us. We sank back against the tree and exhaustion spread through every inch of my body. We were silent and motionless for several minutes.

Leuk turned his head towards me. He was fingering the buttons on his shirt and looked half asleep. His voice had fallen to a whisper again, and he looked down at the ground. "Mr. Ho was very good to us," he said. Before replying, I watched a small red-winged bird alight, high up, at the tip of a stalk.

"Yes, he was," I murmured. The bamboo waved in the warm green air. I listened to the insects, but even that tired me. The breeze whispered through the leaves and I saw Mr. Ho's face appear before me, floating in the grass until he faded away, the sound of rustling coming from his open mouth.

"I hope the ferryman takes him back to his village," whispered Leuk. "I hope he makes it back."

"I hope we do too," I said. I had lost track of what Leuk was saying. I felt the immense weight of sleep on me, and in my chest I felt something I imagined as a whirlpool.

There were several younger bamboo stalks next to me, and as I turned my head to rest, I watched them moving in the breeze. Two round black beetles were crawling up one of the stalks. I leaned forward to watch them. They were a deep black, though their wings had a bluish-green lustre. They had mandibles like little wrenches, and above these, protruding from the middle of their faces, were long green snouts like needles. The beetle near the top scuttled around one of the joints between the bamboo segments, gripping the stalk with its barbed limbs, and settled on a spot just above the joint.

It tested the bamboo with its mandibles for a moment and shifted its body up the stalk. It put the tip of its needle against the young stalk and drove it in. I thought I heard the tiny cracking of the fibres as they split open. Its face was almost touching the stalk, and it was very still for a few moments except for a slight shaking of its abdomen. Then it slowly withdrew the needle and shifted over to look for a new spot. Below it, the other beetle was doing the same.

They were sucking the sugary sap out of the young shoots. More beetles emerged from the soil and started climbing up the other stalks. I guessed that we had chased them off when we first appeared. Now they seemed content to ignore us.

The beetle below was now drawing from its own segment, while the first was still probing for its second drink. I reached over carefully and picked it up. One of its wings fluttered beneath my finger that was holding down the other wing, and it wriggled its legs and mandibles at me. I pulled off the wings and legs and quickly put it in my mouth. I bit down. The sweet bamboo sap burst onto my tongue, and I chewed it up quickly and swallowed. Then I plucked off the other one. It was still drinking, and its needle snapped off in the stalk. While I chewed on it, a tiny drop of sap appeared at the end of the broken needle.

I told Leuk to move over, and together we plucked the beetles off the bamboo and ate them. Others continued marching up the stalks as they probed the fibres for an opening to the sap. They traced little dark lines against the pale green, heedless of our waiting fingers. The sweetness of the sap persisted for the first several bites until a bitter taste built up in my mouth and I stopped.

We lay there until the sun drifted into the afternoon, and we both slept in turns. I fell asleep with my hand on my buckle, and when I woke, it was still there.

The road leading to the village intersected with a much larger one, and we heard vehicles and horses on it even before the road was in sight. I sat down on the roadside and Leuk leaned against a tree.

Soon a truck came down the road. We hid behind two trees in case it was Japanese. From the way it roared and sputtered, we knew it couldn't be military, and we craned our necks out to look. When the truck rounded the bend and came into view, Leuk stepped into the road and waved it down.

It was a rattling old delivery truck with the windshield blown out. One man was behind the wheel, another had mechanic's tools strapped to his belt. He was standing on the step outside the passenger door, hanging on to a bar. He saw us, waved back at Leuk, and told the driver to stop. Then he stepped down and asked us where we were going.

"To Hong Kong!" said Leuk. "Or a place just outside it. I think it's called the Chung Shan gardens." The truck shook and backfired as it idled.

"I know it," said the mechanic. "We'll give you a ride there if you want."

My brother and I looked briefly at each other and said yes. The mechanic went around to the back and I opened the passenger door.

"Not in here," said the driver. Inside, taking up the whole passenger side, was a strange contraption. They had rigged up a kind of second engine inside the cab, almost like a wood stove that fed fuel into whatever engine remained under the hood. Next to the driver were several glass whiskey bottles that, he explained, were full of alcohol that he fed slowly into the engine as he drove. The mechanic came back up front and showed off his invention proudly. He said he'd rigged it himself because of the shortage of fuel and engine parts.

He took us to the back of the truck and helped us in. It was piled high with heavy bags of salt that reached higher than the truck walls. When we got up on top of the bags, we were well above the safety of the truck's walls, and when I looked over the edge, the ground seemed unnervingly far down.

"Lie as flat as you can," said the mechanic. "Hold tight to the bags."

I was a little frightened of falling off at first, until Leuk shifted one of the bags to help me get a better grip. The fumes of burning alcohol stung my nose and eyes as the truck started and shook, and then we took off.

For the first time in months, I felt free of danger. The dust from the salt burned my nostrils, so I lay with my face on my forearms and closed my eyes. In the dark, and feeling how tired my muscles were, I could think only of seeing the girls and my mother again.

About a half-hour into the rocking, bumpy ride, I had to pee badly. I didn't want to ask the driver to stop, so I just unbuttoned carefully while lying down and peed into the bag of salt beneath me. I poked Leuk in the arm and told him what I was doing, and he laughed hysterically. A moment later I shouted, "I'm still peeing!" and he laughed even harder. The mechanic on the outside heard us and looked over and waved, though I knew he couldn't make out what I'd said. We giggled like idiots. Leuk wanted to do it too, and he unzipped himself and made a face, though he had peed on the roadside just before leaving and couldn't make anything. He kept wiggling and making faces, and when he said a drop had finally passed, we laughed even harder and tears ran sideways down my face onto the bags. It never occurred to me that the salt would eventually end up in someone's food.

We drove for what seemed like an hour, taking just one short break where the mechanic and the driver shared their food with us. They had cold red rice mixed with dried shrimp and pickled mustard, and we each devoured a bowl of it. The truckers seemed like close friends and they teased us a lot. I said I was thirsty and the driver took one of the whiskey bottles full of fuel and pretended to take a long swig from it before holding it out to me as though I should drink some too.

The driver took us to a stream a few yards off the road that he said was safe to drink from. The four of us walked down to it and filled water canteens and drank, and Leuk and I did our best to wash ourselves. Even when we were all wet, I don't think we looked much better, and the driver laughed at us. He went back to the truck and returned with a cloth and a bar of soap. He got us to sit down on a rock by the stream, and from the cloth he unwrapped a straight razor. We soaped our hair as much as we could, and the driver carefully shaved our heads.

He shaved Leuk first. When the first long, soapy lock fell on the rock with a plop, I laughed because it looked and sounded so disgusting. Leuk washed his head in the stream again while the driver shaved me. I thought I would keep laughing, but when I felt his left hand carefully holding my neck and scalp, gently pulling my ears, and rubbing his thumb over my skin to look for spots he'd missed, I grew very quiet and a little sleepy. He told us he'd been a barber before the war and wanted to open a shop again when it ended. When he was done, I rinsed off in the stream, and as we walked back to the truck, Leuk and I ran our hands over our heads to feel our clean skin.

We climbed back up onto the salt bags as the mechanic started the engine. The driver said he would go for two hours now without a break. I tried to sleep, but the constant shaking of the truck and slight movement of the salt bags kept me awake. It was too loud for Leuk and me to talk.

I had imagined what it would be like to see Hong Kong come into view, but the road took us to a side of it I didn't know, and in any case it was dark when we arrived. We stopped just inside the gates of what had once been a separate village. The mechanic and the driver came around to the back and helped us both down. They gave us a canteen full of water to take with us.

"Do you know where you're going?" the driver asked.

"To a quilt factory," said Leuk. "Do you know it?"

He clapped his hand on the end of a bag of salt. "No idea. But you'll find it."

We thanked them again and they drove away. I waved at them until they were gone. It was so strange to be dropped off like that, and hear no sounds of warplanes or gunfire, and believe that it was safe to be on our own again. It was as though Chow had just dropped us off at the movies. I shouldered the canteen, and Leuk teased me about my bald head as we started walking.

The northern end of Hong Kong still looked like an old farming village. The roads were dirt and the houses were older-style village dwellings like the one our aunt and uncle had in Tai Fo, and there were no tall buildings anywhere. It looked almost untouched by the war.

We walked down the main street in the evening lamp-light. Had it not been for my shoes, we would have fit in pretty well. The people out walking were more like the city people we'd grown up around, and many of them were out either enjoying the cool air or lining up at the ration station. While we walked, I got distracted by the sign over a bookstore and bumped into an older woman carrying a bag of vegetables. She turned and snapped at me before going on, and while I was turning back to apologize, I nearly ran into someone else. It reminded me of home again, the impatience, the movement of people, the voices. I half expected to reach into my pocket and find a bag of candy.

We had only vague memories of where the factory

was. We had accompanied our father there on a few business trips, and I remembered seeing the quilts piled up in stacks so high there were ladders to reach the top. I recalled the sound of looms and sewing machines farther down a long corridor, clicking and whirring in an oddly muted way as their sound faded into the piles of thick cloth.

We passed a small shop that sold blankets and other cloth goods including quilts, and my brother asked the owner where they came from. At first he told us to get lost — he was closing up for the evening and was doing a final sweep of the flagstone steps outside the store; only one light was left on inside. Everywhere around us, the other stores were closing as well, dimming, sweeping, the lids of normal life shutting as for sleep and the hope of darkness.

Leuk asked the store owner again, begging him this time to help us. The man stepped out into the street and waved an arm towards the far end, telling us to turn there and follow the road to the factory. We didn't fully understand him but didn't want to ask a third time. He shut his shop door behind him as we ran down the street.

The factory was in a very old building with heavy wooden doors over which a single lantern hung. I pounded my fist against them so hard it hurt, and yet I seemed to make only a soft thud. We both pounded on them, four hands, shouting towards the high windows that we were here to see Mrs. Yee-Lin Leung and her little sister and friend. *Take us in too*, I thought. *Let us come off the road at last.*

The irate old woman who opened the door held a

lantern so close to her face I thought she might be blind. She questioned us carefully and looked around to see if we were alone. Then her expression changed and she let us in.

They were sitting in a small, comfortable room on the second floor, with landscape paintings on the walls. It was a kind of living area for the senior factory staff, isolated from the noise by the stacks of quilts below. Yee-Lin was sitting with a cup of tea, looking out a window, and next to her was my little sister, reading as though she were back in her room at home. We ran to meet them and Wei-Ming leapt up as I hugged her.

It had been maybe only a week since they left us at the horse farm. But it had been much longer since I had felt such joy—weeks, months, time stretched out into emptiness on the road away from home and from my mother. I held Wei-Ming and wept to see her and Yee-Lin, and to be safe at last.

At first I didn't say anything about Ling, and it wasn't until the next day that I asked my sister-in-law where she was. It troubled me for many years that I was so slow to ask. I had cared for Ling while I knew her. Her life had been far harder than mine, and she had no one left to look out for her. I worried what it was in me that could suddenly let go of someone in such need, and as I grew older the question disturbed me even more.

Yee-Lin told me that they had walked a similar route to mine and Leuk's, though they hadn't gone down the river. One morning before dawn, Yee-Lin woke to the sound of Ling whispering in her ear. She told Yee-Lin that she was leaving to find the way back to Shantou. She rolled her things up in a blanket and walked away, and though my sister-in-law had asked her to, Ling sent no message back. Like so many people in those years, she wandered back into what we saw as a dark mist but she herself saw as her only hope. It was no rasher or more dangerous than our own journey back to the city. For a few days after Yee-Lin told me about Ling's departure, I felt I had a real choice to go back and find her, to retrace a road I now knew and save her from her solitary walk. But I didn't do that, and even years later I regretted it.

I never forgot her and often wondered where she was, and my memory of Ling was forever intertwined with my doubts about myself. Even now I feel that pang, though the worry has retreated into grief. I can see her only as a girl still frozen at sixteen, a ghost, searching the roads alone because her only friend, in a moment of rare joy, has turned away from her.

Yee-Lin, Leuk, Wei-Ming, and I spent six months at the quilt factory. Mr. Chin, the owner, put us up in his home and paid for us to attend the nearby school. He tried many times to take us home, but the fighting near the harbour and in other parts of the city was still too intense. Yee-Lin sent a message to Sheung. We had no way of knowing if it was ever delivered.

It was difficult to be the closest we'd yet been to home yet be unable to go back. We had no news of my mother, and the cruel words of the Hunan boys echoed in my dreams so that I woke up crying at night from visions of their fulfillment. I slept next to Leuk, and he was very patient with these interruptions. He never knew what to say until I settled down, and then he would simply ask if I was warm enough.

We ate our meals with Mr. Chin in his living room, along with his servants and several staff who had lost their homes. The dining room and one of the bedrooms had been converted into a makeshift hospital run by Methodists. It was very crowded, much like our own house had been before we left. Mr. Chin told us many stories about our father, and he always praised our mother and reassured us that we would return to her.

There was still very little to eat in the city. Our meals were cobbled together from rice rations and the limited vegetables growing in Mr. Chin's yard and improvised gardens in the neighbourhood. The water supply was often poor because the Japanese still controlled it.

Finally, in January 1943, Mr. Chin sat down with us for a talk.

"There still isn't much news. All I hear is from tradesmen in the city. From what they say, things are a bit better. There might be a lull in the fighting right now. You can stay longer, of course, though this might be a good time to make your way home."

While he spoke, he fiddled with a little bead bracelet that Wei-Ming had made him. He didn't seem very confident in what he was saying, but he talked to us every day and it was the first time he'd raised the possibility of us leaving.

Yee-Lin, Leuk, and I talked about it briefly. We had no idea how reliable Mr. Chin's news was, but we wanted desperately to go home. We packed our things and left the next morning.

It was a strange departure. Mr. Chin had the driver from the factory take us part of the way into the city, and then we had to walk for a couple of hours. Luckily, he had dropped us off in Tsim Sha Tsui, and we knew the way from there to the Hong Kong Island ferry and the road to Happy Valley. It was sad and wonderful to walk those streets again. The destruction was even worse — collapsed buildings, streets littered with glass and scorched vehicles, shelters improvised in empty lots. We looked out everywhere for soldiers, but the area was so desolate that even they seemed to have abandoned it. Yet as we walked, I smelled the same trees and heard voices from buildings I knew, and walking through those ruins was like discovering a fragment from a broken vase, with the image of a flower still intact.

We arrived at Wong Nai Chung Road at sunset, and the minute we turned onto it, Leuk took my hand. Yee-Lin was walking slowly with Wei-Ming, so she told us to go ahead. Leuk and I ran up the road even though my legs ached. We pushed open the broken gates and entered the courtyard. At its far end, by a leafless orange tree, my mother sat.

We ran to her shouting and crying. She turned and stared with a puzzled look, and shook her head and waved us off. I stopped. She rose quickly and waved us off again, pointing to the street. Leuk took a nervous step, but our mother yelled at us to leave. She started walking towards us with that irritated gait I knew too well, her finger aimed squarely at the entrance, and my heart caved in despair. Then she stopped with a stunned expression and stammered part of my name. I called her again and moved towards her, and she recognized at last who we were.

Later, she explained to us that we were so thin and changed, she thought we were boys from the country selling firewood. When she finally recognized us, she could barely say our names as she ran to us. I won't describe it any further. The memory of that moment overwhelms me still, and it seems I've spent my whole life caught inside it. When I recall it, everything falls behind a curtain of sensation, and every memory from the war years is drawn behind it too, formless, ecstatic, and corruptible, bathed in evening light.

The end of a life is the end of memory, and so few of us are left now. Sheung and Tang have been dead for many years. Chow outlived them both, and he wrote to me once after he returned to his old village. If I recall correctly, it was five years ago this spring that my niece phoned me around midnight to tell me of Wei-Ming's death in a care home in Kowloon. Yee-Lin had died twelve years before her, apparently from a fall.

My brother Leuk is the only other one of us still alive. He used to write me detailed letters every week, but a stroke has curbed his routine, and now I get a short note once a month, obviously written with assistance. The old letters—how I miss them. For all their banality, they were comforting, they were reliable, and they gave me a picture of the old city. He always opened with the usual greetings and well-wishes, and sometimes a short list of complaints. And then came the meat of it: the solo gambling trips to Macau, his opinion of current events, and the weather. And there's the restaurant. Three times a week he goes to the same place for lunch with the same group of five old friends, a number unchanged over the decades. They usually order the same items, but if the manager persuades them to try a new dish, this gets its own paragraph.

Now the letters are brief, and in the willowy writing I can detect here and there some characters corrected by another hand, maybe a woman's. One of these corrections was overwritten again in his hand—repeating the error—as if relinquishing something so personal as a mistake was wrong. *Good for you*, I thought, and even though the sentence meant nothing, it cheered me and confirmed he was still his old self.

How many of us are still alive who are marked by our worst mistake, the year of our birth? There are few of us left who lived through the war, and fewer still who fought it, and we are all old. Those who came after us have heard us talk a little, but for them it's a time long past, and they see its images mostly in books and films, sometimes in their thoughts, never in their dreams.

Dear youngest brother:

I hope my letter finds you well. It's been five weeks since I wrote. I'm better than when I last wrote, as I'm walking more steadily. If it improves I'll go back to Macau. There's a new casino there, and the restaurants are said to be excellent. But let's see how I do first.

Very hot in Hong Kong now, soon it will be as hot as Malaysia. I had the air conditioner replaced in the spring and that was a good decision. When the heat gets bad the malls and restaurants are always full, which is good for business. You're used to hotter weather, so I guess I shouldn't complain. I wonder sometimes if you yearn for the cooler air here.

The old gang still meets for lunch even though I missed two in a row while I was in the hospital. Since I'm not the sickest of the bunch I must make an effort to attend. The next lunch is in three days. When I was there yesterday, we tried a new dish of razor clams with chili, caught just off Lamma Island. Not too spicy for me. I hope we can try them together one day.

Shun-Yau also returned at that lunch. He's very lucky. His children pay for a woman from the Philippines to accompany him, but yesterday his granddaughter came instead. She's a very nice girl, studying in Australia. He couldn't eat the halibut. She ordered some rice and steamed eggs for him, and helped him lift the spoon. It made me think of that time long ago when he lived with us. He'll miss her when she goes back to Sydney.

I'll try to get back to my old writing habits now that I feel better. I always look forward to your letters. A few letters back you said you were going to see your doctor, so I hope everything is well. Do you still walk in the park across from your flat? I remember the beautiful flower beds there when I came to visit in '09. That seems like yesterday, but really it was years ago.

I'm going to watch some television now. They still carry the Sunday morning church broadcasts from St. Paul's, and I like the sermons from the new minister more. He reminds me of our days at school together.

Wishing you good health,
Leuk

TWENTY-NINE

The photograph taken on my twenty-second birthday, which I lost after moving away, was like a reversal of the one taken on my third. I am there at the table and Leuk is beside me again, and the cake is much plainer, as it should be for a young man. This time it's my brother who's excited. He's just finished his first year of teacher's college—specializing in physics already—and he's looking enthusiastically at the piled-up cream and strawberries fresh from the reopened bakery. I am next to him, dressed more casually, my hair neatly parted, and the expression on my face, overexposed by either the flash or the light from the windows, is at odds with how I think now any young man should feel on his birthday. Which is to say I should look happier.

The photo also shows Ah-Ming, still standing behind us and much older, though still graceful. Her hands rest on the back of my chair as though to encourage me. Her hair is cut shorter and is brushed back in the manner of old women, which may explain the small freedom in the smile on her face. Among all the photos my older brother took, it is one of the few I kept from the years after the war, while I was still living in Hong Kong.

In some ways I was lucky to have been a child during the war. Time moves so differently at that age that a year seems like forever. By the time of that birthday, it was the summer of 1951 and it seemed to me that the war had ended a lifetime ago. Maybe I felt some distance from it, too, because no one ever talked about it. Once the house was repaired and the family firm had been brought up off its knees by Tang and Sheung, and all of us were accounted for and living under one roof, it seemed again that life could flow uninterrupted.

But outside the house, if we were at church or the Jockey Club or visiting other families, I felt as though a darkness hung over us that only others saw and felt. We were all alive. The last death in our family had been my father's, and for all our sorrow, we had reunited intact. I had friends whose mothers or fathers were alone or whose brothers and sisters had disappeared, and when they came to visit, or if we saw them in public and started a conversation, it was never long before their losses clouded over us. Once, in the summer of 1948, after he finished high school, I went to visit Shun-Yau and his mother and Shun-Po in their new flat. I brought Mrs. Yee a gift from my mother, and we talked a little. But after I responded to her polite questions about my family, about the summer or Tang's wedding, she collapsed in tears. The gift, a porcelain cup still wrapped in pale green paper, fell from her hands and shattered, and as it broke, I wished that I too could turn to dust and disappear completely. So many times I walked away from people we knew, feeling as though I were the ambassador of fortune's cruelty. I felt it everywhere, and it was around that time that I began to see I couldn't stay in Hong Kong much longer.

The day after my birthday, in late July, I was sitting with my mother in the rooftop garden, and she was doting on her grandson, Tat-Choy, in his pram. Yee-Lin sat on the other side, one finger extended to let her son grasp it while she looked out over the valley.

From across the road, the sound of a crowd cheering at the horse races rang over the houses and apartments, and the announcer's voice echoed from the speakers like a distant bell. All faded and yet familiar. It was Saturday. I was slouched back in my chair with my right hand shoved in my pocket, worrying the corner of a piece of paper that had been there for two straight days and which I'd been reluctant to take out.

Ah-Tseng came up and set down a tray with tea and fruit and a bowl of rice porridge for my nephew. She took a folding stool out from behind one of the planters and set it beside the pram and then took the bowl of porridge and handed it to Yee-Lin. She dipped the tip of her finger in to check its temperature, even though Ah-Tseng had already let it cool off in the kitchen. Ah-Tseng took it back from her and began to feed the baby. Little threads of egg white wrapped around the porcelain rim and then stuck to his lower lip, and Ah-Tseng brushed them into his mouth with her finger. My mother leaned over and cooed at him every time he took a mouthful of the bland pearl-grey mixture. I fingered the paper again and stopped when my nail tore through one of the folds.

...

A week later, I was cleaning out my room. The letter, now with a few more worried rips in it, lay folded on my dresser, and I avoided looking at it. I went through my room and found books and clothes I would no longer need. Most of what I had still descended from that time before the war, and I told myself my nephew might want some of it one day. I filled a box with things to discard. The old corner of the yard where we had once thrown our trash, and where the British had once dumped all their guns, had been cleared out and turned into a vegetable garden. I put the box in the hall, knowing Chow would take it out later.

At the back of my closet, I found a small cloth bag. I picked it up and it felt very light, so I flipped it over and dumped the contents onto my bed. A polished rock fell out, and with a little extra shaking my old belt landed on the quilt.

My body went numb, and I stared at the belt for several minutes. My right hand drifted ghostlike over my stomach and plucked at my shirt. I hadn't seen it for years. Against the taut, crisp floral print of the quilt, it was pitifully dirty and old. I picked it up and examined the strap. The leather was cracked and frayed, and when I ran my thumb along its edge, a small shower of dirt sprayed onto my hand and sleeve. I stared at the dirt and tried to imagine where it had come from.

The tarnish on the buckle was unchanged, still no darker after many years. I pressed my thumbnail against it, wanting to scrape it and see the gold shine through, but I hesitated and instead rubbed my thumb over the brownish metal, feeling it warm in my hand. It was strange to see again this lifeless thing that had accompanied me in silence all that time. Though I had never used it, during that time it brought me both comfort and worry, and it was my guardian, my monument, and my wound. I toyed with the pin for a moment and rolled the belt back up. I weighed it in my hand a final time before putting it back in the bag.

I brought it to Sheung and showed him. He stretched it out and looked at the strap with faint disgust, then looked closely at the buckle.

"My God, I remember this thing," he said. "I guess you won't need this where you're going." He put it down and looked at me gravely. "You should talk to her soon."

I shook my head in response to his first comment. "Yes, I'll talk to her." I took the belt from him and said, "Let me deal with this."

I was surprised how easily the strap and buckle came apart. I only had to pull slightly against the old seam that wrapped around the buckle, and the strap split open and separated from the gold. Even the metal there was tarnished.

Sheung took the buckle and placed it casually on his desk. He said he would take it to the foundry our family owned and have it melted back and purified. That was the only way to remove the tarnish. I looked at the strap for a moment, and then I tossed it into the empty wastebasket by his desk. It lay half coiled and dead against the wicker, and I tapped the basket lightly with my shoe as though to confirm I was done with it. It went out with the same garbage I had put outside my room. Most likely it was all burned.

The next morning after breakfast, I took the envelope off my dresser and went downstairs to find my mother in the library. I found her drinking tea and looking out at the garden, and I sat down on a stool across from her.

I opened up the letter and handed it to her, though she could not read English. I told her I'd been accepted at a university in America and would be moving to California to study. I would be the first in our family to leave. I already had the ship's ticket and would be going in a few weeks, I said.

She couldn't have been surprised, but she wrung her hands in her lap and blinked many times and looked away towards the garden. After a long silence my mother, that artist of serenity, said she was very happy for me. She said she hoped one day to visit.

My coat was the last object left in my room, and the ticket was sticking out of the right pocket. It lay folded on my bed while I was in the hallway with Chow, carrying my steamer trunk downstairs. It was a green metal box with brass rivets all around and my romanized initials, *CML*, in plain white letters on the top. I had locked it and the key was in my pocket on a small chain. We carried it down the three flights of stairs to the entrance, and Ah-Tseng followed with my coat. Then we took the trunk outside and put it in the boot of the Daimler.

All my brothers, including Leuk, were working and I had said goodbye to them earlier. My mother, Wei-Ming, and Ah-Tseng were coming with me to the port. I rubbed my eyes in the sun.

I was tired. I usually slept badly and during the day would often nod off while sitting or reading. Sleep didn't come easily to me. Mostly I persisted at its edge late into the night, touching its dark outer foliage but never entering. And when I did sleep, it might be the deep rest I needed, but too often it was a time of visitation. Then I was relieved to waken from dreams alone in the quiet emptiness of my room, though drenched in sweat and shaking.

It was time to go. Yee-Lin walked through the doors down to the car and put her arms around me. She was pregnant again, and when I felt the small bump beneath her housedress, it unnerved me.

"Good luck," she said. She held my hands in hers for a moment. She asked me to make good use of my new camera and send photos of California, and I said of course I would. Then I got into the car with my mother, Wei-Ming, and Ah-Tseng, and Chow drove out through the gates.

No one spoke on the drive to the port, but Wei-Ming held my hand. She had told me earlier she had a list of things she wanted from America for her eighteenth birthday next year, but she never produced one and said nothing in the car. The port appeared too soon, and Chow inched the car like a tram through the crowds and jumbled carts until we got to the landing where a huge

American liner was docked. A porter rolled his trolley towards us, but I insisted on helping Chow get the steamer trunk out myself, feeling my mother's eyes on me.

Sheung had made all the arrangements — my ticket there, my tuition, my lodgings and an allowance, and a list of some other Chinese students at the university. The coming months were all planned out without impediment, yet I moved slowly as though wading through mud. The ship's horn sounded, and a man on a megaphone announced that boarding would end in fifteen minutes.

I said my last goodbyes. Chow and Ah-Tseng bowed quickly and I thanked them for everything and promised I would write. I hugged Wei-Ming and she kissed me on the cheek, holding on to my hand even as I said goodbye to my mother. I had been hoping that my farewell with her would be quick, but when the moment came I embraced her tightly and my whole chest seemed to cave in, and I sensed her hand trembling on the back of my neck until she released me. I was relieved when the horn sounded a second time even as we exchanged our last few words. Then I turned and went up the gangway onto the ship. On deck, a steward offered to show me to my room, but I said I would wait until we were farther out. I crammed the ticket back into my pocket with a sweating hand and quickly found a spot where I could see my family standing outside the car.

The last horn sounded as the engines roared and spewed, and we parted from the dock. I stood at the stern and watched the quay. My mother was still there in a posture of enclosed silence, and Wei-Ming was crying.

Ah-Tseng stood behind them, leaning against the car out of my mother's sight. Wei-Ming ran to her and took her hand. I placed mine stiffly on the wooden railing and waved goodbye to them.

As the ship left the harbour, I held the railing and walked carefully around the edge because I didn't want anyone to see my eyes or hear the short sounds I tried to lock inside my throat. Gulls hovered near the prow, and I stood there and let the mist conceal my face. A young couple were holding hands a few feet away from me, and when I saw how they looked at one another, how the woman touched the man's neck, I knew they wouldn't notice me. I didn't want to be seen. I watched the sea farther out where it lay undisturbed. The deep salt water, nourishing and numbing, stretched out indifferently. It offered nothing and took nothing, it was only cold and brutally alive. Gulls hung patiently over the water, knowing it would give up its bounty. A knot formed in my chest like the weight of an anchor, and suddenly I wanted to throw myself into the sea, to be freed by its destructive force. I saw the waves break my body apart, and all the pain drift from it in a momentary foam. A part of me now belonged out in the water's violence. It was a broken thing, a second self I wanted to be rid of and see sink beneath the waves. But I could not cut it out. It would not escape through my tears or wash out in my dreams, all the joys of my future life could not displace it. It was there and would never leave; it was me. The ruined and forgotten bodies, the plumes of burning villages, the pungency and weeping of the lost, were sealed inside me.

Near the prow the gulls turned slowly through the mist. The sea chased them off as it whispered and rumbled against the hull. *Now*, I thought, *now*—and I braced myself to jump. I put my foot against the ledge, gripped the railing and looked down into the foam, and the water seemed to calm as though to greet me. But I stayed standing on the open deck, and my body, heart, and memory fought each other once again, as I knew now they always would.

ACKNOWLEDGEMENTS

This novel draws on my father's memoirs and his few oral stories from the Second World War. While this is a fictional work, nearly all the core incidents in the narrative are based on real events. Unlike twelve-year-old Chung-Man, my father was only nine at the time. As J.G. Ballard often said when asked about his "extraordinary childhood" that inspired *Empire of the Sun*, experiences such as these in Asia and Europe were the norm rather than the exception.

Writing is not as solitary as people say it is. I owe a huge debt to my friend and fellow author David Annandale for his constant encouragement and to Rozelle Srichandra for her support. I'm also greatly indebted to both my agent Robert Lecker and my editor at GLE, Bethany Gibson, who believed in my initial manuscript and saw what it could become.

Michael Kaan was born in Winnipeg,
the second child of a father from
Hong Kong and a Canadian mother.
The Water Beetles is his first novel.